SAVAGE

BY DAVID MEYER

ACKNOWLEDGEMENTS

My thanks go out to E.W. Hildick, Peggy Parish, Beverly Cleary, Gordon Korman, C.S. Lewis, every author who wrote under the Franklin W. Dixon pseudonym, Clive Cussler, and many, many others. Your books stirred a young boy's imagination in countless, incredible ways.

Also, thank you to Julie for editing this novel as well as for your loving support. Ryden, thank you for your happy peekaboo squeals. Dad, many thanks for helping me get this book out into the world.

The curtains are about to open. So, take your seat. Get nice and comfortable.

Welcome to the world of *Apex Predator*.

Welcome to *SAVAGE*.

CHAPTER 1

Date: Nov. 23, 2017, 9:02 p.m.; Location: North Maine Woods, ME

Zach Caplan tightened his grip on the steering wheel as a distant roar accosted his ears. It lasted no more than a few seconds before giving way to eerie silence. There was no response. No sudden bursts of gunfire, no rushing jets, no booming explosions. All of those noises had ceased months earlier. Which could only mean one thing. The war between mankind and beast was over.

And mankind had lost.

He'd never actually seen the battlefields. But the initial radio reports had painted vivid images of them. Long stretches of city streets, suburban neighborhoods, and open countryside, all littered with death and destruction. Multitudes of soldiers and civilians, crushed underfoot. Cars, tanks, and armored vehicles, broken and smashed. The burning wreckage of jets and helicopters. Shattered skyscrapers, demolished buildings, and ruined houses, all charred over from endless napalm attacks. Some remnants of mankind had survived the war, of course. Caplan and his friends. The Danter colony. Probably a few other survivor communities as well. But ultimately, it didn't matter. Things would never go back to normal. Modern society, for all intents and purposes, was finished.

No more civilization. But hey, look on the bright side, he thought with a dark, silent chuckle. *No more taxes either.*

Indeed, events of the last seventeen months had squashed that old adage about death and taxes. After all, what kind of numbskull paid taxes in the middle of the apocalypse?

As for death, well, that part of the adage still held true. But he didn't dwell on that fact. It didn't pay to think about the war, about the HA-78 virus, about the Holocene extinction, about the billions of people who'd lost their lives. Instead, he focused on what was controllable. Namely, the here and now.

Maintaining an even speed, he directed the van farther down the dark road. He drove without headlights, lest he attract one of *them*. Fortunately, the stars, unobscured by clouds, provided decent lighting. So, he could see pretty much everything. Windswept litter, the remnants of a once-carefree species now fighting for its very survival. Patches of brown grass, uncut for months. Dying trees and bushes, all victims of the ongoing mass extinction event. Animal carcasses, hollowed out by starvation and scavengers.

A dull ache, driven by raw and unrelenting hunger, appeared in the pit of his belly. Taking a deep breath, he resisted the urge to dip into his evening rations. Better to save them for later. For when he might really need them. *Forget thriving*, he sang in his head. *Just keep on surviving.* Maybe they weren't the most uplifting verses of all time. But hey, they'd kept him and his friends alive these last seventeen months. As such, he was determined to stay the course even though—his mouth twitched—not everyone agreed with it.

"We're coming up on a cross street." Derek Perkins, situated in the passenger seat, squinted at the windshield. "Ellicot Road, I think."

"Got it." Bailey Mills, kneeling in the cargo space, leaned over a large map. She aimed her flashlight beam at the crumpled paper. "Two miles to go."

Caplan nodded and continued to drive. No one would ever mistake him for tall, dark, and handsome. Indeed, he stood an inch under six feet. His skin, despite years of toiling under the sun, remained unusually fair. His face, rugged and weathered from a life spent outdoors, lacked any trace of refinement.

And yet, he wasn't blonde and blue-eyed either. Instead, his hair was jet black and curly. His piercing eyes were as green as freshly watered grass from the old days.

After a short distance, he spotted a large section of cracked, sunken pavement. It was shaped like a rough circle with thin lines stretching away from it. His brow cinched tight. It was a pawprint. One of *their* pawprints.

The van rocked from side to side as Caplan eased it off the road and around the massive pawprint. It was an old vehicle and often felt like it was splitting apart at the seams. But it was spacious and didn't consume much gas, which served them well on supply runs.

He'd found it two months earlier while searching a local campsite for food. He still remembered throwing open the rear doors and casting his gaze upon the previous owner. All of the signs—her fingers wrapped around her throat, her glassy and moist eyes, her purple and foam-covered lips— pointed to death by infection. Specifically, by the HA-78 virus.

Once upon a time, her corpse would've shocked him. But not these days. Premature death, either by the dying ecosystems, by HA-78, or by *them* was the norm in this new world.

He drove back onto the pavement and continued forward. A one-story structure, backed by dark, craggy hills as well as a forest of sagging spruce trees, appeared on the right side of the road. Unlit letters mounted above the front doors spelled out, *Carlson Market*. A couple of gas pumps sat off to the side. The parking lot held five or six heavily-damaged cars, some of which had been flipped onto their roofs.

"It's still standing." Perkins' voice wavered with excitement. "I can't believe it."

"Me neither." Mills gazed at the vehicles. "Especially since one of *them* definitely came through here. Why'd it only attack the cars?"

"Who knows?" He licked his dry, parched lips. "And honestly, who cares?"

Perkins had a point. Food didn't come easily in this strange new world. And unfortunately, that wasn't going to change anytime soon. Not when the death of nature was thousands of years in the making. Wild game still roamed the forests, but in much smaller numbers. Most of the indigenous animals had died out when their ecosystems started to collapse. Foraging was an option, but for how much longer? Fruits, mushrooms, roots, and berries were becoming increasingly difficult to find. And they couldn't even eat most of what they gathered. It needed to be set aside, preserved and stored for the icy months ahead.

Salvaging was even more problematic. The North Maine Woods didn't contain a lot of stores or houses. And most of the existing buildings had been pulverized by *them*. So to find a still-standing store with no obvious signs of looting wasn't just a welcome surprise.

It was a miracle.

Caplan pulled the van to the side of the road and turned off the ignition. The engine fell silent and various internal lights darkened.

Perkins chuckled. "Nice spot, Zach. But do you think you could, I don't know, park in the actual lot this time?"

"And make things easy on you?" He grinned. "Not a chance."

With his gaze locked on the store, Caplan climbed out of the vehicle. A fierce wind, cold as ice, blew into his face. Ignoring it, he produced a pair of binoculars and studied the parking lot. Amongst the vehicles, he saw sections of crunched pavement along with a number of dark stains. Probably blood splatter. Most likely, survivors had been gathered at the store when *it* arrived. Maybe they'd tried to fight, maybe they hadn't. It didn't matter.

They never stood a chance.

He turned to the storefront and adjusted the lenses. The glass doors and windows were still intact. A veritable wall of old advertisements and community notices—*Veal Cutlets dirt cheap at just $9.99/lb!, Lost Cat: Have You Seen My Whiskers?, The Bunt Roaches: Maine's Premiere Jam Band rocks the Upright Boogie Bar on Saturday, June 18 at 9:00 p.m.*—kept him from seeing the interior.

He lowered the binoculars but his gaze lingered on those signs, those fragments of the past. He missed the old days. Days when sales, pets, and concerts actually existed. Days when first-world problems—*why is the Internet soooo slow?*—had seemed ultra-important.

He'd never appreciated civilization until it was gone. And he doubted he was unique in that respect. The greatest of epochs were almost always hated by those lucky enough to live within them. They were only considered shiny and golden in hindsight. That is, after all hope had faded away, leaving nothing but stretching tentacles of despair and darkness. *Such is the strange fate of mankind*, he thought. *To have it all. To hate it all. To lose it all. To miss it all.*

Mills climbed out of the van. She clutched a collapsible bow, procured from the mangled wreckage of a sporting goods store, in her right hand. Even without fancy clothes or personal stylists she was a knockout. Her tanned body, outfitted in studded long boots, leggings, and a black leather jacket, was sculpted to perfection. Her hair, blonde and dirty, was fixed into boxer braids. And staring into her big blue eyes reminded him of swimming in an endless—and totally forbidden—sea.

Seventeen months ago, Mills had been widely known in the press by such names as *Billionaire Bailey* and *the Boozing Bad Girl*. Her supermodel looks, incredible wealth, and self-destructive antics had titillated folks on a daily basis. That, of course, was before *them*. Before HA-78 and the Holocene extinction. Before civilization had ceased to exist.

She hiked to Caplan's side. "See anyone?" She arched an eyebrow. "Or anything?"

A deep sense of awe and unease came over him. It felt like he was being swarmed by apparitions. By the ghosts of all those who'd died these last seventeen months. He shook his head and the odd feeling melted away. "No," he replied. "It looks deserted."

Returning the binoculars to the van, he grabbed his rifle. He slung the strap over his shoulder and checked the sheathed axes that hung from his belt.

She nodded at the rifle. "Just so you know, that's the last of your ammunition. Derek's almost out, too."

"I was afraid of that."

"On the bright side, you're packing some pretty good stuff. Those cartridges use tungsten penetrators in copper jackets." She brushed a few strands of hair out of her eyes. "In other words, they'll pierce body armor."

Mills had taken to the apocalypse like most people took to food and water. She lived it, breathed it. Maybe even, as Caplan suspected, enjoyed it.

Ducking down, he and Mills made their way toward the store. Perkins, armed with a long pistol, joined them at the halfway point. His hair, black and curly, whipped with the wind. His mocha-colored face, pockmarked and gaunt with hunger, reflected a mixture of blind hope and deep-seated desperation.

They stopped outside a pair of solid glass doors, lined with layers upon layers of ads and notices. Caplan tried the knobs. They were locked.

Reaching into a pocket, he grabbed hold of a small flashlight. He turned it on and aimed the beam between a pair of ads. The store contained several aisles of tall shelves. But it was too dark to see what—if anything—was on them.

"Allow me." Mills placed her bow on the ground and grabbed a set of lock picks from her jacket. In less than a minute, a soft click filled the air.

Caplan extinguished his light and grabbed one of the knobs. This time it turned easily, if a bit noisily, in his hand. He checked to make sure the others were ready. Then he pushed the door open.

Pistol drawn, Perkins rushed into the store and took up position on the left. With an arrow fitted into her bowstring, Mills passed through the doorframe and proceeded to scan the right side of the store. Caplan, rifle cradled in his arms, followed them inside and closed the door behind him.

For a moment, they stood absolutely still. Then Caplan flashed a series of hand signals. Spreading out, the trio headed deeper into the store, clearing the aisles and searching the back rooms.

After a thorough check, they joined up and paced along the aisles, stunned by what they saw. Tiny flies swarmed rotten cuts of meat. The dairy section smelled of spoiled milk. Vegetables, once fresh, had wilted into piles of mushy liquid. But the center aisles were an entirely different story.

"Crackers. Pretzels. And what have we got here?" Perkins ripped open a large bag and began stuffing ranch-flavored waffle-cut chips into his mouth. "Oh my God. I've died and gone to heaven."

Mills smiled. "Slow down or that might just happen."

He laughed, spitting out tiny particles. "Yeah, but what a way to go, right?"

"I can't argue with that." She rounded the bend and walked into the neighboring aisle. It was stocked with canned beans, fruits, and vegetables. Stuffing her bow under her armpit, she aimed her flashlight beam at the shelves. Then she picked up a can of lima beans and pulled off the ring tab. She gave the can a quick sniff. Her eyes bulged. Tipping the can to her mouth, she began to gobble up its contents.

Caplan watched her with a wry smile. "What happened to taking it slow?"

Caught in mid-swallow, she choked. Then she started laughing. "Okay, I deserved that." Wiping her lips, she held out the can. "Try some."

"No, thanks."

"Try some." Her lips curled into a small, flirty smile. "Or do I have to make you?"

His heart beat just a little faster, but he quickly forced it back into its regular rhythm. Mills was off-limits. Not because of anything she'd done, but because of that other *she*.

His stomach growled. He'd never cared for lima beans. But food was food and anyway, maybe starvation had changed things. Maybe foods he'd once despised—lima beans, mushrooms, olives, avocados, grapefruits—tasted different in this new world. And so he took the can and tipped it toward his mouth. A couple of beans, slimy and pungent, slipped down his throat. *Well, that settles it*, he thought. *Taste buds don't change.*

He handed the can back to her. "How can you eat this crap?"

"It's delicious."

"You mean gross."

"Suit yourself." She smiled one of her most dazzling smiles. "But you're missing out, Zach."

Don't I know it, he thought. While she finished the beans, he studied the many cans and other packages lining the shelves. "Ready to start moving this stuff?"

"Already?" She made a face. "You're no fun."

"Maybe not here. But elsewhere?" He gave her a sly smile. "That's a whole different story."

Indeed, Caplan was all-business when it came to the outside world. He rarely let his friends leave the cabin and then, only for supply runs. And he never let runs last longer than absolutely necessary. He was, after all, the leader. And in this day and age, that meant keeping his people safe above all else.

"Now, you've got me curious." A thoughtful look crossed her visage. "You know, I think I saw some boxes in the back."

Caplan and Perkins followed her to one of the back rooms. Inside, they found containers of all shapes and sizes. They grabbed as many as they could and returned to the aisles. Perkins started with the chips and crackers while Mills focused on the canned goods. Meanwhile, Caplan paced the store for a second time, aiming his beam down each and every aisle. He didn't find any ammunition. But he did see lanterns, batteries, knives, camping gear, clothes, and plenty of other goodies.

It was enough to make him want to jump into the air. To pump his fist like he'd just won the lottery. Because, in a way, that's exactly what had happened. The store changed everything. It solved their food problems, their supply shortages. It might even stop all that foolish talk about joining up with the Danter colony.

He retraced his steps and tossed his containers into one of the aisles. Then he filled two of them with boxes of cereal and oatmeal along with packaged breakfast bars. Grabbing the containers, he hiked to the doors.

A sudden coldness welled up in the pit of his stomach. It crept outward, stealing through his veins and blood vessels. He shivered involuntarily as a creepy feeling came over him. It was the sort of feeling one experienced in a dark, dank basement or while hiking through a graveyard on a black night. The sort of feeling that someone—or something—was watching. *Don't look*, he told himself. *You know there's nothing there so don't you dare look.* Of course, he looked.

A gray mist, vaporous and without much shape, floated in the semi-darkness. It was about ten feet away, compressing a bit before expanding back to its original size. It didn't look like a person. It didn't look like much of anything. But it was there. It was real.

Well, you finally lost your marbles, Zach, he thought with a sigh. *That ought to make the end of the world just a bit more interesting.*

The mist shifted backward, then forward. Abruptly, it morphed and an airy tentacle appeared at its side. The tentacle unfurled, stretching toward Caplan.

The ice in his veins and vessels got colder, harsher. He faced the gray mist head-on. Blinked and …

And nothing.

It was gone.

"Are you okay?" Mills asked.

The iciness faded. Caplan blinked again and looked around. He saw Mills carrying a heavy box of cans and packages. But he saw no sign of the gray mist. *What's worse?* he wondered. *Seeing a ghost? Or only thinking you've seen one?*

"Yeah, I'm fine," he replied. "Just tired."

"Poor baby." Smirking, she nodded at his cereal-laden containers. "Want me to carry those for you?"

"Nah." He hefted them with one hand and shot her a wink. "Leave the heavy stuff to me."

Spinning around, he walked to the glass doors, pushed them open, and strode outside. The wind, cold and hard, raked his skin like a giant claw. But he barely noticed it. Instead, he thought about what he'd seen, what he'd felt. It was so real, yet it couldn't have been real.

Maybe he really was tired. He'd barely eaten or slept for months. And every bit of energy he possessed had gone into keeping his little band of survivors alive. So, maybe that explained the mist. Maybe it was just a delusion of his tired, starving self.

"Zach." Mills' voice lacked its usual spunk and sassiness.

Turning around, he saw her looking above and beyond the store. Following her gaze, he saw something he'd hoped to never see again.

The dark hills just beyond the building transformed into a giant mass of shifting, thumping blackness. The mass surged upward and Caplan saw it clearly. It was a dire wolf, similar to the many reborn megafauna that now stalked the planet. But this wasn't the same species he'd fought in the Vallerio Forest all those months ago. This dire wolf was different. It was gigantic. It was monstrous.

It was one of *them*.

CHAPTER 2

Caplan's mind whirled, flashing back to seventeen months earlier. He recalled the first behemoth he'd ever seen, a genetically-engineered saber-toothed tiger of massive proportions. He recalled its lava-orange eyes, hotter than fire. He recalled its sharp, curving teeth. But most of all, he recalled its size. At some thirty feet in height, it had towered over him. He'd escaped with his life, but just barely.

"This way." Sliding behind a crushed car, he set his containers upon the ground. Then he grabbed hold of his rifle and peered over the dented roof.

The dire wolf stood at the edge of the forest behind the store. As far as Caplan knew, there was just one behemoth per species. Awhile back, he'd started giving them names in order to differentiate them from the normal-sized reborn megafauna. The saber-toothed tiger behemoth, for instance, was now known as Saber. As for this dire wolf, he'd nicknamed it Dire. Admittedly, it wasn't the most creative naming scheme in the world. But hey, it did the trick.

Dire's shoulders stretched some thirty feet off the ground. Its golden brown coat, streaked with black, blended into the shadows. Its eyes, lava-orange, burned holes through the darkness.

Thoughts flooded Caplan's brain as he gazed upon the ungodly creature. The events that had brought him to this moment had a dark, distant past, much of which had taken place long before he was born.

Some ten to eleven-thousand years ago, vast amounts of Pleistocene megafauna—giant animals—mysteriously died out across the globe. Mastodons, mammoths, giant ground sloths, saber-toothed tigers, short-faced bears, glyptodonts, and many other creatures all went extinct during this period, now known as the Quaternary extinction event.

Their deaths left gaping holes at the top of the food chain. The chain, along with the world's many and varied ecosystems, proceeded to unravel over thousands of years, leading to large-scale extinctions across the globe. This phenomenon had been known amongst the scientific community as the Holocene extinction. But what those scientists hadn't known seventeen months earlier was that the Holocene extinction was about to kick into high gear.

Only one person—James Corbotch—was ahead of the curve. For years, he'd experimented with ways to fix the food chain in the confines of the enormous Vallerio Forest. First, he'd introduced proxies—horses, bison, elephants, and others—in place of the original megafauna. When this failed, he'd set out to breathe life into the past. Using his fabulous wealth, he'd recruited the world's top scientists to a secret facility and set about recreating the entire spectrum of long-deceased Pleistocene megafauna.

For some unknown reason, these creatures exhibited unusual bloodlust. Even worse, a few of them began to experience enormous growth spurts. These new creatures, behemoths, set out across the Vallerio. They'd eventually broken free from the forest and, with behemoths from Corbotch's many other facilities around the world, set forth on an epic rampage.

Humanity might've—should've—stopped them. But one of Corbotch's other research teams had created a deadly viral compound called HA-78. Caplan and his friends, against their will, had actually been turned into asymptomatic carriers of the compound. That was why they'd fled to the North Maine Woods in the first place. To avoid people, to avoid infecting them. But it hadn't mattered. Corbotch had just released HA-78 into the general population, killing billions of people in the process.

Some had survived it. They'd survived the behemoths, too. But could they survive the death of nature? Theoretically, the reborn megafauna—the normal-sized ones, not the behemoths—should've fixed the food chain. In turn, that should've stopped the Holocene extinction dead in its tracks. But for some reason, that hadn't happened.

Caplan did see some evidence of a slowdown. However, the various ecosystems comprising the North Maine Woods continued to fail and he suspected that held true across the globe. All in all, the last seventeen months had been hell on Earth and the future looked even bleaker.

Mills slipped behind the vehicle and placed her containers on the pavement. She clutched her bow tightly, but didn't bother retrieving an arrow from her quiver.

The twin doors flew open and banged against their stoppers. Perkins strode outside a moment later, carrying a large container. "Hey guys," he called out. "Where'd you—?"

"Quiet," Caplan hissed. "And get down."

Perkins looked over his shoulder. A shudder ran through his arms. Carefully, he lowered the container to the ground. *What now?* he mouthed.

Not sure, Caplan mouthed back. *Hang on.*

Perkins hesitated, licked his lips. *Hurry.*

Caplan's mind raced. He hated leaving the food behind, but he saw no way to save it. *And all you ate was lima beans?* he thought. *For shame.*

"It's just sitting there," Mills whispered. "Why isn't it attacking us?"

"Good question." Caplan studied Dire's massive head, its claws, its teeth. Why had James Corbotch created behemoths anyway? Were they part of his plan to stop the Holocene extinction? "Maybe it can't see us."

"That—oh, no."

Following her gaze, he saw something streak away from the store. "Derek," he called out. "Stop."

But it was too late. Perkins was already scampering toward one of the wrecks. Dire's lips curled into something resembling a grin. Growling, it paced around the building.

The ground rumbled. Caplan lifted his rifle and took careful aim. Squeezing the trigger, he directed gunfire at the behemoth. But the armor-piercing bullets merely bounced off its thick hide.

Teeth bared, Dire bore down on Perkins. A wrecked car went airborne as the massive creature ripped through it.

Caplan's magazine ran empty. He reached into his pocket for another one. But that was it, the last of his ammunition.

Backing away, Perkins raised his long pistol. He squeezed off a few shots. Dire didn't stop, didn't even slow down. Instead, it opened its jaws and lunged.

At the last second, Perkins dove to his right. Enormous teeth grazed his waist before crunching into the pavement. He spun in mid-air like a helicopter blade and crashed with a sickening thud into an overturned SUV.

Caplan ran out from behind the vehicle with Mills just steps behind him. His powerful arms pumped hard and his breaths came short and fast. He ran with an awkward, strange gait. But he possessed quiet, antelope-like speed.

Dire lurched in his direction. But its jaws, embedded deep into the cracked pavement, kept it anchored. Grunting and growling, it fought to free itself.

Caplan skidded to a stop next to Perkins. The man's sweatshirt, stained and covered with dirt, hung in tatters. Entire layers of flesh had been sheared off his left side, exposing fat and muscle. He was losing blood fast and from multiple places.

Perkins' eyes fluttered open. He winced, clearly in great pain. "Where is ... and how long ...?" His jaw hung in the air for a moment, quivering. Then his eyes closed and he fell limp.

Caplan's gaze turned steely. Perkins needed serious medical attention, the type they couldn't hope to provide by themselves. Their best bet was to staunch the bleeding and get him back to the cabin. Hopefully, Morgan, the closest thing they had to a doctor, could help him.

He grabbed Perkins under the armpits. Mills took hold of his feet and together, they hurried toward the van.

Claws clicked on pavement. With a mighty yank, Dire pulled its teeth from the rubble and rolled onto its side.

"It's loose," Caplan shouted. "How much farther?"

Mills looked toward the van. "Too far."

"Then head for the store."

Shifting directions, they hustled toward the market. Dire's powerful muscles coiled up. Its massive eyes blinked rapidly. Then it jumped up and bounded across the parking lot.

They ran to the front doors and Caplan wrenched one of them open. Quickly, they dragged Perkins into the store. The door closed over just as the behemoth arrived. It stopped outside the structure and lowered its massive head to the ground, trying to peer through the windows.

Caplan and Mills set Perkins down behind a checkout counter and threw themselves to the floor. "What if it attacks the building?" she whispered.

Caplan studied the thin walls, the leaky ceiling. "Then we're in trouble."

Hunkering down, they waited. Waited for the creature to attack, to shatter the glass, to stick its long snout into the store. But nothing happened.

He chanced a look over the counter. A shadow shrouded the glass panes, but it was light in color. He hurried to the window and looked outside. Dire had backed up about twenty feet. Now, it paced back and forth, denting and cracking the pavement.

Mills gritted her teeth. "It's blocking us."

Indeed, the behemoth had cut them off from their van. And the other vehicles were far too damaged to run properly. Without wheels, they were as good as dead. Under different circumstances, Caplan would've waited out the creature. After all, the store had plenty of food and supplies. It could keep them alive for months. But they didn't have months. They needed to get back to the cabin—to Morgan—as quickly as possible.

Perkins' life depended on it.

CHAPTER 3

Date: Nov. 23, 2017, 9:56 p.m.; Location: North Maine Woods, ME

"This isn't working." Mills removed a bloodied, wadded-up shirt from Perkins' side and tossed it onto the checkout counter. Immediately, she pressed another shirt against the man's injuries. Within seconds, it was soaked through with blood. "What about a tourniquet?"

Perkins lay on his right side behind the counter, propped up by heavy bags of flour. His eyes were closed and his mocha skin had taken on a sickly yellow tinge. Despite their best efforts, he continued to bleed profusely. The risk of exsanguination, already high, was growing by the second.

"On his entire side?" Caplan shook his head. "Keep up the pressure. I'll be back in a second."

He ran down several aisles. Using his beam, he located a metal trash can, a bunch of *Cy Reed* comics, a lighter, a bottle of lighter fluid, a long wooden spoon, masking tape, and some rubbing alcohol. He returned to the counter and stuffed the comics into the trash can. After filling the lighter, he set the colorful pages ablaze. Smoke shot up to the ceiling, but there were no ringing bells, no sprays of water. Like so many other things in this world, the sprinkler system was dead.

"You're going to cauterize it?" Mills peeled another bloodied shirt off of Perkins' side and replaced it with a fresh one. "Is that safe?"

"No. But we've got to stop the bleeding."

He unsheathed an axe and wiped its blade on one of the clean shirts they'd gathered from the clothing aisle. Then he stuck the blade into the fire and waited for it to heat up.

Cauterization utilized protein denaturation. Essentially, the heated blade would cause Perkins' hydrophobic proteins to lose their solubility. They'd cluster together, binding tightly and stopping the blood flow. Even though it was effective, it was still a last-ditch type of treatment. The biggest problem with cauterization was that it raised the risk of infection to astronomical levels. While the heated blade would kill bacteria, it would also leave second and third degree burns in its wake, creating the ideal environment for even more bacteria.

"Tape that spoon into his mouth and get rid of all the cloth." He flipped the blade over and began to heat its other side. "Then hold him down. Whatever you do, don't let him move."

Grabbing the spoon, she slipped it into Perkins' open jaw. She wrapped one side of the spoon in masking tape, extended the tape behind his head, and proceeded to wrap the other side as well. She secured the spoon with even more tape. Then she removed the cloth, exposing Perkins' wounded side to fresh air. Finally, she pulled away the bags of flour and laid him flat on his back.

Blood poured out of the man's side, making it nearly impossible to see the actual wounds. The sheer scale of the injuries worried Caplan. Could Perkins survive that much blood loss? Could he survive the amount of cauterization necessary to stem it?

Caplan flipped the blade again and yet again. Finally, he pulled it away from the flame and nodded at Mills. Returning the nod, she grabbed hold of Perkins' shoulders.

He took a second to wipe away gobs of blood with a spare cloth. Then he pressed the blade against Perkins' side. Skin sizzled and the odor of burnt flesh filled his nostrils.

Perkins' eyelids shot open. Gasping, he tried to gnash his teeth, but the spoon kept him from doing so. His body attempted to wiggle and squirm. But Mills had a good grip on his shoulders and held him down.

Caplan kept the blade steady for a few seconds. Then he pulled it away, flipped it over, and pressed it against the man's side for a second time.

Perkins froze. His eyes rolled to the back of his head and he passed out.

Caplan pressed the blade against Perkins' side over and over again, reheating it several times in the process. He worked in sections, starting with the areas that emitted the most blood. Soon, the red liquid started to slow. And then it stopped altogether.

Afterward, he laid his blade on the floor. The air stank of blood and smoke. Perkins' side, black and crusty, looked like the inside of a barbecue grill. Even worse, his burnt flesh emitted a soft crackling noise. Like the crunching of charred paper.

Steeling himself, Caplan checked the man for a pulse.

Mills took a deep breath. "Well?"

"He's alive. For now."

Exhaling, she started to remove her hands from Perkins' shoulders.

"No, keep holding him." Caplan picked up the rubbing alcohol. He pulled off the cap and proceeded to pour the liquid over the injured flesh. Perkins' eyelids bolted open. Gasping and moaning, he tried to move without success before falling unconscious for a second time.

Mills gave Caplan an unsure look. He nodded and she pulled her hands away from the man's shoulders. "What now?" she asked.

"We need to get him home. But first, we need meds."

"What about Dire?" She glanced at the front doors. At the giant shadow that cast a light pall over the store's interior. "It's still out there."

"One step at a time."

While she watched Perkins, Caplan raced back into the aisles. He stuffed his pockets with bandages, aspirin, pain killers, and other medical supplies. Then he ran back to the counter. He and Mills quickly wrapped bandages around the entirety of Perkins' torso.

When they were finished, Mills sat back on her heels. "Maybe we can sneak out the back door. Head into the forest and circle around to the van."

"We might make it, but we'll never get away. It'll be on us as soon as we fire up the engine." He frowned. "Maybe we can find another car."

"There's nothing around here for miles. Believe me, I've practically memorized that old map. It's either the van or we hoof it."

"Then I guess it's the van."

She stood up and turned in a half-circle, casting a sad look around the store. "I really thought this was our break. I really thought this place was going to save us."

"Me too." Caplan glanced at the unconscious Perkins. The man's body was covered in bandages and surrounded by piles of blood-soaked clothing. The smell of burnt flesh hung heavy in the air. Nearby, the small fire crackled, licking at the edges of the metal trash can and throwing a little light onto the floor. He stared at it for a few seconds, entranced by its orange and yellow flames, its ever-shifting shape, its warm heat. "And maybe it still can."

"How?"

"Simple." He picked up the trash can. "As a distraction."

CHAPTER 4

Date: Nov. 23, 2017, 10:31 p.m.; Location: North Maine Woods, ME

Multiple fires erupted, spreading from aisle to aisle, helped along by rubbing alcohol and other incendiaries.

Smoke billowed outward as the fires joined together, creating a mid-sized blaze. The blaze expanded, spreading to the walls and ceiling. Within a few short minutes, it had turned into a full-blown inferno.

"Outside." Caplan coughed as black smoke filled his lungs. "Now."

Quietly, Mills opened the rear door and hurried out into a small section of parking lot. The rising inferno sent sharp rays of light across the pavement, illuminating a dented dumpster and scattered car parts.

Caplan threw Perkins over his shoulder. Then he followed Mills across the lot and into a patch of dead grass. They kept going, sprinting past the tree line and into the depths of the forest. Only then did they slow down and take stock of what had once been a vibrant ecosystem.

The trees, mostly black spruces, measured nearly one hundred feet tall. Some remained standing although a significant number had fallen prey to soil erosion and root rot. Large patches of speckled reddish-brown bark had peeled away from the trunks, making room for dark green moss. Branches, withered and pointing at the ground, were largely barren.

As they hurried through the area, Caplan fixed his gaze on the ground. It was hard and covered with twigs and branches. The little grass that remained was long and brown. He saw no signs of life. No nests, no tracks, no scat. Even bugs and spiders were nowhere to be seen. *Not much left in this world,* he thought. *Just death and monsters.*

"Look at that," Mills whispered under her breath. "It's just standing there. Like it's not even afraid of the fire."

Twisting his neck, Caplan saw the enormous dire wolf, bathed in shadow and light. It stood on all fours, growling at the inferno. Seeing it like that reminded him of Saber. It too had showed little respect for fire.

Multiple explosions pierced the air. Bits of fire scattered in all directions with many of them landing amongst the dead and dying vegetation. New blazes sprang up, filling the night sky with crackling cinders and dense smoke. *Correction*, he thought. *Make that death, monsters, and forest fires.*

From a certain standpoint, fire wasn't such a bad thing. It would clear away the dead trees and renew the soil. Maybe, just maybe, it would even bring life back to this desolate place. But at the moment, it was just another obstacle to face, another threat to him and his friends.

He shifted his grip on Perkins. The man twitched and groaned. Beads of sweat covered his rail-like body and nearly all of the rich color had drained out of his gaunt face. Suddenly, his eyes popped open. His cheeks puffed in and out as he took a few deep breaths. "The keys," he wheezed. "Where are the keys?"

That's more like it, Caplan thought. It was good to see Perkins moving and talking again. "Don't worry." His free hand patted his pocket. "I've got them."

"What about my passport?"

"Passport?"

"The plane … I can't miss it. I …" Perkins' features twisted with confusion. "I need to catch my plane."

Caplan clenched his jaw. This was no physiological recovery. This was something else. Something dark and foreboding. The last rays of a setting sun, so to speak. A sun that, without Morgan's help, would rise no more.

He doubled his speed. Mills matched the pace and after another minute or so, he caught a glimpse of the road beyond the dying spruces. The mere sight of the dilapidated pavement warmed his heart while chilling him at the same time. The road was their ticket home. It would lead them back to the cabin, back to Morgan and the others. At the same time, this simple mixture of tar and compressed gravel served as a haunting reminder of all that had been lost. Of a once-mighty civilization, now shattered to pieces.

They hustled out of the forest. Turning left, they saw the van, still parked alongside the road.

"That's strange," Mills said.

"What's strange?"

"Dire. I think it's ... well, I'm not sure what it's doing."

To his left, Caplan saw the massive dire wolf striding around the back of the building. Growling, it stared at the flames. "Maybe it likes the heat?"

"Maybe." Kneeling down, she waited for Dire to circle around to the front of the building. As soon as its back was turned, she darted to the van. Opening the rear doors, she hopped into the cargo area.

Caplan checked the behemoth and saw it was still focused on the fire. Swiftly, he carried Perkins to the vehicle and placed the man into the cargo area with Mills. Then he closed the doors and climbed into the front seat.

Mills glanced out a side window. "Look at its paws."

Still circling the fire, Dire crossed the front of the store. And Caplan now saw what Mills had seen. Indeed, the massive creature was stomping at the edges of the fire, extinguishing the flames and sending puffs of grayish smoke into the starry sky. *Well, how about that?* he thought. *A firefighting behemoth.*

Dire left the store and trotted to the edge of the parking lot. Carefully, it began stomping out the burning vegetation.

Caplan inserted the key into the ignition. He turned it and the engine sputtered to life. The behemoth rotated its head. Its lava-orange eyes knifed through the darkness.

He threw the vehicle into a one hundred and eighty-degree turn. Then he pushed his boot against the accelerator. For a couple of tense seconds, his eyes were glued to the rearview mirror.

Dire twisted around to chase them. Just then, a new fire sprung up around the gas pumps. The pumps exploded and flames spat into the air.

"Whoa," Mills said.

Fire rained down on the massive dire wolf. A normal-sized creature would've fled for safety. But not Dire. It started to battle the flames even as its thick fur burned brightly for all to see.

Caplan was awestruck. The behemoths had withstood mankind's deadliest weapons. And this one hadn't even flinched at the sight of fire, easily one of the most destructive forces of nature. What could possibly stop these massive beasts?

Nothing, he realized. *Absolutely nothing.*

CHAPTER 5

Date: Nov. 24, 2017, 12:06 a.m.; Location: North Maine Woods, ME

"He stopped breathing," Mills whispered frantically.

The cabin was close, less than a mile away. But the distance felt more like a light year. "Do you know CPR?" Caplan asked.

She shook her head.

"Push hard and fast in the center of his chest. Do it thirty times." He waited for her to finish, checking her form in the rearview mirror. "Now, tilt his head back. That's good. Lift the chin and pinch his nose. Cover his mouth with yours and blow until his chest rises. Do it twice."

She followed the instructions. Afterward, she checked his mouth. "Nothing," she said.

"Do it again." While she continued CPR, he pressed harder on the accelerator. They'd left the main road a few miles back and were now zipping through a dense section of coniferous trees.

He skirted around a fallen spruce and past a patch of moss-covered rocks. Ahead, he spotted a large wood cabin in the center of a sizable clearing. It was almost completely dark, thanks to thick curtains hanging in the windows. A light trail of smoke spat out of a short chimney. Trashcans and other containers, partially filled with rainwater, surrounded the structure. A Rexto 419R3 corporate helicopter, heavily dented and covered with scorch marks, sat off to one side.

He drove up to the front door, hopped out, and ran to the back. "How is he?"

"He just started breathing." Mills grabbed Perkins under the armpits. Carefully, she lowered him into Caplan's arms. Then she ran to the cabin and opened the front door, causing soft light to fill the clearing. "Amanda," she barked. "We need help."

Caplan lifted the unconscious Perkins over his shoulder and made a beeline for the cabin. A blazing fire, warm and bright, greeted him as he raced through the front door. Off to one side, Brian Toland lounged on a couch, a paperback book clutched in his grubby hands. Tricia Elliott sat in a wood chair, head down, mending clothes with thread and needle.

"You didn't find any food, did you?" Toland's voice, annoying and abrasive, filled the cabin. "You know, this is starting to become obnoxious. While you're out there playing games, the rest of us are—"

"Shut up, Brian." Mills pointed toward Perkins' bedroom. "Amanda's in there."

Caplan carried Perkins into the bedroom and saw Morgan. The apocalypse hadn't been particularly kind to her. Or rather, she hadn't been particularly kind to herself. Her once-perfect posture had turned into awkward slouching. Dirt and grime caked her skin. Her long blonde hair looked like it had been shocked with a brutal jolt of electricity. Only her eyes, blue and sharp as ever, hinted at any semblance to the woman he'd once loved.

"Put him there." Morgan pointed at the bed. "Tricia, I need you."

Caplan did as she said. "How can I help?"

"By leaving." Her voice was cold, clinical. Like usual.

He nearly ran into Elliott on his way out. She recoiled, as she always did when someone came too close to her. He gave her a wide berth to pass. Then he strode into the common room and closed the door behind him.

Seventeen months ago, Caplan and his little group had flown the Rexto to the cabin in their ultimately vain effort to avoid spreading the HA-78 virus. The cabin, along with the accompanying land, had been in his family's possession for decades. He'd visited it often as a kid and could still recall collecting water from the nearby stream, beating dust out of the rugs, and gathering firewood from the forest. Ahh, those were the days. Now, the stream had dried up, necessitating their dependence on rainwater. And beating dust out of the rugs didn't seem so important in the face of starvation. But hey, at least there was firewood. In fact, with so many dead trees around, it was their most abundant resource.

"What happened to Derek?" Toland smirked. He was a grizzled older man who'd once found work as an author. He wore thick glasses, which he protected with his life. His face, once fat, was now quite thin. But it was difficult to tell under his scraggily gray beard. "Did he get a boo boo?"

Mills exhaled. "A behemoth tried to eat him."

"Well, at least something's eating around here."

"Okay, that's it. You're—"

"Let's go outside." Caplan tugged her sleeve. "I need some fresh air."

She glared at Toland. Then she followed Caplan out into the clearing, slamming the door behind her. "Can you believe that guy?" she seethed. "Next time he complains about hunger, I'm going to feed him a knuckle sandwich."

He smiled.

"He doesn't even help out," she continued. "Tricia sews. And Amanda tries to help in her own way. But not him. He just sits around, complaining. He's dead weight, Zach."

"Yeah. But he's our dead weight."

She fell silent.

He ventured away from the cabin. Lifting his nose, he sniffed the air. Once upon a time, the clearing had smelled of blooming flowers, morning dew, and fresh cut grass. But now, all he smelled was death. Dead grass, dead trees, dead animals, dead everything. *Nothing like the smell of death to get you going in the morning,* he thought with a dark chuckle. *That and body odor, of course. Can't forget the body odor.*

The stench of body odor hung heavy around the cabin. It wasn't that they didn't have ways of cleaning themselves. Indeed, he'd fixed up a pretty ingenious solar-heated shower many months earlier. No, the real issue was getting their hands on soap, shampoo, and deodorant.

Mills paced back and forth across the starlit clearing, blowing off steam. Then she produced a deck of playing cards. "High Thirty-One?"

"I thought you'd never ask." They sat down on the patchy brown grass and she dealt out six cards. He picked up three of them. *Two of Hearts, Ace of Clubs, Six of Clubs,* he thought. *Not bad.*

The goal of High Thirty-One was to get as close as possible to thirty-one points. Aces and face cards counted for eleven and ten points, respectively. All other cards were counted at face value. The trick was that points could only be added together if they came from the same suit. So, two face cards and an ace in separate suits only yielded a total of eleven points. But in the same suit, that hand was worth thirty-one points.

He discarded the Two of Hearts and drew a new card. *Nine of Clubs*, he thought with a hidden smile. *This game's in the bag.*

Besides books and each other, cards served as their only source of entertainment. Not that Caplan minded. The one bright spot of this new world was that it had brought an end to television, video games, computers, cell phones, and social media. His little band of survivors actually talked to each other, did things together. He stole a look at Perkins' window and caught a glimpse of Morgan's shadow. Well, most of them anyway.

Mills drew and discarded. On his next turn, Caplan knocked on the ground instead of drawing a new card. She arched an eyebrow and drew one last card. Discarding it, she held out her hand. "Fourteen," she said.

Caplan did the same. "Twenty-six."

"You got lucky."

He adopted a snooty expression. "I make my own luck."

"Do you now?" Smiling lightly, she handed the deck to him. He dealt out another hand and they continued to play. After a few games, she glanced toward the cabin. "I hate this."

"Hate what?"

"Waiting."

"If we're waiting, that means he's still okay."

"I know. It's just ..." She trailed off. "What if she can't help him?"

"Then we'll find someone who can."

"Does the Danter colony have a doctor?"

"Yes. Sandy Pylor. If the roads were better, I would've taken Derek straight to her." He shrugged. "Obviously, I may still take him to her."

Danter was located twenty miles north of the cabin. But the roads leading that way were a veritable mess. Navigating them safely could take hours.

Besides, Caplan wasn't all that eager to go to Danter. Roughly three-quarters of its four-hundred residents had passed away during the last year and a half. As a result, Mayor Mike Zelton had begun to recruit new people to the little colony. And the last thing Caplan wanted was to endure yet another sales pitch.

Making matters even more difficult, he liked Mayor Zelton. In fact, he liked many of Danter's residents. He'd gotten to know them while vacationing at the cabin over the years. By and large, they were good people and a part of him hated to reject their entreaties. But what choice did he have? Above all else, he had to protect his people.

Ever since Mayor Zelton's first sales pitch, a debate had raged within the cabin. Namely, should they stay put? Or should they join up with Danter? Caplan led the stay-put faction. Their survival, he believed, was all that mattered. And the best way to survive this dangerous world was to remain in the middle of nowhere, hidden away from monsters, animal and human alike.

Morgan led the opposing faction, contesting mere survival wasn't enough. They had a greater responsibility to what remained of mankind. A responsibility to keep fighting. To cure HA-78. To defeat the behemoths. To end the

Holocene extinction. And they couldn't do that by secluding themselves in the middle of nowhere.

Mills, Perkins, and Toland saw fit to join Caplan's faction. Elliott, surprisingly enough, had thrown her lot in with Morgan. Since Caplan's faction had the numbers, their will prevailed. But Morgan wasn't happy about it. In fact, the debate had driven an enormous—and possibly permanent—wedge between them.

Mills looked thoughtful. "Guess I'd better pack a bag. You know … just in case."

He shook his head. "No matter what happens, I need you here, protecting the cabin."

"We stick together, remember? No matter what happens, we stick together."

Ahh, his own words, used against him. Truthfully, sticking together was the optimal survival strategy. But so was staying out of sight. If he had to drive Perkins to Danter, he'd prefer to do it alone, to leave the others in the safe confines of the cabin.

But deep down, he realized that would never happen. If he left, Mills would insist on coming. Morgan and Elliott, already eager to leave, would join them. And there was no way Toland would stay behind by himself. No, they'd all drive off together. And just like that, their fates would change. "We could die out there," he said.

"Better together than apart."

He exhaled. "Let's just finish this hand, okay?"

She drew, shuffled her cards, and discarded. Then she looked away. "I keep thinking about the store."

He picked up a card from the pile and immediately discarded it. "What about it?"

"Why was it still standing?"

"Luck?"

"Dire didn't attack the store even when we were inside it. Almost as if …"

"As if what?"

"As if it was using the store as a trap."

Numerous animals, such as cougars, acted as ambush predators. And behemoths were far smarter than them. "It's possible," he conceded. "If you're right, it raises another question. Why do behemoths care so much about us?"

"What do you mean?"

"James told us the reborn megafauna would end the Holocene extinction. It hasn't worked, but at least I get what he was trying to do. However, I can't figure out why he created behemoths. As far as I can tell, they aren't fulfilling any ecological niche. All they do is prey on people."

She picked up another card and added it to her hand. "Maybe that's the point. Maybe they're supposed to keep us in check."

"Maybe. But that's not all that bugs me. If James wanted to dial back time ten or eleven thousand years, he should've stopped with the reborn megafauna. Behemoth-sized creatures haven't walked this planet since the dinosaurs went belly-up."

He drew and discarded several more cards. Then he glanced at his hand. He held a Seven of Hearts, an Eight of Hearts, and a Jack of Diamonds. After four draws, he'd accumulated just fifteen points. So, he drew again and picked up a Five of Diamonds. After a moment of hesitation, he decided to rebuild in Diamonds and discarded the Seven of Hearts.

Mills snatched it up and discarded a Two of Hearts. *Not good*, he thought, reaching for the deck. *I need a miracle.*

The cabin door banged open. Morgan, looking tired and bedraggled, walked outside.

"Well?" Mills asked, rising to her feet. "How is he?"

Morgan didn't say a word. But her teary eyes and drawn cheeks spoke volumes.

Perkins was dead.

CHAPTER 6

Date: Nov. 24, 2017, 8:14 a.m.; Location: North Maine Woods, ME

I don't know how we're going to make it without you, Caplan thought as he stared at the thick plank of wood positioned at the edge of the clearing. *But we will. That's a promise.*

He shivered. Stuffing his hands into his pockets, he watched his breath form little clouds in front of his face. He hadn't slept much. And the little sleep he'd gotten had been plagued by bad dreams. Dreams of ghostly apparitions and behemoths. Dreams of Perkins, of blood, of the horrible pain he'd inflicted upon the man. And all of this backed by surreal images of a dying world. A world of vast wastelands, modern ruins, and charred, cracked streets lined with corpses.

The cabin door banged against the stopper. Mills walked outside. She carried steaming mugs in either hand and a portable radio under an armpit. Wordlessly, she handed a mug to him. Then she set the radio on the ground and took a few halting sips from the second mug.

The faint aroma of coffee filled Caplan's nostrils. When they'd first arrived at the cabin, he'd mixed up daily batches of fresh pine needle tea. The concoction, rich in Vitamins A and C, was both healthy and delicious. But when the trees began to die, he'd stopped making it. Now, they drank filtered rainwater, flavored with whatever they managed to scrounge up from campgrounds, homes, and stores.

He sipped the coffee. It was beyond weak. But hey, it was hot and at least it had *some* flavor. "How are your arms?"

"Sore. But my hands are worse." She studied her calloused, swollen fingers. "What I wouldn't give for a manicure right now."

A few hours ago, they'd dug a grave for Perkins at the edge of the clearing. Then they'd fashioned a gravestone out of wood and Caplan had carved the man's name upon it. They'd gathered the others and each of them—even Elliott— had said a few words on his behalf. It wasn't much, wasn't nearly enough.

But it would have to do.

"Are the others up?" he asked.

She nodded. "Brian's reading. Tricia's fixing breakfast. And I'm sure you can guess what Amanda's doing."

He glanced at the cabin. The curtains were thrown wide open, welcoming in early rays of sunlight. As such, he could see Morgan sitting at his father's old desk. A large logbook, made of fine leather, was spread out before her. It was slightly charred, but still very much intact. "Working on something none of us will ever understand?"

"Ding, ding, ding!" She took a long draught from her mug. "Congratulations, Mr. Caplan. You're our grand prize winner!"

"Yeah? What's my prize?"

She reached into the pocket of her leather jacket and pulled out a small object. With a wink, she tossed it to him.

He caught the brightly-colored plastic package. His eyes widened and his stomach emitted a low growl. "How ...?" he asked. "When ...?"

"Last night, before Dire. They were racked near the checkout counter and I remembered you liked them."

"Like?" He ripped open the plastic and pulled out a large Chidler's Peanut Butter Cup, wrapped in metallic orange paper. "You mean love."

She laughed and time careened to a halt. Her laughter was wonderful. It made him feel warm and toasty on the inside. Like maybe this world wasn't so bad after all. Like maybe it had more to offer than just death and despair.

But the moment was doomed before it even began. And as it faded away, awkwardness descended on the clearing. He glanced at Morgan again, wondering if she was watching them. But no. She was hunched over the desk, still reading the logbook, still scribbling away in its margins.

He stuffed the candy into his mouth and his taste buds exploded with glee. Textured hard chocolate, gooey peanut butter … this was, as far as he was concerned, the absolute pinnacle of culinary delight.

He grabbed a candy from the bag and tossed it to Mills. Catching it, she arched an amused eyebrow. "Are you sure?"

"No." He grinned. "So, eat it fast."

She unwrapped the paper and bit off a piece of chocolate and peanut butter. Her eyes rolled to the sky and she looked like she might faint. "Wow," she said. "That's just … wow."

The door banged against the stopper again. Elliott appeared, bowls of hot, watery stew in her hands. Her close-clipped hair, once dyed canary yellow, had long ago reverted to a light brownish color. A tight red sweatshirt and jeans covered her skeletal form. Her eyes, gleaming with almost inhuman intensity, flitted constantly in all directions.

She offered them the bowls and, without a word, marched back into the cabin. Not because she was angry. But because that was her way. She was quiet and stuck to herself. Her problems ran deep as Caplan had discovered awhile back. One night, her screams had awoken him and he'd raced into her room only to find her fast asleep, evidently suffering from night terrors. But not in her bed. No, she was curled up on the hard floorboards in the far corner of her room. The following night, he'd peeked in again and saw her in the exact same spot, trembling and distraught.

He'd never said a word about it, not to her or to anyone else. They all had problems stemming from the events of the last seventeen months. And those problems, like it or not, weren't going away anytime soon.

Mills finished the candy. Then she sat down and began eating spoonfuls of stew. Meanwhile, she played with the radio, causing static to fill the air.

Caplan groaned. "Can't that wait?"

"We always listen for traffic at breakfast."

"Believe me, I know. It's just …" He exhaled. "We never hear anything."

"We will."

"You can't really believe that."

"I have to."

"Just be happy we're alive." He waved a hand at the cabin. "We've got shelter, water, a little food. Trust me. This is as good as it gets."

"God, I hope not."

"Hey, it's better than dying." The words left his mouth before he could reel them back in. Lips tight, he glanced at the wooden headstone.

Mills offered a small shrug. "Maybe. But not by much."

He recalled his little song. *Forget thriving*, he sang in his head. *Just keep on surviving*. He thought she agreed with that point of view. But maybe not.

Sitting down, he dove into his stew. It contained little chunks of precooked sausage. He gobbled up this rare treat with enthusiasm. When he was finished, he set his bowl upon the ground and wiped his lips. His stomach started to growl, eager for more food.

For the next ten minutes, Mills worked the radio, listening for voices amongst the static. Finally, she silenced the device. Raising the bowl to her lips, she drained the rest of her breakfast. Then she swiped her finger along the plastic surface and licked it clean. "I still can't believe he's gone," she said with a furtive look at Perkins' grave.

"Me either." Left unsaid was a cold, hard truth. Perkins had been a hard worker and a good hunter. His loss was going to hurt them in more ways than one.

"It's my fault."

Caplan sighed, shook his head. "No."

"I saw it first. I should've warned you guys right away. But I hesitated."

"And I should've bided my time, circled the store before going inside. Derek should've kept his cool instead of sprinting into the parking lot. The others should've been there with us, helping out."

She nodded silently. Then she cocked her head. "Do you hear that?"

"Hear what?"

"I think she's referring to me." The masculine voice, downtrodden yet still boisterous as a carnival barker, ripped across the landscape.

Caplan whirled around. A short, muscular man with charcoal-colored skin and close-cropped black hair stood at the edge of the clearing. His name was Noel Ross and he wasn't really a carnival barker. Before the fall of civilization, he'd owned an ice cream shop in the middle of tiny Danter. But he was full of frenetic charm, a trait that served him well in his current role as Deputy Mayor.

Caplan still recalled the first time he'd barged into Ross' shop, his youthful eyes all aglow. The wonderful scents of chocolate, strawberry, and vanilla had swirled in his nostrils. Stammering, he'd thrown down some change and ordered a scoop of chocolate, laced with Chidler's Peanut Butter Cups. He'd expected a small dish for his pittance of money. But Ross, because he was that kind of guy, dished him out the equivalent of a feast.

"Hey, Noel." Caplan rose to his feet. "I appreciate the visit. But we're just not interested."

Ross strode across the clearing. "You might be when you hear what I have to say."

"Did you walk here?" Mills asked.

"No, I drove. I left my car back at the road." Ross stopped in front of the makeshift tombstone. A long sigh left his lips. "When did this happen?"

"Last night."

"Was it *them*?"

Mills and Caplan exchanged looks. "I don't know who *them* is," Caplan said. "But Dire sliced him up on a supply run. We tried to save him, but it wasn't enough."

"I see. I'm sorry for your loss."

"Thanks." Caplan gave the man a curious look. "So, who's *them*?"

Ross tore his gaze away from the tombstone. "Four days ago, a bunch of soldiers appeared in Danter. They came out of the woods, out of buildings. There must've been a hundred of them, all packing heat. They had us surrounded before we could get our hands out of our pockets."

Caplan sensed a slight waver in the man's voice. "What'd they want?"

"Food and supplies." He sighed. "They disarmed us and gave us a list. Then they took five of our people, including Mike, away at gunpoint. We've got until the first of the month to get them what they want. Otherwise …"

He trailed off, but the implication was obvious. If Danter failed, Mayor Zelton and the other four residents were as good as dead. Caplan winced internally at the thought.

Zelton was a classic small-town politician, well-versed in the art of pressing flesh and kissing babies. But it wasn't all for show. There was a genuine kindness beneath the façade, as Caplan had discovered many years ago.

Mills cleared her throat. "What are you going to do?"

"These people are vultures. They'll blackmail us forever if we let them. So, we're going to pretend to comply. When their guard is down, we'll strike back." He gave them a meaningful look. "But to do that, we're going to need help."

"I'm sorry about Mike," Caplan said. "I really am. But count us out."

"Being alone doesn't make you safe. What if they come for you next?"

"They won't find us."

"They might." He sighed. "Numbers matter in this new world, Zach. A big population is the only way to stand up to bullies."

"A big population also gets you noticed. And being noticed is tantamount to death." He shook his head. "Staying small is a much better strategy."

Ross cast his gaze at the tombstone. "How'd that strategy work out for Derek?"

Caplan's gaze hardened. His fingers curled into fists.

"Sorry," Ross said quickly. "I didn't mean that."

His fingers stiffened, then slowly relaxed. "I know."

"What if you just help us out for this one fight?" Ross asked. "After that, you can come back here."

"I'm not going to put my friends in danger."

"I guess I can respect that." Ross glanced at the sky. "Well, I'd best be going. I've got a lot of ground to cover today. You folks be safe now."

Turning around, he strode across the clearing. Moments later, he vanished into the forest.

Mills watched him with an arched eye. "I hate to admit it, but he's got a point. If those soldiers come this way, we won't be able to stop them."

"They won't come here. Blackmailing a tiny group like ours would be a waste of time. They're better off picking on the Danters of the world."

A cold breeze swept through the clearing, causing Mills to don a pair of gloves. "I hate to bring this up. But without Derek, it's just us tonight. Coupled with Noel's news, we might want to stay close to home. I was looking at our maps and saw a small cabin we haven't hit yet."

"Tonight's a hunting night," Caplan said.

"We're out of ammo."

"You've still got your bow."

"Sure. But what about you?"

"Don't worry about me." Ignoring his still-growling stomach, he rose to his feet. "I don't need a gun to hunt."

CHAPTER 7

Date: Nov. 24, 2017, 9:05 p.m.; Location: North Maine Woods, ME

Caplan crouched on a thick branch, his unblinking eyes fixed on the dark, dying forest. Big game was nearly impossible to find these days so he searched for rabbits and squirrels. But he wasn't picky. He'd take chipmunks, snakes, anything really. Anything to alleviate the gnawing hunger that slowly consumed him and his friends.

He shivered as a stiff breeze sprang up from the north. Winter was getting close. A harsh New England-style winter that would leave the landscape drenched with snow, ice, and freezing temperatures. Everything—salvaging and hunting included—was about to get harder, tougher.

But he was determined to stick it out, to make it work. At least they had the cabin and the van. At least they had their meager supplies and food. *Still, Florida would be pretty sweet right now,* he thought. *No, wait. Hawaii!*

Black flies, attracted to the carbon dioxide in his breath, swarmed Caplan's face. Only a mask of mud, topped with a thin layer of pine resin harvested from a still-living tree, kept them at bay. More mud and pine resin covered his black field jacket, cargo pants, wool socks, and sturdy boots, effectively masking his scent.

At first, thoughts of Perkins and Zelton consumed his brain. But as the night slipped by, he found himself thinking of *her*. He still missed Morgan sometimes, most of all at moments like this one. Misty, quiet moments where the world seemed almost normal. Where the horrors that now stalked the earth felt more like distant nightmares than everyday reality. Why'd they have to fight like this? Why couldn't she recognize the futility inherent in trying to fix an irreparably broken world?

A tiny rustle filled his ears. Twisting his head, he saw Bailey Mills. The former socialite rested in the crook of a fungus-covered eastern white pine tree. She clutched her collapsible bow in her right hand. Her left hand reached into her jacket pocket and pulled out a small chunk of beef jerky, a sizable portion of her evening rations. She gave it a good, long look. Then she rubbed it carefully in her hands and took a small bite. She chewed slowly, deliberately, savoring the taste. When she was finished, she lifted the rest of the meat to her nostrils and inhaled it. A smile flooded her visage.

Caplan's belly rumbled softly and he started to reach into his cargo pants for a bite of food.

A branch cracked. Dry leaves crunched.

Snapping to attention, he shifted on the balls of his feet. A sliver of moon hung in the sky, providing a bit of light to his otherwise dark surroundings. It was nighttime, a few hours before midnight. Not that it mattered. Time had little meaning these days.

To the west, he spotted the lumbering gait of a large creature. A woolly mammoth to be precise, one of the normal-sized ones. But that didn't mean it could be taken lightly. The very fact it had survived this long was a testament to its strength and killing prowess.

His gaze turned downward as the beast passed about ten feet beneath his position. Its curving tusks were chipped and cracked. Its hide was scarred in numerous places. Flakes of dried blood coated its coarse fur. Like all of Corbotch's reborn megafauna, it was clearly driven to fight. To maul anything and everything it faced.

He shot Mills a quick look. She gave him a tight-lipped nod. He knew what she was thinking. Woolly mammoths were dangerous, unpredictable opponents. But they were rich in meat and their hides could be used to make all sorts of things. Simply put, the beast was an opportunity that couldn't be missed. But how to take it without guns? He touched his axes and an idea came to him.

He flashed her a hand signal. Then he dropped to the ground, landing quietly on some grass. Stealing forward, Caplan grabbed the mammoth's short tail with both hands. He swung his legs up, bracing them against the beast's rear end. It jolted and twisted around. Its trunk lifted to the sky and it trumpeted out a series of angry notes.

Gritting his teeth, Caplan fought to maintain his balance. Once he'd stabilized his footing, he removed his left hand from the tail, grabbed one of his axes, and began to chop away at the beast's legs. The hide was stiff and tough but soon gave way to the sharp blade.

The mammoth howled as the axe sliced through a layer of fat and nicked one of its tendons. Rearing up, it bucked wildly. Caplan went airborne and only his strong grip on the tail kept him from being thrown off completely.

His body reversed course, thudding against the mammoth's backside. Grunting softly, he lifted his left hand. Still holding the axe, he wrapped the tips of his fingers around the tail.

The mammoth, sensing an opening, bucked harder and faster. Caplan fought to get his footing, but the beast's frenzied movements made that impossible. Slowly, his sweat-drenched fingers began to slip.

A soft thump sounded out and the mammoth froze in place. Taking advantage, Caplan kicked his feet up, replanting them on the beast's backside. In the process, he noticed a still-quivering arrow sticking out of its forehead.

Glancing up, he saw Mills, bow in hand, leap onto a rickety branch. She sprinted forward and leapt again, crossing to the branches of a second eastern white pine tree with graceful ease. She ran a little farther and then grabbed an arrow from her quiver. Fitting it into the bowstring, she took aim and let it fly. The projectile soared straight and true, slamming into the mammoth's skull at top speed.

Caplan wasted no time. Swinging low, he hacked away at the beast's legs. The hide ripped wide open in various spots, spilling fatty tissue and blood onto the soil. The beast began to sag.

After a few more chops, he jumped clear and the mammoth flopped onto the ground. Still defiant, it blurted out notes of fury.

He pulled the second axe from his belt. Mills climbed down from the tree, produced a sharp arrow, and joined him.

Without a word, they attacked the mammoth's neck until it fell still.

Afterward, they gazed upon the bloodied carcass. Caplan's heart thumped softly against his chest as his adrenaline began to fade. With Perkins gone, he didn't feel much like celebrating. But the mammoth, with its bounty of fresh meat, was still a major victory in a world sorely lacking in them. They could preserve the meat via drying, curing, and smoking techniques. With careful rationing, it would feed them for weeks. Of course, that didn't solve the longer-term food problem. But it bought them time.

Forget thriving, he sang silently. *Just keep on surviving.*

CHAPTER 8

Date: Nov. 24, 2017, 11:18 p.m.; Location: North Maine Woods, ME

Wrinkling his nose, Caplan went to work cleaning and harvesting the carcass. Meanwhile, Mills scaled the lower limbs of a black ash tree. She grabbed hold of their plastic sled, originally designed for ice fishing, and lowered it to the ground. She dragged it back to the carcass and they loaded it up with meat. Then they cached the rest of the dead animal in a shallow hole.

She grabbed a rope on one side of the sled. "Nice takedown. Where'd you learn to do that?"

He grabbed the second rope and helped her pull. The sled jerked and began to slide over dirt and dry brush. "From the history books. That's how some African warriors used to hunt elephants."

The wind picked up speed until it felt like sheets of ice were slamming into his mud-covered cheeks. His strength waned and his arms started to hurt.

Moonlight filtered through the overhanging branches, casting long shadows along the ground. Piles of decaying leaves covered the hard soil. A small brook, filled with scarce amounts of iron-gray water, weaved in and out of the sparse vegetation. Fallen trees, hollowed out and rotting away, crisscrossed the brook.

After a long walk, they exited the forest and dragged the sled onto a paved road. Mills released her rope and hiked to the van. She hopped into the cargo area, shook out a plastic tarp, and laid it down. Then she and Caplan proceeded to load the meat into the vehicle.

After they were finished, she studied the rope burns on her fingers. "My hands look like hamburger meat," she complained. "Can't we park a little closer next time?"

He shook his head. "Too many trees."

"Then I say we hunt right here from now on."

"That sounds great." He cracked a grin. "Now, you just have to convince the animals to cooperate."

"We use the roads." She faked an annoyed look. "Why can't they?"

Occasionally, they'd spot a squirrel or rabbit hanging out on the side of the road. But most animals, especially the larger ones, stuck to the depths of the forest.

They gathered up the sled and dragged it back to the carcass. For the next hour, they hauled meat to the van. Then they tossed the sled into the rear, climbed into the front seats, and began the short drive back to the cabin.

Mills spent most of the ride lounging in the passenger seat, knee-high boots propped up on the dashboard. Her head was turned toward her window, her gaze fixed on the outside world. "The sky is nice tonight," she remarked as they drew close to home.

"It's okay."

"That's the one thing that hasn't changed. Well, that and your feelings toward lima beans."

He laughed.

She glanced at him. "I like when you laugh."

A tingling sensation ran down his spine. *Say something,* he thought as the seconds ticked by. *Anything!* "You know who had a great laugh? Derek."

"Yes. Yes, he did." Shifting to the window, she resumed gazing at the sky.

Nice one, Zach, he chided himself. *But next time, just for kicks, could you make things a bit more awkward?*

A few minutes later, he pulled up in front of the cabin. The thick curtains were pulled shut. But the windows still glowed and flickered.

"Looks like someone made a fire." Mills kicked her boots off the dashboard and sat up. "That's going to feel so awesome."

Caplan agreed. He was cold, hungry, and exhausted. A fire would help with one of those things. Maybe a second one since they could use it to smoke the meat. And maybe even the third one if he slept on the couch. He used to do that back in the early days. He'd stay awake as long as possible, waiting for Morgan to finish working. And when he could take no more, he'd curl up under a blanket on the old cushions. When had he stopped doing that anyway? Ah, well, the exact date didn't matter. What mattered was that at some point he'd stopped waiting for her. Instead, he'd gone off to bed by himself and she'd joined him when she was finished. And then they'd started fighting about whether to go to Danter or not and she'd stopped coming to bed altogether.

A lot had changed over the last seventeen months. He glanced at Mills. A lot, indeed. "I think one of us can unload the meat," he said, parking the van just outside the cabin.

She arched an eyebrow. "You mean it?"

"Yeah." He grinned. "Come find me when you're done."

She laughed and swatted him on the arm. Then she climbed outside and opened the rear door. "Do you want to cure this stuff? Or smoke it?"

He preferred the flavor of smoked meat. But it was nice to have some variety. "Both," he replied. "Half and half."

Nodding, she grabbed a thick slab of meat and hoisted it over her shoulder. Then she walked to the cabin and entered the front door. Within seconds, faint cheers rang out.

Caplan grabbed a slab of bloody meat and hauled it into the cabin. The others—even Morgan—stood around Mills, looking tired but excited. "Well, you finally came through," Toland remarked. "Maybe we'll actually eat a real meal one of these days."

"The sooner, the better," Mills replied. "But first, we have to prep this stuff."

"Of course." Toland backed away. "Let me know when you're done and—"

"If you want to eat, you'll get your butt out to that van right now." Her gaze narrowed. "That goes for all of you. Everybody helps tonight. No exceptions, no excuses."

Toland studied her eyes and apparently, didn't like what he saw. "Fine." He exhaled in exacerbation. "But you owe me."

"Yeah," she said, following him outside. "I owe you a punch in the face."

Working together, they unloaded the meat. Afterward, the group split up. Elliott filled a bucket with their supply of rainwater, grabbed a bit of liquid soap and a sponge, and scrubbed down the van. Mills and Toland went inside and prepped the meat by cutting away the fat, skin, and bone. Meanwhile, Caplan and Morgan tossed charcoal into the fire. Then they walked into the forest and harvested wood from a fallen green ash tree. By the time they returned, the fire had burnt down to a hot coal bed.

Mills and Toland salted half of the prepped meat and began to hang it around the common room. Caplan and Morgan used sticks from the green ash tree to fashion a tripod over the smoking coal bed. Then they lashed individual sticks to the tripod and racked strips of unsalted meat on them. A few flies buzzed around at first. But the smoke and heat kept them at bay and eventually, they lost interest.

Caplan tossed a little extra wood on the fire and then sat back. The smoke and heat repelled bugs. But it also helped dry the meat, a necessity for long-term preservation.

"Nice job." Morgan knelt next to him. "I don't know what we'd do without you."

"You'd figure it out." She'd cleaned herself up a bit and as a result, smelled like lavender instead of body odor and grime. Even her hair, normally a stringy mess, looked shiny and smooth. "Say, I've got a question for you."

"Shoot."

"Have you ever seen a ghost?"

She shook her head. "Why?"

"Because I saw one. Yesterday, before Dire showed up. On the way into the store, I had this really weird feeling of awe and unease. And then on the way out, I felt something watching me. I turned around and saw a gray mist. It hung around for a few seconds. Then it disappeared."

Curiosity flashed across her face. "Where was Dire?"

"Just behind the store. Why?"

"Because I think it explains your symptoms. You know how I didn't want you to get rid of that audio equipment we found in the van? Well, that's because it's specialized ornithology equipment, designed to detect infrasound."

He cocked his head.

"Infrasound is low-frequency sound outside the realm of normal human hearing. But that doesn't mean our bodies can't detect it. Some people experience anxiety, sorrow, or chills when exposed to it. And at the right frequency, it can cause eyeballs to vibrate, which might explain your ghost sighting."

"And you think Dire had something to do with this infrasound?"

"Lots of large creatures—whales, elephants, rhinos—use it to communicate over long distances. For a while now, I've suspected behemoths do the same thing. Of course, I'll need to run some tests to be sure." She trailed off, then paused for a long moment. "But that can wait. Right now, we need to talk. About us."

The moment felt utterly surreal to him. He couldn't remember the last time they'd had an actual conversation about their relationship. Or much of anything else, either.

"I'm ... well, I'm leaving, Zach."

He stared at her.

"Tricia and I talked it over. We're going to Danter."

He blinked. A memory, long forgotten, seared its way across his brain. He recalled sitting in Ross' shop as a kid, chowing down on delicious ice cream, surrounded by his parents, Mayor Zelton, the Pylors, a young Connie Aquila, and many other chattering folks. And just like that, the memory ended. There was no conflict, no argument. It was just him and his parents, enjoying a sunny afternoon in tiny Danter. He had lots of those memories. Happy little snippets of simpler times.

He blinked again. "Are you out of your mind?"

"I've taken my research as far as I can go by myself. Frankly, I'm stumped. I need other sets of eyeballs studying the logbook and looking at my work."

"Didn't you hear what I said this morning? Danter's dealing with blackmailers right now."

"That's part of the reason I'm going. They need help."

"You could die."

"And if I don't go, other people could die. Including your friend, Mike."

His gazed tightened an imperceptible amount. He didn't want Mayor Zelton to die. He didn't want anyone to die. But facts were facts. If he wanted to protect his friends, he needed to stay away from Danter. *Forget thriving*, he sang silently. *Just keep on surviving.* "The town's a good twenty miles from here. How are you going to get there?"

"I'm hoping you'll drive us."

"And if I refuse?"

"Then we'll walk. But one way or another, we're leaving tomorrow."

Competing urges tugged at Caplan's brain. If he let Morgan and Elliott leave, he wouldn't be able to protect them. But leaving the cabin on foot meant entering the open world. A world of behemoths, reborn megafauna, and soldiers. And he couldn't protect *anyone* in that world.

He sighed. "Is there anything I can do to change your mind?"

"No."

"Why does Tricia want to leave?"

"I'm not sure. But she's adamant about it."

He stared at the embers for a long time. "I really hope you reconsider this. But if you don't, I'll drive you to the edge of Danter sometime tomorrow."

Her face brightened. "Really?"

"Yes. But you'll have to walk from there. I'm not leaving the tree cover under any circumstances. Agreed?"

"Agreed." She sighed. "Look, I know you probably think I'm crazy. But I have to do this."

"Do what? It's too late to stop HA-78. And no one is going to stop the behemoths."

"But we can still stop the Holocene extinction."

He focused his gaze on a single chunk of reddish, smoking charcoal. "And you think working with other people can change that?"

"I do. The solution's in there." She glanced at the charred, leather logbook. "I just need help digging it out."

Seventeen months ago, Mills had gotten her hands on the logbook while holed up deep within the Vallerio Forest. Bronze-colored text upon the cover read, *Apex Predator*. While the interior was heavily damaged, it still possessed tantalizing information about the Apex Predator project.

Apex Predator was James Corbotch's multi-stage plan to defeat the Holocene extinction. The logbook, which contained hundreds of memorandums, letters, notes, drawings, and diagrams, was part history book, part scientific manual. It detailed the project's origins, its various stages, its breakthroughs, and more.

Caplan had tried to read it a few times. More than a few times, actually. But much of the material, prepared by a vast array of brilliant scientists, went way over his head.

However, it seemed to make sense to Morgan. She spent every single day poring over the book, adding little notes in the margins.

"How do you know the solution's in there?" he asked.

"Because *everything* is in there. I've learned so much, Zach."

"Like what?"

"For one thing, I can now say for sure that the behemoths aren't some kind of mistake. They're essential to ending the extinction."

His ears perked. "How so?"

Mills and Toland finished hanging meat strips and walked over to join the conversation.

"The secret lies deep in history." Morgan paused. "We all know something happened ten to eleven thousand years ago. Something *strange*."

Caplan nodded. "You're talking about the Quaternary extinction event."

"Yes. Simply put, entire genera of large mammals went extinct in the blink of a geological eyeball. And it didn't just happen in one small corner of the world. No, it happened almost *everywhere*. North America, South America, Australia, Europe. Only Africa and parts of Asia were spared."

"So, they died at the same time." Mills shrugged. "What's the big deal?"

"The big deal is we can tie dinosaur extinctions to historical events. The same can't be said of the Pleistocene megafauna. Until recently, nobody knew why so many of them died out at the exact same time."

Caplan's eyes widened. "You figured it out?"

"Not me. James' scientists deserve the credit." She glanced at the logbook. "He told us the truth in the Vallerio, but it was only a partial truth."

"So, what caused the Quaternary extinction event?" Caplan asked. "Was it hunting?"

She shook her head. "If that were the case, we'd expect to see a strong correlation between the rate of extinction and the growth of the human population. But no such correlation exists. And on a separate note, just consider the case of ancient North America. How many people could've lived here ten thousand years ago?"

"Thousands?" Mills guessed. "Tens of thousands?"

"Exactly. Far fewer than would've been necessary to drive *entire genera* into extinction. And ancient hunters didn't even have guns. They used arrows and spears, which weren't easy to make but quite simple to break. Furthermore, while some ancient Americans were nomads, many others lived in defined areas, leaving massive amounts of land unoccupied. Ancient hunters, lacking cars or trains, had no easy way of accessing that land." Morgan paused for a moment. "No, it wasn't overhunting. And climate change doesn't work either. Global temperatures did increase during that period. But many of the animals that went extinct had survived similar temperature changes in the past."

Mills crossed her arms. "Enough stalling, Amanda. What caused the Quaternary extinction event?"

"Simply put, it was a reaction to an even earlier event." She paused. "Sixty-five million years ago, the dinosaurs died out. Land mammals took over Earth. But none of them were big enough to fill the dinosaurs' shoes, so to speak. Usually, evolution has a way of sorting these things out. And sure enough, mammals underwent a growth spurt for the next thirty million years. *Paraceratherium transouralicum,* for instance, reached a shoulder height of sixteen feet. Its neck was another seven to eight feet long, giving it a total height in excess of twenty feet. This growth spurt was nature's way of filling an ecological niche."

"Or not." Toland looked bored. "Mammals never reached the size of dinosaurs. At least not until the behemoths came around."

"And that's exactly the problem. Mammals hit a plateau—James' scientists refer to it as the Mammalian Plateau—about thirty-five million years ago. As a result, an entire ecological niche went unfulfilled. That was when the food chain truly started to unravel. It caused the Quaternary extinction event, which in turn, led to the present Holocene extinction." Morgan paused to take a breath. "We thought James was trying to reel back time to the Pleistocene epoch. But he was actually trying to arrange things as if the Mammalian Plateau had never happened."

"I see," Caplan said slowly. "Mammals should've evolved to dinosaur-like sizes. When they didn't, it caused a ripple effect through history."

She nodded.

"I don't buy it," Toland remarked. "If Mother Nature changed her mind, she had to have a good reason for it."

"You'd think so. But if one exists, James' scientists never found it. Bottom line, mammals should've kept growing. They didn't and now everything is dying."

"So, we can't kill the behemoths," Mills said. "I mean, even if we were capable of killing them, we couldn't do it."

Morgan nodded. "That's correct. They're absolutely essential to stopping this extinction."

"Then why haven't they worked yet?"

"I'm not sure. Maybe James didn't engineer enough of them. Or maybe the problem is the bloodlust we've witnessed in all of his creations. Or maybe it's something else I haven't even considered yet. That's why I need to go to Danter. If they can help me figure out what went wrong, I might be able to fix it." A slight smile cracked her lips. "Maybe, just maybe, that'll end the Holocene extinction once and for all."

CHAPTER 9

Date: Nov. 24, 2017, 11:46 p.m.; Location: Belkop, NH

The saber-toothed tiger, known by some as Saber, stared across the ruined landscape, undisputed king of all it surveyed. And yet, it was bewildered. Bewildered and torn by strange, conflicting purposes. It didn't fully understand the many bizarre things that surrounded it. But it wasn't entirely ignorant either.

For instance, it understood that it was, in some peculiar way, too large for this world. It knew this because its prey, full of bony meat and pungent red blood, was much too small for even a tiny snack. It also understood that its desire to eat went deeper than mere hunger. It wasn't out to just fill its belly. It didn't even like the taste of prey all that much. What it really desired was the slight relief it received every time that pungent red blood touched its tongue. Relief from that infernal ringing noise, relief from those weird sensations in its head. Eating prey caused it to feel, well, normal. At least for a little while.

Saber heard familiar bursts of noise along with growls, roars, and screeches. Angling its sixty-foot tall body, it cut between two dark structures, pausing only to peer inside the little gaps. Prey liked to hole up inside them so sometimes it found food this way.

Seeing nothing, it continued toward the noises. Before long, it saw frenzied activity, bright lights, and thick smoke.

Farther back, it saw prey lined up behind barricades. Each one was just a fraction of its height and nowhere near its length. They carried little objects, weapons of some sort, that did no real damage. A couple of those annoying fire spitters sat near the prey. They were all aimed at an enormous four-legged beast with roundish ears, a light mane, and coarse fur. The fur was colored dark orange with faint black stripes.

Looking past the beast, Saber saw two more behemoths. One creature possessed long legs. Parallel horns stuck out of its skull. Another one walked in a hunched manner on four legs. Occasionally, it would rise up on its back legs before falling back to the earth with a resounding crash.

All around these beasts lay the remains of a vicious battle. Dead prey lay strewn about the ground, some crushed underfoot, others eaten. Fire spitters, smashed to pieces, spat smoke into the sky. Tall structures, damaged but not destroyed, leaned precariously in all directions.

The beast roared as fire continued to assault its thick hide. It tried to swipe at one of the spitters, but was driven back by even more fire.

Saber cocked its head. It wasn't related to this particular beast or any of the other ones for that matter. But it could sense them, even communicate with them.

Claws clicking loudly, it raced onto a hard, dark surface. Prey spun toward it and their features, so visible to its ultra-keen eyes, recoiled in fright. Immediately, the spitters twisted its way. Fire slammed into its legs. Undeterred, it leapt onto the front end of a spitter. The spitter went airborne, spinning on end. Extending its paw, Saber slapped the spitter, sending it flying into a group of prey.

Prey scattered and tried to surround Saber. But their weapons—even the spitters—were of little use. Blood and sparks flew as the behemoth continued its attack.

Afterward, Saber lurched upward and roared at the moon. The other beasts wandered out onto the battlefield and started to feast on the dead prey.

And that was when Saber struck.

It launched itself at the beast, sinking its long teeth into coarse fur and thick hide. The confused beast whimpered and flopped on the ground. Another fierce bite put it out of its misery.

Saber turned on the other two behemoths. It dove at the horned creature, knocking it to the ground. Swiftly, it clawed a couple of gaping holes in the creature's belly. The creature exhaled a loud gasp, then fell still.

Seeing this, the hunched behemoth tried to retreat. But Saber pounced on it and pinned it to the ground. It swatted at the behemoth's face and then bit down on its neck, instantly killing the animal.

Afterward, Saber rose up on all fours. Then it crisscrossed the battlefield, sniffing at the prey and feeding on them. Some prey were still alive and tried to fight. It liked eating them most of all. Never mind the taste. The blood of the still-living, for whatever reason, provided the most relief.

It ate a little more and continued to sniff the ground, searching for the scent. The one that had plagued it for as long as it could remember. The one that had somehow triggered that infernal ringing noise. But it was unable to pick up even a trace of the smell.

As Saber turned to leave, it caught sight of the three dead behemoths. As was its practice, it didn't feed on them. Instead, it moved onward, in search of the scent.

Always in search of the scent.

CHAPTER 10

Date: Nov. 25, 2017, 7:53 p.m.; Location: Danter, ME

"I can't believe this." Mills' jaw fell slack as she stared out the side window. "I mean, I knew it was bad. But actually seeing it …" She trailed off.

A yawn, borne from frenzied nerves and sheer exhaustion, escaped Caplan's lips. The drive, which would've taken maybe a half-hour in the old world, had lasted nearly four times that long due to blocked and mangled roads.

He stopped the van at the edge of the woods and cut the headlights. Up ahead, a large bonfire illuminated the remains of Danter. Short buildings and small homes sat in crumbling states. The streets were ripped apart and filled with smashed and abandoned vehicles. Parking meters, mailboxes, and stoplights lay scattered amongst brown grass and dying vegetation.

Graves lay on the outskirts of Danter. Dozens of them from the looks of it. Many of the residents had succumbed to HA-78. Others, he knew, had been killed by behemoths and reborn megafauna.

He exhaled. It pained him to see Danter like this, more dead than alive. From his vantage point, he could just make out the charred remains of Danter Library. He'd spent a lot of wonderful afternoons in that musty, old building, consuming strange books on legends and mysteries under the distrustful eye of Head Librarian Luann Cordell. Now, the building was gone, living on only in the memories of those who'd crossed its hallowed threshold.

Exhaling again, he snuck a glimpse at Morgan. She sat to his right, nestled between him and Mills. Her lips were pursed, her eyes were focused on her future.

Danter meant a lot to him. But in all honesty, it was nothing, a mere blip on the map. And yet, it had been ravaged by behemoths and targeted by soldiers. And Morgan and Elliott wanted to live there? Were they crazy?

"Are you sure you want to go through with this?" he asked quietly.

Morgan nodded.

"Then hurry up already," Toland muttered. "It's cramped back here."

Caplan shot him an annoyed look. "Knock it off, Brian."

"No, he's right." Morgan waited for Mills to exit the car before climbing outside. She grabbed a duffel bag, which was filled with several sets of clothes, some personal items, and the logbook, and hiked around to Caplan's window. "Take care of yourself," she said quietly.

"You too." He hesitated. "Do me a favor. When you get to that bonfire, shoot me a wave. Just so I know you're okay."

"Will do." She leaned in and kissed his cheek. "Take care of yourself."

She said her goodbyes to Mills and Toland. Then she and Elliott began walking toward Danter.

Caplan placed his elbow on the windowsill and sank into his seat. He felt raw and numb on the inside. He'd miss Morgan. Elliott, too, of course. But he and Morgan had a much longer and richer history together. Life wouldn't be the same without her.

"We're wasting time," Toland barked. "Let's go."

"Keep your drawers on," Mills retorted. "We're just making sure they're okay."

"What's the point? They'll be dead soon anyway."

Caplan's lips drew tight, but he refrained from saying anything. Instead, he watched Morgan and Elliott hike all the way to the bonfire. Morgan turned to wave. But at the last second, she hesitated. Adopting a fast pace, she and Elliott hurried across the intersection and passed out of view.

Mills frowned. "What was that?"

"I don't know." Caplan leaned forward. A couple of tense seconds passed as he waited for Morgan's wave. But she didn't reappear. "Something's wrong."

"Nothing's wrong," Toland said. "They just forgot about us. Which, incidentally, is exactly what we should be doing about them."

Caplan gave Mills a look. She arched her eyebrows.

Quietly, he turned the ignition. Keeping his window down and the headlights off, he edged the van out of the woods and drove into Danter.

"Not much of a welcome wagon," Mills remarked. "Where is everyone?"

Tension built in Caplan's shoulders as he drove down Main Street. Ahead, he saw the bonfire. Constructed from dead trees and long, dry branches, it was positioned at the intersection of Main and Maple.

Dim noise rose up from the night. He heard rushing wind, flickering flames, and burning leaves. But he heard chatter as well. The words were difficult to distinguish, but they were fueled by ire and disdain.

You should turn around, he told himself. *Before it's too late.* But of course, he kept driving anyway.

The glow brightened as they neared the bonfire. At the corner of Maple Street, Caplan hung a right. Immediately, he hit the brakes and gawked at the sight before him.

Dozens of Danter residents were lined up on one side of the street. Soldiers, dressed in combat uniforms and bulletproof vests, stood in front of the civilians. Long rifles, slung around their necks, filled their hands.

Farther back, Caplan saw the old baseball field. Three transport helicopters, rotors stilled and lights darkened, rested in the middle of it.

Switching his attention back to the civilians, Caplan saw Ross. He spotted Morgan and Elliott as well. They stood spread-eagled up against a wall with their bags at their feet. Two soldiers were busy patting them down.

He shifted his gaze back to the street. His pulse quickened as he spotted five other people. They lay on the pavement, their bodies riddled with bullets. One deceased man in particular caught his eye.

No, he thought, his lip curling in fury. *Not Mike.*

A woman twisted toward the van. Her almond-shaped eyes stared at him like he was some kind of bug. Unlike the soldiers, she wore jeans and a gray shirt. A dark red cloak hung over her shoulders and draped down to her ankles. She looked gritty, but regal. Like a warlord of the streets.

A man stood next to her. He wore a bulletproof vest and carried a rifle. Red-faced and overly muscular, he reminded Caplan of a gym rat with a penchant for the needle.

Mills exhaled. "It looks like Danter's blackmailers decided to swing by a little early."

Caplan nodded. "They must've caught wind of Noel's plan."

"Who cares?" Toland hissed. "Get us out of here."

The warlord called out an order. Soldiers rotated toward the van. Their faces hardened. Their rifles swung into position.

Caplan hesitated for a split-second. He couldn't just leave Morgan and Elliott with these monsters. Anyway escape was impossible. The soldiers would fill the van with bullets long before he drove out of harm's way. So, he did the only thing he could do. He gritted his teeth.

And stomped on the gas pedal.

CHAPTER 11

Date: Nov. 25, 2017, 8:11 p.m.; Location: Danter, ME

Gunfire filled the cold night. A series of tiny sparks flew up from the pavement. Caplan yanked the steering wheel to the left, then to the right. The gunfire lessened as soldiers dove out of the way.

He slammed the brakes, halting the vehicle next to Morgan and Elliott.

"Get in," Mills yelled.

Morgan shoved a soldier. He bumped into another one and they fell into a heap of limbs.

"Now's our chance." Ross' voice, loud and fierce, filled the air. "Run for it!"

The Danter residents scattered in all directions. Some ran down Maple Street. Others ducked into alleys, doorways, or scampered over rubble. Still others attacked the soldiers, wrenching away their rifles. Fists flew and more gunfire pierced the air as small, pitched battles rang out.

Morgan grabbed her duffel bag. Then she and Elliott raced to the back of the van. Throwing open the door, they climbed into the cargo space.

"Go," Mills shouted.

Caplan sped to the end of Maple Street and hung a right. He shot a quick glimpse at the helicopters and was relieved to see their rotors were still quiet. Gunning the engine, he raced out of town.

And into the waiting night.

CHAPTER 12

Date: Nov. 25, 2017, 10:06 p.m.; Location: Danter, ME

Caplan slammed the brakes, bringing the van to a screeching halt. He dimmed the headlights and shut off the engine. Perking his ears, he listened for whirring rotors and buzzing engines. But the night sky remained quiet.

"Take us to Danter, she said," Toland muttered. "Everything will be fine, she said."

"Shut up, Brian." Mills nodded at Morgan. "This isn't her fault."

"No? Then how else did we get into this mess?"

"We're not in a mess." She stared at the sky. "Not yet."

"Oh, I feel *way* better now."

"Stop arguing." Caplan swiveled his head toward the cabin. "And start packing. Grab only the things you need. Plus, as much food and water as we can carry."

"At last." Toland smiled. "Mr. Survival chips in with a rare bit of sound thinking."

Mills gave Caplan a look. *Can I punch him?* she mouthed.

Sure, he mouthed in response. *Just aim for his head. There's nothing in there to hurt anyway*.

She chuckled.

Morgan shrugged off her duffel bag. "Obviously, I'm already packed so I'll help with the food and water. How long before we leave?"

"We're not leaving," Caplan replied.

"And just like that, Mr. Survival returns to dolt status," Toland quipped.

"They've got helicopters and we'll be easy to spot on the road," he explained. "For now, it's better to keep a low profile. We'll park the van in the woods, all packed up in case we need to make a quick escape. We'll use branches to cover up the Rexto. If we do it right, this place will look vacant in no time."

Toland gave him a weary look. "You're happy about this, aren't you?"

"What makes you say that?"

"Because you get to keep us here, under your thumb. Living like cavemen, fulfilling your pathetic survivalist fantasies."

"I didn't see you volunteering to go to Danter," Mills said.

"What can I say? I don't care for losers."

Caplan opened his door and stepped outside. Morgan climbed out of the back and joined him in front of the cabin. He could see crushing disappointment etched into her exhausted, dirty features. Clearly, Danter's demise had brought an end to her hopes, her dreams. Well, it was better off that way. *Forget thriving*, he sang silently. *Just keep on surviving*.

He led the others into the cabin. He packed a few things. Then he grabbed a spare backpack from his room and began to fill it with strips of smoked meat.

"Hey," Elliott shouted from outside.

Caplan's ears perked. Elliott never raised her voice. She barely *used* her voice. If she was shouting, something was definitely wrong. "What is it?" he called out, rising to his feet.

Her reply came quickly. "We've got company."

CHAPTER 13

Date: Nov. 25, 2017, 10:18 p.m.; Location: North Maine Woods, ME

A helicopter, outfitted with camouflage paint, paused about fifty feet above the clearing. Its dark windows revealed nothing of its interior. Its sleek metallic sides cast off blinding streaks of moonlight.

Caplan started for the van, but a sudden burst of gunfire cut across the soil, inches from his feet. Bitterness filled his mouth as he came to a halt. For seventeen long months, he'd fought to protect his people from the dangers of this new world. He'd procured supplies amongst raging behemoths and herds of reborn megafauna. He'd dealt with countless liars, crooks, and murderers who lived along the open road, preying upon the weak and innocent. And all the while, he'd endured hunger, thirst, and exhaustion. It hadn't been easy. But he'd managed to keep his people safe, to maintain at least some control over their precarious situation.

Between Perkins' death, the events at Danter, and the helicopter's arrival, he felt that control spinning away from him. Had he ever had control in the first place? Or was it all just an illusion?

The chopper descended toward the clearing. The landing gear touched ground. The whirring blades slowed to a halt.

Then the side door opened and six soldiers emerged from the rotorcraft. They wore bulletproof vests and other gear. Long rifles were slung around their necks.

The warlord emerged from the helicopter. Taking the lead, she walked forward with strong, purposeful strides. She was middle-aged and of Native American descent. Her dark hair was tied back into braids. She sported a round face, a severe nose, high cheekbones and heavy earlobes. Her almond-shaped eyes were hooded and her lips were long and plump.

Engines rumbled softly from within the surrounding forest. Caplan couldn't see the vehicles or their occupants. But he knew they were there. Like it or not, he and his friends were surrounded.

Elliott slid to his side. Others emerged from the cabin. He gave them a quick look, seeing everyone but Mills. Part of him hoped she was making a run for it. The other part knew she'd never leave them behind.

"If it isn't the one and only Zach Caplan," the woman exclaimed. "We've been looking for you for a long time."

Shockwaves roiled his gut. Who was this woman? And how in the world did she know his name?

"Just so you know, an autograph will set you back a cool twenty," he replied.

She smiled. "Is that why you went to Danter? To share your fame with the little people?"

"It definitely wasn't for the night life." He shrugged. "What can I say? Executions just aren't my thing."

"And here I thought we had so much in common."

"At least we'll always have Danter."

"Ahh, memories."

She spoke to him in a familiar tone, almost as if she really knew him. Had he met her before? He racked his brain, but couldn't recall her face.

"My name is Chenoa Roberts," she continued. "I run Frontier Rising. Perhaps you've heard of it?"

"Can't say that I have."

"I have." Toland's visage darkened. "Frontier Rising is a private military company based out of Boston. It's part of the Corbotch Empire."

A lightning bolt shot down Caplan's spine. The Corbotch Empire was the colloquial name for the vast business holdings of James Corbotch. Originating in the seventeenth century, it had eventually grown into the world's mightiest conglomerate.

All of them, at one point or another, had run afoul of the Corbotch Empire. Corbotch, in turn, had tried to murder them. Seventeen months ago, he'd dumped Morgan, Elliott, and Toland in his killing ground, a field inhabited by reborn saber-toothed tigers. And he'd secretly infected Caplan with HA-78, expecting this would spread the disease to Morgan. Fortunately, they'd all survived, due in part to Perkins' help.

The last time Caplan saw Corbotch, the man was in the middle of the Vallerio Forest, surrounded by fire and facing the behemoth known as Saber. All this time, he'd figured the man for dead. Could he have been wrong? Had the elderly patriarch of the Corbotch family somehow survived?

"That's correct," Roberts said.

Morgan tossed back her hair and tied it into a ponytail. "I figured the Corbotch Empire would've dissolved by now."

"Without completing the Apex Predator project?" She shook her head. "I don't think so."

The more she talked, the more Caplan's muscles tensed up. He had no illusions about the situation. Roberts was there to kill them.

He'd spent the last seventeen months living by a simple principle. Namely, that there was no way to fight the terrors of this new world. So, he'd hidden from them instead, squirreling his friends away in the middle of nowhere. And it had worked.

For a little while.

"I've been looking for all of you ever since you inadvertently launched the Apex Predator project." Her gaze flitted amongst them. "You're Brian. You must be Amanda. And I'm pretty sure you're Tricia. Where's Derek Perkins? And Bailey Mills?"

"Derek died a few days ago." That was true, of course. But what about Mills? Where was she? "We lost Bailey a long time ago," he lied.

"Is that right? Then I suppose you won't mind if I take a look inside your cabin?"

"Would it matter if I did?"

"Not really. Why don't you give me the tour? Your friends can wait here. Oh, and one more thing. I don't like liars. So, if I find Derek or Bailey in there, I won't just kill them." Her smile turned cold as winter. "I'll kill you, too."

CHAPTER 14

Date: Nov. 25, 2017, 10:27 p.m.; Location: North Maine Woods, ME

"What's that smell?" Roberts sniffed as she strode into the cabin. "Columbian mammoth?"

"Woolly," Caplan replied.

"Impressive. How'd you kill it?"

"You wouldn't believe me if I told you."

Static buzzed. A masculine voice filled the common room. "Commander Roberts? Over."

"I need to get this." Keeping her gun steady, she unclipped a radio from her waist and pressed a button. "Go ahead, B-Box. Over."

Caplan scanned the cabin, searching for signs of Mills. He didn't see her. So, where was she?

"One of our drones spotted a colossus. It's about eight miles south of here. Over."

"What type is it?" Roberts asked. "Over."

"Dire wolf. Over."

"Try to steer it away. If you can't, we'll cut short and retreat. Over."

"Roger. Out."

As Roberts returned the radio to her belt, Caplan rubbed his jaw. "A colossus, huh?"

"What do you call them?"

"Behemoths. We ran into that dire wolf behemoth two nights ago. That's how Derek died." His heart twinged just a bit. "But it was a lot farther away than eight miles."

"It could've tracked you here. They can do that, you know. Colossi are regular bloodhounds." Pushing Caplan ahead of her, she conducted a quick search of the cabin. Afterward, she took him back to the common room. "It looks like you were telling the truth."

"I've been known to do that sometimes." He adopted a bored look even as his brain worked in overdrive. "So, what now? Are you going to execute me here or outside?"

"Oh, I'm not going to execute you, Zach."

He arched an eyebrow. "You're letting us go?"

"I didn't say that." She paused. "I work out of Savage Station. Ever heard of it?"

The name meant nothing to him, but he recalled Corbotch's plan to save a small slice of humanity. The best, brightest, and youngest, as the man had put it at the time. Were those people now living at Savage Station?

"No," he replied. "But it sure sounds warm and cozy."

"It's got food, water, electricity, recreation ... everything you could ever want."

"And we're going there?"

"Going? Yes. Staying? No." A light smile crossed her lips. "Savage Station is the last bastion of civilization on Earth. Or at least it will be come December Third."

December Third? That was just a week away. "What happens then?"

"Stage Three, of course."

His brow furrowed. According to Morgan's research, Apex Predator consisted of three stages. Stage One had centered around the creation and global dispersal of reborn megafauna and behemoths. Stage Two had focused on the deadly HA-78 compound. Unfortunately, all information about Stage Three had been lost to fire damage. But he was pretty sure it didn't involve sunshine and rainbows.

"What's Stage Three?" he asked.

"You'll find out soon enough."

"Can't wait," he said, as she prodded him toward the door. "I've got a question for you. How'd you end up in Danter? It's not exactly a booming metropolis."

"The same way we found the other cities, towns, and outposts. Namely, satellites and drones."

"And you're targeting all of those places during Stage Three?" He shook his head. "That's dumb. Who are you going to steal supplies from once they're gone?"

"Blackmailing Danter was a temporary solution to a temporary problem." She shrugged. "Frankly, we thought we'd be living in a more abundant world by now. But Stages One and Two merely slowed the Holocene extinction. Stage Three, fortunately, will end it."

As he neared the doorway, Caplan looked around the cabin, his gaze lingering on light fixtures, old paintings, and that little spot in the corner where an eight-year old version of himself had secretly carved initials into the baseboard. He had lots of memories of this place, both old and new. He didn't want to leave it. But what choice did he have?

Roberts grabbed her radio. "B-Box, are you there? Over."

"Yeah, I'm here. Over."

"We've got four newcomers. We'll be taking them aboard shortly. Over."

"Roger. Out."

Using her rifle, she prodded Caplan outside where he rejoined Morgan, Elliott, and Toland. With several guns upon them, they made their way to the chopper.

A soft whistle caught Caplan's ear. Swiveling his head, he saw Mills hiding in the shadows just outside the clearing. Her quiver was slung over her shoulder and she held the collapsible bow in one hand. Her lips moved silently, mouthing the same sentence over and over again.

It's him.

CHAPTER 15

Date: Nov. 25, 2017, 10:43 p.m.; Location: North Maine Woods, ME

Him? His brow furrowed. *Wait. Is she talking about …?*

Alarm bells blared in his head. He wanted to run, but there was nowhere to go.

Hemmed in by soldiers, he and the others followed Roberts to the helicopter. And all the while, he tried to think of a plan. But after months of beating the odds, he drew a complete blank.

The helicopter's cabin door slid open and a man emerged into the night. He was tall and middle-aged. A tailored white shirt, topped off by a gray sport coat, covered his muscular form.

Caplan would've recognized the man anywhere, even without the seamless and substantial plastic surgery. It was the man who'd tricked him, who'd secretly infected him with HA-78. The man who'd single-handedly obliterated the human race. "So, you're alive." He stared into James Corbotch's eyes. "What a shame."

CHAPTER 16

Date: Nov. 25, 2017, 10:44 p.m.; Location: North Maine Woods, ME

"Hello, Zach." Corbotch smiled, causing his face to wrinkle ever so slightly. "Long time no see."

"Not long enough," Caplan replied.

"Amanda. Brian. Tricia." He nodded at each of them in turn. "Where's Bailey? And that turncoat, Derek?"

"We found no sign of them," Roberts replied. "Supposedly, they're dead."

"Too bad." He glanced at the Rexto. "Is that my helicopter?"

"The one and only." Toland cocked his head. "By the way, that's some impressive plastic surgery. Don't get me wrong. You're still ugly. But at least you look younger."

"I don't look younger. I *am* younger." He touched his cheek. "Not all of my genetic engineering efforts went toward megafauna, you know."

Morgan recoiled in horror. "You genetically engineered yourself?"

"I was going under the knife anyway, thanks to that forest fire." He spoke in a calm, relaxed tone. Like they were lifelong friends. "Anyway my drones have been searching for you for months. I can't tell you how ecstatic I was when you popped up in Danter. Even now, I can barely believe we're together again."

"It's like a high school reunion," Caplan said. "With that jerk you always hated showing up at the last minute."

Roberts gave him a nasty look. "Show some respect. Mr. Corbotch is saving the world."

"Could've fooled me. Last I checked, he was busy wiping out our species."

Corbotch's mouth formed a thin smile. "You say that like it's a bad thing."

"Mass murder? Yeah, I'd say that's a bad thing."

"For Earth to heal, humanity must die."

"Nice slogan. You could've made a fortune in the greeting card business."

"Why does humanity have to die?" Morgan asked. "We didn't cause the Holocene extinction. The Mammalian Plateau did."

"That's true." Light glinted in his eyes. "I see you've been studying that logbook Bailey stole from me."

"You didn't answer my question."

"No, I didn't. The problem with humanity is that it only exists because of the Mammalian Plateau. The colossi, if nature had been allowed to take its course, would've kept the *Homo* genus from ever expanding past the archaic phase. In other words, we're a mistake."

"You're part of that mistake."

"Yes, but a small contingent of people is necessary to end the Holocene extinction as well as to keep a watchful eye on the natural world."

"You're insane."

"Not to mention delusional," Toland added. "You've created Franken-nature and you don't even know it."

"Oh?" Corbotch gave him a fleeting glance. "Then why don't you enlighten me?"

"Your behemoths or colossi or whatever you want to call them didn't come about via millions of years of evolution. And so they don't have millions of years of instincts to draw upon. The same goes for the reborn megafauna. All of these new creatures are blank slates, unleashed upon a foreign world they can't possibly understand." He shook his head. "No wonder they've got bloodlust."

"You're assuming that bloodlust, as you call it, is natural."

Morgan frowned. "You're manipulating them?"

"Yes, via very complex microchips. There are a variety of reasons for this but in general, we're helping the current generation of animals adapt to the rigors of this world."

"You sound like you've got everything figured out," Caplan said. "Except, that is, how to actually stop the extinction."

Corbotch's face twisted just a bit and for a brief moment, Caplan saw frustration in the man's eyes. Then he blinked and the frustration was gone. "It's taken a bit longer than we expected," he admitted. "Fortunately, Stage Three will solve everything."

"What is Stage Three?" Morgan asked. "Is that where you finish off the human race?"

"You'll learn all about Stage Three soon enough." He gave them a broad smile. "Are you ready to go?"

"Where are we going?" Toland asked.

"Savage Station." Corbotch's smile widened. "It's in the Vallerio Forest."

"Do we have a choice?"

"I'm afraid not."

Roberts snapped her fingers. A couple of soldiers produced metal restraints.

Caplan steeled up. He couldn't allow his friends to get on that helicopter. To do so, he knew, would bring them certain death.

He lunged at Corbotch. A powerful fist struck him in the jaw. Another one caught his belly. Stunned, he crumpled to the ground.

"My scientists didn't edit my genes to merely heal me," Corbotch said, rubbing his knuckles. "They *improved* me. Take my bones, for instance. My LRP5 gene underwent a slight modification. This caused my bones to harden a great deal. In fact, they're virtually unbreakable. I'm more resistant to disease now. Stronger and faster, too."

"But definitely not smarter." Caplan dug his fists into the soil. Flinging them upward, he sent dirt into the air. It mixed with soil already churned up by the rotors. The result was a small dirt cloud, which cut visibility to inches.

"Run!" he shouted.

CHAPTER 17

Date: Nov. 25, 2017, 10:48 p.m.; Location: North Maine Woods, ME

A stampede broke out as Caplan's friends sprinted for the tree line. He tried to follow suit, but Corbotch's blows had left him winded.

A hand reached under his armpit and jerked him to his feet. Looking back, he saw Mills' determined visage. "Come on," she whispered.

Holding his breath, he let her lead him away from the helicopter. Their options, he knew, were limited. They couldn't go back to the cabin and his axes and her bow weren't much good against rifles. No, their best bet was to head for the forest. Find their friends. Flee the area.

But that was easier said than done. Having heard the engines in the forest, he figured the area was crawling with soldiers. Could his friends slip through the noose? Morgan was probably okay. But what about Elliott and Toland? *Well, maybe just Tricia*, he thought with a dark, silent chuckle. *They can have Brian.*

One by one, his senses vanished under the dirt onslaught. Soil filled his eyeballs and ears. Then his nostrils and mouth. He couldn't see, hear, smell, or taste. He could only feel. And what he felt were millions of tiny pinpricks as dirt assailed his face, neck, and hands.

He rubbed caked dirt out of his eyes and followed Mills to a moss-covered black ash tree. They headed deeper into the forest and he saw other trees. Eastern hemlocks, white spruces, paper birches, and more.

The dirt cloud began to thin and he caught glimpses of the landscape. Silently, they moved past jagged rocks, dead bushes, small hills, and fallen trees.

Mills darted to a patch of eroded soil and a large mass of exposed, tangled roots. Crouching down, she entered a little cubbyhole formed by the roots.

He slid into the cubbyhole. "Any sign of the others?"

"I think ... yes, that's Brian." She pointed sideways. "Over there."

Looking through the roots, he saw Toland. The man's back was plastered to a corky, black ash tree. He stared in their direction, breathing quietly.

Swiveling his neck, Caplan searched the rest of the forest. But he didn't see Morgan or Elliott.

The sound of beating blades grew deafening. Turning toward the clearing, he watched dirt swirl around the helicopter. Shadowy figures hoisted themselves through the cabin door and disappeared.

"They're leaving." Mills' brow tightened as the helicopter lifted into the air. "Not that I'm complaining, but why?"

The rotors continued to send dirt back and forth, up and down. But for a split-second, the debris parted and Caplan caught a tiny glimpse of the cabin. "Oh, no."

"What's wrong?"

"He's got her." He could barely breathe. "James has Amanda."

He flew out of the cubbyhole and sprinted through the forest. But the helicopter was already well out of reach by the time he ran into the clearing. All he could do was watch. Watch as the rotorcraft rose high into the sky. Watch as it took Morgan away from him.

"I'll find you," he whispered softly. "No matter what it takes, I'll find you."

CHAPTER 18

Date: Nov. 25, 2017, 10:56 p.m.; Location: North Maine Woods, ME

As dirt returned to the earth, Caplan became aware of a disturbing fact. Corbotch might've flown away. But the soldiers who'd arrived by vehicle had stayed behind, as evidenced by the two-dozen shadowy figures sweeping through the forest.

Toland darted into the clearing. Mills scurried out from the darkness. Moments later, Elliott appeared as well.

"The door." Mills pointed into the sky. "It's opening."

Caplan squinted into the night. The helicopter had halted above the clearing. A familiar figure, shrouded in darkness, leaned out of the cabin. "That's Chenoa. She's holding something. She's—"

Roberts released a small object and vanished back into the cabin. The door slid shut. The helicopter gained altitude.

The object hurtled to the ground. Caplan couldn't identify it, but it looked small. Roughly the size of a baseball. Shifting his gaze, he realized the object, whatever it was, was heading straight for the van.

Oh, crap, he thought. "Down," he shouted. "Get—"

And then the clearing exploded.

CHAPTER 19

Date: Nov. 25, 2017, 10:58 p.m.; Location: North Maine Woods, ME

A powerful shockwave slammed into Caplan and he crashed to the ground. Rolling onto his side, he lay still. His head swam as a fiery wind washed over him. Without even looking, he knew the van was gone, blown to bits by some kind of incendiary device.

Painfully, he propped himself up on his elbows and looked around. Toland and Elliott lay on their backs, their chests heaving up and down. Mills was sprawled out on her stomach. Trickles of blood ran down her cheeks.

Cold darkness grabbed hold of Caplan, dragging him by the feet and hands into its deepest depths. He could feel it everywhere, laughing at him, mocking him. It centered onto his chest, pressing hard. Smothering him, crushing him, ripping the breath right out of his lungs.

Heat seared his back, burning up some of the darkness. He twisted around. A roaring blaze lit up much of the clearing, stretching and licking at the night sky. As he watched the flames dance, the tiniest ray of light flickered deep inside him. It didn't extinguish the darkness. But it was something good, something that could help him struggle back to the light. *She missed*, he thought. *The easiest target imaginable and she missed it.*

Incredibly, the van was still parked right where he'd left it, its unblemished sides shining brightly in the fiery light.

The Rexto 419R3 helicopter was undamaged as well. Not that it helped much. Without Perkins at the helm, they'd never get it off the ground.

He shook the pain out of his limbs and regained his footing. A crackling inferno engulfed the cabin, sending columns of gray smoke shooting into the sky.

As he watched the fire eat through the old dwelling, he felt memories stir within him. Memories of his childhood, of his parents, of long vacations in these woods. He recalled running through and around the cabin as a kid, exploring everything and making up games on the fly. Ahh, those were the days. Carefree days when he'd felt safe and happy. When the world had seemed so full of life.

"Good riddance." Toland took a few steps, testing his legs. "That cabin of yours was the worst."

Slowly, relentlessly, the flames cut through the dwelling. Caplan had no real desire to stop them, not after all that had happened. But he sort of liked the idea of sticking around, of watching it burn. Of seeing so many of his tangible childhood memories turned into smoke and ash. Unfortunately, there was no time.

"Come on." He ran to the van's front door and threw it open. The key was still in the ignition. He gave it a quick turn and the vehicle roared to life.

Wincing, Toland climbed into the passenger seat. Meanwhile, Mills and Elliott clambered into the cargo area. Wrenching the wheel, Caplan stepped on the gas pedal and directed the van in a half-circle. Then he drove through the forest and out onto the main road.

"Where are we going?" Mills asked.

"Anywhere but here," he replied.

As the seconds ticked by, his adrenaline began to fade. He sagged slightly in his seat and became aware of other things. The taste of salt on his lips. The smell of dirt in the upholstery. The beads of sweat dripping down his cheeks, contrasted by the chilly air.

Bright lights appeared, illuminating the van's interior. Caplan squinted at the rearview mirror. Four armored vehicles raced after them, filling both lanes of the road.

"What now, Mr. Survival?" Toland asked. "Because as far as I can tell, this is wide-open road. Forest on both sides and I don't see any turns or cross streets."

Caplan's mind reeled. Perkins and Zelton were dead. Danter residents had scattered. Morgan was gone. The cabin had been reduced to ash. Now, armored cars were chasing down their rickety van. Everything was spinning out of control and he saw no way to stop it.

Should we stick to the road? he wondered. *Or take our chances with the forest?* The road, he knew, was in relatively good shape. While this ensured them a smooth drive, it also meant the same for their pursuers.

The forest, in contrast, had plenty of obstacles. But one wrong turn would kill them all.

Forget thriving, he sang to himself. *Just keep on surviving.* The mantra had gotten him this far. Surely, it wouldn't fail him now. Thriving—that is, getting away with the van intact—wasn't going to happen. But they might survive if they lowered their expectations.

"There's only one way out of this," Caplan said. "We need to abandon ship."

Toland eyed him with disdain. "That's your plan?"

"It's too big, too bright. Those soldiers could spot it with their eyes closed. But if we leave it, if we split up and sneak off into the forest, we've got a chance."

"So, we go from one big target to four smaller ones." Mills nodded thoughtfully. "I like it."

Caplan pressed on the gas. Picking up speed, he raced down the long road.

"Tell me something," Toland said. "What happens after we escape? Are we supposed to spend the rest of our lives wandering the forest like dolts?"

"This road runs for miles. When the coast is clear, walk back to it." He rubbed his jaw, picturing the route in his mind. "There's an abandoned gas station ten miles north of here. We'll meet there."

"Unless those goons get us first."

Caplan ignored him. "As soon as I stop, split up. Run fast and hard. Don't stop for anything. Got it?"

Toland fell silent. Mills and Elliott nodded in agreement.

He drove through a slight turn and then hit the brakes. At the same time, he yanked the steering wheel to the left. Gasping and squealing, the van's rear tires slid across the pavement. Swiftly, he hit the gas again and the vehicle shot into the forest.

The pursuing headlights vanished. Dirt and branches kicked up off the ground and began to pelt the windows and siding. Driving as fast as he dared, he directed the van between trees and bushes. "Get ready," he called out. "Three. Two—"

Dazzling light filled his eyes. Gunshots roiled the still air. Glancing in the rearview mirror, Caplan saw two armored cars shoot over a small hill.

Muscles straining, he wrenched the wheel to the left. The vehicle shifted in that direction, but not by much.

Windswept debris struck the van. Then new light pierced the van. Heart pounding, he shot a glance to both side windows.

"They're surrounding us," Mills said.

"Speed up." Toland's voice cracked around the edges. "Before it's too late."

More gunshots rang out. Metal exploded. The van jolted, then jerked to the left. Clenching the wheel, Caplan tried to force it back into position. But the steering refused to respond. "Brace yourselves," he shouted.

The van crashed into a thick tree. Caplan slammed into his seatbelt and air vacated his lungs. He gasped for oxygen, but came up empty. Dimly, he was aware of the armored cars screeching to a halt.

Desperately, he unbuckled his seat belt, cracked his door, and threw himself out into the night. Rolling onto his back, he struggled to breathe.

"Hello, Zach."

This new voice, masculine and clipped, rattled in Caplan's eardrums. He gulped in some oxygen and turned his head. A cold, blustery wind struck his face. The air smelled of dirt and death.

A couple of feet away, he saw Roberts' companion from Danter. The guy's face was bright red and his overly-muscular arms bulged beneath his shirt and bulletproof vest.

As he caught his breath, Caplan saw more soldiers. They stood silent and stone-still. Their rifles, although held tightly, were aimed at the ground.

The man eyed Caplan up and down. "You're pretty scrawny for a survival expert."

"Hey, we can't all be steroid abusers."

The man's cheeks brightened a few shades. "Get the prisoners into my vehicle," he called out. "And—"

A loud blast rang out. A bullet hole appeared in the man's forehead. Stammering quietly, he fell to the soil.

More gunshots filled the darkness. A couple of soldiers froze up, then pitched to the ground. Other soldiers turned to fight. But they quickly disappeared under a wave of screaming attackers.

Bones snapped. Blades plunged into bodies. Shrieks erupted into the night.

When the last soldier had fallen, a man stood up. Sporting a thin grin, he approached Caplan. "Fancy seeing you again."

Caplan blinked. "Noel?"

CHAPTER 20

Date: Nov. 26, 2017, 2:06 a.m.; Location: North Maine Woods, ME

"Sydney is just about done with your van." Plopping down on a tree trunk, Ross offered Caplan a plastic water bottle. "How're you feeling?"

Caplan took the bottle in his grubby hands. It felt warm to the touch. Gently, he rubbed it against his cold forehead. "As good as I look."

"That bad, huh?"

He chuckled. A fierce ache erupted in his side, transforming the chuckle into a grimace.

"Bailey told me about Amanda." Ross produced a second water bottle. Uncapping it, he took a small sip. "Tough break."

"Tell me about it."

"I'm sorry we got you into this mess."

Caplan uncapped his bottle and choked down some warm water. "So, what happened? I thought they gave you until the first of the month."

"They did. Unfortunately, they changed their minds." His eyes took on a glazed look. "All of a sudden, these bright lights appeared. I ran outside and saw the helicopters. Then soldiers flooded the streets. Next thing I knew, I was face-to-face with this woman in a red cloak. She called herself Chenoa Roberts. She said she'd used drones to spy on us. She said we needed to be punished for trying to build an army. She—"

A shudder passed through Ross and he paused. His face scrunched up. "She … she shot Mike. Right in the forehead. Then she shot the others. It was …" He choked up.

Caplan turned his gaze to the ground. Zelton had been one of those larger-than-life characters. The kind of guy who did things other people only dreamt of doing. The kind of guy who would live on in the memories of all who'd known him.

He liked Zelton, but he hadn't been particularly close to the man. Still, he knew how it felt to lose a close friend. So, he fully understood Ross' grief.

Ross cleared his throat. "Afterward, Chenoa said she had big plans for us. That she was taking us to a place called Savage Station. I gathered it wasn't to honor us, if you know what I mean. Anyway that's when you showed up." He gave Caplan a sideways glance. "I don't know why you changed your mind about joining us. But I'm sure glad you did."

"Actually, I didn't. I was just dropping off Amanda and Tricia."

"Regardless, I'm grateful."

"I'm the one who should be grateful. How'd you know where to find us?"

"We took some radios off of those soldiers before we escaped. We've been listening in on their traffic."

"Have you heard anything about Savage Station? Like where I might be able to find it?"

Ross shook his head.

Disappointment crept over Caplan. He suspected Corbotch had taken Morgan to Savage Station. Furthermore, he knew Savage was located somewhere within the Vallerio

Forest. But the Vallerio was gigantic. And although Caplan had worked within its borders for several years, he'd never heard of Savage Station.

"Something bad is about to happen," Caplan said. "It's called Stage Three. I don't know the exact details. But when it's over, Savage Station will be the last place standing. Everything else—cities, towns, outposts—will be gone."

He chuckled in disbelief. "I guess it's a good thing we're nomads now."

"Honestly, I'm not sure it matters. They found you before all of this. I imagine they'll find you again."

"So much for optimism." He sighed. "When's this Stage Three supposed to happen?"

"One week from now."

"Cripes, that's not a lot of time."

"I know."

The tools ceased clanking. Moments later, a short woman of Asian descent strode into view. Grease stained her high cheekbones and her eyes were hooded with exhaustion. Her name was Sydney Teo and she ran an auto body shop out of her house. She and Caplan were roughly the same age and they'd played together as kids. Even then, she'd been a wizard with a wrench.

"Hey, Zach," she said. "Your van's ready to go."

"Thanks, Sydney." He looked into her tired eyes. "By the way, did you get a chance to check out the audio equipment in the back?"

"Sure did. It's operating just fine. You know, I would've killed for a system like that back in the day."

He breathed a sigh of relief. If Morgan was right, the behemoths mostly likely communicated via infrasound signals. The audio equipment, developed for the practice of ornithology, could identify these signals. In other words, it was a behemoth detector.

"Can you teach my friends how to use it?" he asked.

"No problem." She hesitated. "By the way, what's with that Tricia girl?"

"What about her?"

"She's just … quiet. Don't get me wrong. She seems nice. But she's really, really quiet."

"She's been through a lot."

Teo's brow furrowed. She gave Caplan and Ross a nod. Then she walked back to the van.

Ross twisted the bottle in his hands, causing the plastic to crinkle. "So, you're going after Amanda, huh?"

Caplan nodded.

"Need help?"

"No, thanks."

"We've got a stake in this too, you know. If Stage Three comes to pass, it could mean the end of us."

"Not if you break up into smaller groups and keep your heads down." Caplan shrugged. "Anyway I'm not interested in stopping Stage Three. I just want to find Amanda and get out of there."

"Zach?"

Caplan glanced at Elliott. She stood ten feet away, her posture a mixture of discomfort and determination. "What's up?" he asked.

"I'm … well, I'm not leaving with you. I've decided to stay with the Danter folks."

Caplan shot Ross an angry look. Ross, in turn, raised both hands in a defensive gesture. "This is the first I'm hearing about it."

"It's true." Elliott's squeaky voice gained some strength. "This is my decision."

A sharp pain filled Caplan's chest. The thought of leaving her behind, of not being able to protect her, was almost too much to handle.

"Why?" he asked.

"I'm not like you. I need people. Lots of people. People who can help me get through … whatever it is I'm going through." She toed the soil for a moment. Then she stole away into the night.

Ross waited until she was gone to speak. "We'll take good care of her."

"I know." With an audible sigh, Caplan rose to his feet. "Zach?"

"Yeah?"

"Good luck."

"You too, Noel."

CHAPTER 21

Date: Nov. 26, 2017, 3:45 a.m.; Location: North Maine Woods, ME

"We're running on fumes." Caplan cast a wary eye at the fuel gauge. The little red needle had passed the *E* designation miles back and was now in uncharted territory.

"Just a little farther." Mills, on all fours in the cargo area, bent over one of her maps. "Take your next right."

Caplan coaxed the van another mile or so. A hand-painted sign, mounted on sturdy poles, appeared. It read, *Welcome to Kal's Camps.* A smaller sign, attached to the bigger one, declared *Vacancy … Come On In!*

After leaving Elliott, Ross and the rest of the Danter colony, Caplan, Mills, and Toland had hit the road. With no clear destination in mind, Caplan had aimed the van in the

Vallerio's general direction. When gas started to dwindle, Mills began to look for a place where they could refuel.

He dimmed the lights and gave his eyes time to adjust to the darkness. Then he directed the van, coughing and gasping for sustenance, onto a makeshift road. Maintaining a slow speed, he crept down the gravel until he caught sight of a wood lodge. A couple of trucks and sedans were parked outside the structure. They were caked with dried dirt and covered in bird droppings. Other than a few nicks and dents, they appeared undamaged.

"Bailey," Caplan whispered. "Can you check for infrasound?"

She switched on the audio equipment and began fiddling with switches and dials. "No sign of it. But remember, we don't know for sure that behemoths use infrasound. And even if they do, they probably don't use it all of the time."

"I understand." His gaze turned to the vehicles. "Nobody's driven them for a long time. They might be good for some gas."

She nodded. "How do you want to do this? Fast and dirty or slow and sweet?"

"You two have a secret language?" Toland offered a bored smirk. "How cute."

It had been a long time since Caplan had heard *fast and dirty or slow and sweet*. Perkins, Mills, and him had used that expression often in the early days. But with time and experience, it'd fallen by the wayside.

He rubbed his bleary eyes. For the last hour, he'd driven in near-silence, consumed by shades of light and darkness. Every now and then, he'd snuck glances at Toland and Mills. He'd seen their gaunt cheeks, their furrowed brows, their steady gazes. He was thankful they, along with Elliott, were alive. Thankful they'd escaped Corbotch's grasp. At the same time, he couldn't stop thinking about Morgan. Was she okay? What was Corbotch doing to her?

"You'd know our language if you'd ever bothered to come with us," Mills pointed out.

"I had better things to do," Toland replied.

"Like what? Be a useless lump?"

Caplan shook his head. "You told us you were a big game hunter. We could've used you out there."

"If you weren't so ridiculously incompetent, that wouldn't have been the case," Toland retorted.

"You talk big," Mills said. "But that's all it is … talk."

"Ahh, a cliché." He shook his head. "How amazingly uncreative of you, my dear."

"Ahh, mockery over my choice of language. How utterly original of you."

"Stop it," Caplan said. "Both of you."

With a small smile, Mills folded up the map. Meanwhile, Toland gave Caplan a caustic look. "Well, well, well … our fearless leader has something to say. Tell me, what disaster are you going to lead us into next, Mr. Survival?"

Caplan resisted a sudden urge to pop Toland in the mouth. "Fast and dirty means we go in, get what we need, and get out. Slow and sweet means we scout the land before we salvage. It's safer and more thorough, but eats up clock." His stomach growled. Their reserves, the mammoth meat, everything. … it was all gone, consumed by the cabin fire. "We'll take it slow and sweet," he decided. "We need every scrap of food and water we can find."

He slipped outside. Looking back, he saw Toland still sitting in the passenger seat. "Are you coming?"

"On your little walkabout? I don't think so." He pulled a lever next to him, causing his seat to recline. Leaning back, he closed his eyes. "Wake me when you're finished."

Reaching back into the van, Caplan pulled the keys out of the ignition.

"What's wrong?" Toland cracked an amused eye. "You don't trust me?"

"I have to protect the van."

"From what?"

The corners of his lips turned upward, forming a devilish grin. "From anyone who might try to steal it while you're sleeping."

Toland's eyes bulged. "Wait a—"

He shut the door, ending the conversation. One second later, he heard the soft click of the automatic door locks. The sound caused his grin to widen. *Enjoy your nap*, he thought.

He pulled out his small flashlight and one of his axes. Then he issued a few hand signals to Mills. Quietly, they circled the perimeter, looking for survivors, reborn megafauna, and behemoths. Finding nothing, they gravitated toward one of the cabins.

Mills recoiled in disgust as she opened the door. "Ugh."

Caplan held his breath, but it didn't keep the sickly-sweet stench of rotting flesh from flooding his nostrils. Months ago, he would've gagged at the odor. But he was used to it now.

He aimed his beam into a living room. The space was outfitted with a wooden rocker, a few old-fashioned easy chairs, and a double-benched picnic table. A clothed woman, partially stripped of flesh and covered with a smattering of flies, sat in one of the chairs. Claw marks around her throat indicated she'd been choking shortly before death.

"Another HA-78 victim," Mills said.

Caplan nodded. Together, they performed a cursory search of the cabin, finding two more bodies—an adult male and a little boy—in the process. Seeing the family like that—dead and picked apart by insects—should've caused his insides to hurt. But he'd seen a lot of dead families over the last seventeen months. And nothing about this one was particularly shocking. He wondered about that, about his growing indifference toward death. What did that say about him? About his humanity?

He searched the drawers and suitcases, taking note of the clothes and toiletry items. Next, he checked the cupboards, finding canned goods, a carton of soda bottles, chocolate bars, and marshmallows. The powerless fridge held plenty of food, none of it edible.

Mills grabbed a set of car keys from a side table. They proceeded to search the other cabins. Four of them held bodies. They found three more corpses in the lodge. But it wasn't all death and despair. They also located more food, additional car keys, bottled and canned drinks, batteries, flashlights, matches, and plenty of other stuff.

They headed out to the parking area. While Mills matched the keys to the appropriate vehicles, Caplan studied a wooden signboard. A carved map showed the surrounding area and he took time to memorize it. The local landmarks included Delta River, strings of giant boulders, various clearings, an old road, and a mountain known as Pyre Peak. A separate carved image depicted a close-up of Pyre Peak. The accompanying text indicated it had once been used for logging purposes. While the old road led up to the top, visitors were advised to avoid it due to lack of maintenance as well as loose rock and steep cliffs.

He left the signboard and helped Mills search the vehicles. They found little of interest. Afterward, they fired up the ignitions and examined the fuel gauges.

"Food, water, plenty of gas," she said, climbing out of a weathered, red truck. "Not bad."

Indeed, it was a pretty good haul. The supplies would last them a week, maybe longer. And that gas could take them a considerable distance.

Turning in a slow circle, he studied the remote, deserted landscape. The place, although rather big, would make for a decent home. Of course, the bodies would have to be buried. And they'd have to dispose of the rotten food and use a little elbow grease to get everything spic and span again. But it might be worth the effort, especially with the close proximity to Delta River. Most likely, the waterway was suffering like the rest of the natural world. But if it held liquid, it probably saw a decent amount of animal traffic.

Maybe we can come back here, he thought wistfully. *After … just after …*

Mills cleared her throat. "There's something you should know about Savage Station."

Instantly, his mind shifted back to the clearing. To her whispering silently into the night. *It's him*, she'd mouthed. Obviously, she'd learned Corbotch's identity while spying on the helicopter. But he'd failed to consider the possibility she might've heard other things as well.

"What's that?" he asked.

"After Chenoa took you inside the cabin, I snuck along the edge of the clearing. A couple of soldiers stood guard near the helicopter and I was able to get pretty close to them." She ran a hand over her tightly-woven hair. "One guy complained about howling noises back at Savage. The other guy agreed. He said he could handle the screams, but the howling was freaking him out."

"Anything else?"

"These noises … it was obvious they were the result of torture. And not just of one or two people. It sounded like there were hundreds, maybe thousands, of prisoners."

He shivered and not because of the bristling wind slashing against his cheeks. "That's interesting. Noel told me Chenoa planned to take him and his people to Savage, most likely as a form of punishment. She and James must be running a mass torture program out of there."

"What could they possibly hope to gain from that?"

"I don't know." He stared at the sky, at the still-dark horizon. He hated the feeling of helplessness that pervaded him. "Let's strip the camp," he said. "Then we can bed down for a few hours."

"If you get the gas, I'll start the salvage." She studied the cabins and lodge. "What should I do with the bodies?"

"Leave them." In the beginning, they'd buried every corpse they'd stumbled across. But HA-78's death toll quickly turned this into a gigantic burden. Eventually, they'd abandoned the practice altogether. In fact, Perkins' grave was the first one Caplan had dug in over a year. "Just focus on gathering food and anything else that might help us. Use the suitcases to carry stuff."

"It'd be nice to have some extra hands right about now."

His temper flared a tiny bit. "We don't need them."

"Them?"

"The Danter colony. Who else?"

"Actually, I was referring to Brian. It's about time we put him to work."

"Oh." His ire faded and he found himself wondering why he'd gotten angry in the first place.

He tossed her the keys. She walked to the van, unlocked the passenger door, and wrenched it open. She and Toland argued for a few seconds. Then he climbed out of his seat and, with a sour look upon his face, followed her to the nearest cabin.

Caplan hiked to the lodge and circled around to the rear. He located an old garden hose and used one of his axes to slice off an ample portion of it. Then he strode into the lodge and entered the *Employees Only* door. In the old world, portable gas containers were an absolute necessity for those who lived in remote locations. So, he had no trouble finding a bunch of them on some metal shelving units.

He grabbed a couple of containers and went outside. He popped off the red truck's gas cap and peeled back the spring-loaded flap. Then he eased one end of the tube into the tank. He placed the other end of the tube into his mouth and began to suck on it. Gas flowed in his direction. Spitting out the tube, he stuck it into one of the containers.

He repeated the process with the other vehicles, gathering nearly three full containers of fuel. He used some of the fuel to fill up the van's tank. Then he stowed the rest of it in the cargo area.

Afterward, Caplan hiked to the cabins. He helped Mills and Toland finish gathering supplies. Then they rolled the suitcases back to the van and tossed them into the cargo area. While Mills lashed them down, Toland emitted a loud groan. "My back hurts."

Mills stopped working long enough to roll her eyes. "Poor baby."

Ignoring her, Toland looked at Caplan. "You do realize Amanda's probably dead by now. And if she's not dead, she'll be dead soon enough."

He narrowed his gaze.

"It's time to forget her. It's time to move on, to start thinking about our future."

"You're all heart, Brian."

"Hey, I never claimed to be nice. Nice will get you killed in this world." Twisting around, he walked away.

"Where are you going?" Mills asked.

"To bed," he replied. "If you think I'm sleeping another second in that piece of crap van, you're out of your mind."

He stalked up to one of the corpse-free cabins, yanked the door open, and disappeared inside. Seconds later, the door slammed shut.

Caplan stood still, bathed in jets of cold air. It was early morning and the sun was just starting to breach the horizon. Behind him, he sensed Mills. Sensed her presence, her aching stare. She was close enough to touch. And oh, how he wanted to touch her. To feel her warmth. To wrap himself around it, inside of it.

He turned toward her. Stared deep into her moist blue eyes and started to swim. It was just him, just her. Just them in the middle of nowhere.

A small lock of hair slipped loose from her braids. He reached out to touch it, to brush it away. She recoiled a bit and he hesitated. But then she grasped his hand and pressed it against her cheek. Her skin felt soft, tender. But there were rough parts, too. Scratches, welts, and bumps. Tiny wounds accumulated over the last seventeen months.

She pressed herself against his chest. Releasing his hand, she wrapped her fingers around the back of his neck. Breathing softly, she stared into his eyes. "Are you sure about this?"

He leaned down. Pressed his lips against hers. Their first kiss. It wasn't tender. It was hungry. Like that of two caged animals finally released into the wild. "Absolutely."

CHAPTER 22

Date: Nov. 26, 2017, 8:48 a.m.; Location: North Maine Woods, ME

Dazzling light slanted in through the open windows, bathing Mills in an almost-blinding glow. Caplan didn't shut his eyes or even blink. To do so would break their trance-like gaze. A gaze that allowed them to share unspoken feelings and emotions. Anger. Sadness. Frustration. Fear. Defiance.

Those feelings wouldn't change. Not now, not later. They were permanent, unchangeable features of vast mental landscapes. He knew, accepted that. But for far too long, he'd sat on his feelings, hiding them from his friends. With the world in a state of free-fall, they'd needed a rock to stand on. And so he'd been that rock.

However, it had taken its toll. He could see that now. He could see how much pain he'd internalized. To share those unspoken feelings with Mills, to have her do the same with him, was truly a magnificent gift. It made him feel, well, almost human again.

They rolled back and forth, switching top to bottom and back again. Their toes clenched. Her fingernails dug into his back, deep enough to draw blood. His hands gripped her sides, pinning her just right. This wasn't gentle, delicate lovemaking. This was wild, frenzied fornication. A type of ancient, animalistic intimacy, unknown to mankind since the rise of civilization.

She grabbed his hair, yanking his face toward hers. Locking lips, they kissed passionately, even violently. He broke off the embrace and flipped her onto her belly. She moaned softly.

His emotions and feelings slipped away. His mind went blank. He couldn't think or rationalize or worry about the future. All he could do was obey the carnal instincts buried deep within his brain.

They changed positions again and yet again. Their passion grew until it could be contained no more. And when they finally climaxed in a fit of uncontrollable fervor, their voices rose as one to the heavens. To the Almighty high above, begging Him to give this world another look. To see what had become of His creation. To see why it shouldn't be left to the cold hands of oblivion.

She collapsed next to him, gasping for air. Her body glistened with sweat. She lay there for a moment, her eyes locked onto his. Then she threw the sheet off with both hands. Breathing heavily, she stared at the ceiling.

Caplan was spent, physically and emotionally. A part of him wanted to close his eyes, to dive into dreamless sleep. But he kept them peeled. Turning on his left side, he propped his head up on his hand and watched her. Watched her breathe, watched her body vibrate from head-to-toe.

"A girl could get used to that, you know." She smiled coyly before breaking out into giggles. "Oh, my God. I didn't realize the windows were open. Do you think he heard us?"

"Brian?" Caplan chuckled. "Yeah, he probably heard us. In fact, I'd say anything within a mile heard us."

"I can just imagine what he'll say." She adopted a gruff, overly masculine imitation of Toland's voice. "Better you do it together than with other people. Wouldn't want dolts like you two infecting the gene pool."

Caplan laughed. It felt good to laugh. Screwing up his voice, he mimicked Toland's caustic tone. "Just don't ever have a kid, dolts. The world's got enough dumb and ugly already."

She collapsed into a cascade of giggles. Caplan smiled as she tried—and failed—to get control of herself. This was good. No, this was better than good. This was …

But the thought was interrupted by other thoughts. Thoughts that had been pent-up behind a now-fading wall of carnal desire. Thoughts of Perkins and Zelton. Thoughts of Morgan and Savage Station. Thoughts of Corbotch and the mysterious Stage Three.

Mills must've experienced something similar because her giggles dried up. Her gleeful demeanor vanished into darkness. Silently, she pulled on her clothes. He did the same and together, they walked outside.

How was he going to find Savage Station? It could be anywhere within the massive Vallerio Forest. For a single crazy moment, he considered setting fire to one of the cabins. Maybe Corbotch's drones would spot the smoke and send soldiers after him. Surely, they'd take him to Savage Station.

But he quickly dismissed the idea. It was one thing to endanger himself, something else to endanger Mills and Toland. He'd just have to find another way to locate Corbotch's refuge.

Slight vibrations shot through the ground. Distant thumping and cracking filled the air.

Caplan ran to Toland's cabin and threw open the door. "Time to go," he shouted.

Toland, fully dressed, hustled outside and the three of them raced to the van. Caplan hopped into the driver's seat and ignited the engine. Toland climbed into the passenger seat while Mills scrambled into the cargo area. But when she turned to close the back doors, she froze.

The steering wheel trembled in Caplan's hands. Tree trunks splintered and cracked, louder than gunfire. Glancing backward, he saw a dust cloud roll through the forest. The dust was thick and frenzied. But he could still see through it, all the way to that giant, ungodly mass of heaving, shuddering flesh.

It was Dire. And it wasn't just close.

It was almost on top of them.

"The doors," he shouted.

Mills closed the rear doors. Caplan stomped on the gas pedal and twisted the wheel. The van shot across a stretch of dead grass. He thought about going for the open road, but knew they'd never make it. So, he said a silent prayer and aimed the vehicle at the tree line.

The van burst through a gap. Twisting the wheel, he directed the vehicle around a small rock patch and under a pair of crisscrossing, sagging elms.

A ferocious growl tore through the forest. Glimpsing the rearview mirror, he saw Dire burst into the clearing with the force of an unstoppable hurricane. Dust continued to surround it, vibrating in mid-air as if it had a life of its own.

Stuck with shoddy transportation, they wouldn't make nightfall. *Well, how do you want to go, Zach?* he thought. *Eaten alive? Crushed to death? Ahh, so many choices!*

Dire pulled up in front of the campground. Its snout, long and narrow, lifted to the sun. A grotesque howl pierced the sky. It was raw and vicious and full of ancient rage.

A shudder ran through Caplan as he met its gaze in the rearview mirror. Staring into those swirling orange eyes was like staring into the depths of erupting volcanoes. Volcanoes that would, if they got too close, send him and his friends to an early grave.

The behemoth reared up on its hind legs. Then it raced across the campground, crunching through cabins like they were made out of toothpicks.

Caplan swerved around the thickest part of a fallen pine tree. The vehicle smashed over withered, lifeless branches, causing them to crackle like fireworks. But those noises were swiftly drowned out by the sound of smashing tree trunks.

The tires passed over a soft patch of dirt. Soil kicked up and pelted the windshield. He turned on the wipers. They helped, but the flying debris still limited his visibility.

"Faster." Toland swiveled around in his seat and looked out the back windows. "Go faster, you dolt."

Caplan furrowed his brow. He'd already avoided a half-dozen collisions by the skin of his teeth. If he drove any faster, he'd almost certainly wreck them into a tree.

Still, he shared Toland's urgency. He could practically sense the creature. Sense its speed, its movements. It was almost as if a long-dormant sixth sense, desperate for self-preservation, had roared to life deep inside his brain.

He spun the wheel to his right and threaded the vehicle through a grove of pine trees. An image of the carved signboard filled his brain and he recalled the area's local landmarks. There was a small clearing just ahead. If he continued past it, he'd reach Delta River. If he turned right, he'd be faced with a string of giant boulders. Left would take him to Pyre Peak. He didn't know how much water still ran through the Delta. But even if it were bone dry, the channel would probably be too deep to cross. And those giant boulders made a right turn inadvisable. As for Pyre Peak, it was a non-starter. Sure, an old logging road led up its steep sides. But that road, according to what he'd read, was poorly maintained and bordered by steep cliffs.

Can't run, he thought. *So, we'll hide.*

He drove into the clearing and hit the brakes. Throwing the van into reverse, he twisted the wheel to the left. Swiftly, he backed the vehicle into a thick tree grove and cut the engine. The van fell still.

"Are you stupid?" Toland gave him a wide-eyed look. "You're going to get us killed."

"Be quiet." He watched the dust cloud tear through the forest. Dirt and brown pine needles began to vibrate and swirl in rising circles. Wood gasped and cracked as trees collapsed to either side.

And then it appeared.

Surrounded by airborne debris, the thirty-foot tall behemoth looked like it was emerging from some kind of otherworldly portal. A portal that led to far-off lands and ancient ruins full of sinister magic. But no such luck. Dire was part of this time, this world. And nothing was going to change that.

Stepping into the clearing, Dire focused its gaze on the dark forest. Its neck twisted from right to left and back again.

Adrenaline raced through Caplan's body, ready to restart the engine at a moment's notice. Not that it would help much. Not when this behemoth, this terrifying amalgamation of ancient genes and human ingenuity, was so close.

He held his breath and stayed perfectly still. Dire towered above them, a living, breathing skyscraper with razor-sharp teeth. Ahh, those teeth. So sharp, so gigantic. After seeing what they'd done to Perkins, it wasn't hard to imagine them stabbing through the roof, crunching into flesh and bone.

Dire glared into the dense forest. Ripples ran down its hide, causing its fur to shift and tremble. With a guttural growl, it twisted around.

And marched away.

Mills wiped beads of sweat from her forehead. "Nice thinking, Zach."

"Don't pat him on the back just yet," Toland said. "Dire's still looking for us."

She looked at Caplan. "You saw that signboard, right? What else is around here?"

"There's a river to the north," he replied. "Boulders to the east. A mountain to the west. We won't be able to get past any of it."

"And we can't go south either. Not with Dire hanging around." She furrowed her brow in thought. "Do you remember any hiding places? Maybe a cave?"

He shook his head.

"So, we're screwed." Toland growled. "Nice job, Mr. Survival. First, you got Derek killed. Then you let James kidnap Amanda. Now, you've trapped us with a behemoth. You're like a human wrecking ball."

"And you're a pompous jerk," Mills retorted. "In case you didn't notice, he saved us from Dire."

A clump of trees exploded without warning. Chunks of wood crashed into the van, denting and piercing the sides.

Giant nostrils appeared in front of the windshield. Air vented through them, causing the glass to fog up.

Caplan's heart pounded against his chest as the fog vanished. A pair of giant eyelids slid open. Lava-orange eyes, hotter than fire, met his gaze.

Toland shot Mills a sickly smirk. "You were saying?"

CHAPTER 23

Date: Nov. 26, 2017, 9:39 a.m.; Location: North Maine Woods, ME

Caplan turned the key. The engine shuddered, but didn't catch.

Dire's eyes opened wider and wider. So wide they looked like they'd pop right out of its head. Peeling its lips back, it bared its fangs. Drool dripped from its jaws and splashed against the glass.

He turned the key for a second time. The engine shuddered. Then it coughed and burst to life.

Reaching to the steering column, he flicked a switch. Bright beams shot out of the headlights and straight into Dire's face. Growling, the behemoth twisted away.

Caplan stomped on the gas and the van shot beneath Dire's massive head. On either side of him, he saw giant fur-covered legs, thick and rooted to the ground.

"Look out," Toland shouted.

An enormous paw crashed into the soil, nearly striking the van. A harsh tremor shot through the vehicle, causing Caplan's skull to rattle inside his head.

He twisted the wheel to the right. Another paw slammed into the ground directly in front of him and he wrenched the wheel back to the left.

Paws rained down on the soil as Dire spun in a circle. Caplan dodged right, left, left again, weaving a path through this ever-changing forest of limbs.

A paw struck the soil with thunderous force. Mills shouted and Caplan twisted the wheel to the right. The vehicle scraped up against a gigantic leg and the sudden jolt sent his body careening into his seatbelt. For a moment, he thought he'd lost control. But he managed to keep the wheel steady and the van shot out into open woods.

Almost immediately, he saw a tall, thick tree. Moss covered it and he saw numerous cracks in the wood.

"Turn, you dolt," Toland shouted.

Caplan was a step ahead of him. The van rumbled over exposed roots and shot past the tree. Glancing in the rearview mirror, he saw Dire in fast pursuit, crashing through the dense, sickly forest with relative ease.

He wrenched the wheel, angling the vehicle to the right. Then he wrenched it back to the left. For the next few minutes, he drove in a zig-zag pattern, turning every time the behemoth got close. At first, this confused the creature. But soon, it figured out Caplan's strategy and even began to anticipate it. To make matters worse, the forest grew thicker, denser.

"There's an old logging road around here," Caplan called out. "Find it."

Toland peered out his side window. Mills knelt in the cargo area, her gaze sweeping the forest. "Over there," she said, pointing to the left.

Twisting the wheel, he pressed hard on the gas. The vehicle shot up and over a hill. Its tires left the ground and then smacked it a second later. The jarring thud sent Mills crashing into the audio equipment.

Loud clatters, like pieces of metal repeatedly striking each other, filled the air. The steering wheel stiffened. Gritting his teeth, Caplan fought to control it. But it was like driving an over-sized bumper car and the van began to careen from side to side.

Somehow, he directed the vehicle onto the gravel road. Yanking the wheel, he straightened out the tires.

Mills peeled herself off of the floor. Twisting to the audio equipment, she began flipping switches and turning dials.

Dire raced toward a thick tree grove lining the road. Picking up speed, it dipped its head. Its shoulders slammed into the grove. The trees cracked and splintered. But somehow, they managed to hold firm.

Gnashing its teeth, Dire lunged at the van. Its saliva sprayed over the back window. But its jaws came up short.

Ahead, Caplan saw Pyre Peak, flanked to the southwest by the shorter Mount Gatlor. According to what he'd read, Pyre Peak carried an elevation north of four thousand feet. Thick woods, once prized by local logging companies, had formerly covered the landform. But now, the mountain looked barren.

"What's up there?" Toland asked.

"An old fire tower," Caplan replied. "Maybe some abandoned equipment, too."

"Oh, that's a big help," he said, his voice dripping with sarcasm.

Caplan knew the forest on either side was too dense for driving. And he couldn't turn around, not with Dire on their tail. So, his only option was to keep following the gravel road up the mountainside and pray the behemoth didn't care for heights. But could the van even handle the steep road? What if its steering failed? And what if Dire followed them up?

Quashing his doubts, he drove to the foot of Pyre Peak. Then he directed the vehicle over a large bump and up the steep road.

Dire smashed free of the grove. Leaping onto the road, it galloped across the gravel.

Caplan reached a hairpin turn, the first of many that awaited him. With one eye on Dire, he wrenched the steering wheel. The tires were sluggish, but still turned. Stepping on the gas, he continued up the mountainside.

Dire closed the gap and before long was within striking distance. Extending its jaws, it lunged at the van.

Caplan shifted the stiff wheel. The vehicle jolted to the left. Dire's teeth chomped at empty air.

He drove around another hairpin turn. Looking out his window, he saw a thin metal rail lining the road. It was rusty and looked to be on its last legs. Past it, he saw the forest far beneath him. *You're being chased by a monster. Your vehicle barely functions and you're racing up a mountainside. And oh, yeah, those barricades couldn't stop a tricycle, let alone a van.* He shook his head. *What could possibly go wrong?*

He continued to drive, forging a path up the increasingly precarious gravel road. Every time he approached a hairpin turn, he held his breath, wondering if the steering would hold up. So far, he'd been lucky. But his luck couldn't last forever.

He roared around another hairpin turn. Checking the rearview mirror, he saw Dire chasing after them. Its eyes were fixed on the van and nothing else. Not the road, not the forest far below, not anything.

He raced to the next hairpin turn. At nearly one hundred and eighty-degrees, it was the tightest one yet.

The ground roiled as Dire thundered after them. Its eyes sparked with a gleam of triumph.

Fingers tensed, Caplan stared at the behemoth. He saw its rippling fur, its long snout, its lava-orange eyes.

Dire picked up speed. As it drew close, it lowered its dripping jaws back to the ground.

He reached the curve and wrenched the wheel. The van tipped to one side as it navigated the tight turn.

Metal squealed as Dire tore through the flimsy barricade. Desperately, it dug its claws into the ground. But it was too little, too late. Howling, the beast plunged off the cliff. A distant thump, accompanied by smashing wood, filled the night. The howling died off.

And then all was quiet.

CHAPTER 24

Date: Nov. 26, 2017, 10:01 a.m.; Location: North Maine Woods, ME

Caplan pumped the brakes and the van slid to a halt. He wiped sweat from his visage, then sat perfectly still, inhaling and exhaling deep breaths. Despite the victory, adrenaline raced through his body. Was Dire really dead? Or had it survived the fall?

Wind careened against the van. Gravel skittered across the old road. The engine clattered softly. But he heard no growls, howls, or shrieks.

Releasing the brake, he directed the van in a half-circle. Then he parked the vehicle and popped his door open. Stepping outside, he walked to the edge of the cliff. Far below, he saw Dire trying to get up. But its left rear leg, swollen and misshapen, couldn't support its weight and the behemoth crashed back to the soil.

Toland, looking rather pale under his scraggily gray beard, joined him at the cliff. "Well, we're still alive," he remarked. "No thanks to you."

"I'll take a lucky life over a skillful death any day."

Mills walked out to join them. "Amanda was right," she said. "The behemoths use infrasound."

Caplan arched an eyebrow.

"I switched on the equipment during the chase. Dire was sending out signals the whole time. Not big ones, mind you. Small ones. And …" Her voice trailed off. When she spoke again, her tone reflected angry frustration. "Don't look now, but we've got an audience."

Caplan heard a distinct whining noise. Keeping his head level, he snuck a quick peek at the sky. A small metallic object hovered overhead.

"What's that?" Toland asked.

"It's a surveillance drone. It must've been tracking Dire." Mills exhaled. "And us."

The fierce wind relented. Caplan heard roaring engines and shifting gravel. Seconds later, a string of armored vehicles roared into his field of vision.

"Chenoa must've kept a team in the area in case we popped up again." Caplan gritted his teeth. "Let's go."

As he ran back to the van, he shot a gaze at the summit. Like the rest of the mountain, it appeared devoid of trees. He did see the old fire tower, but that wouldn't offer much in the way of hiding spots. Making matters worse, the road was the summit's sole access point. Fleeing to the top, in other words, was just delaying the inevitable.

The armored vehicles reached the mountainside and began scaling Pyre Peak. Meanwhile, Caplan hopped into the front seat. His only option was to backtrack, to slip past the oncoming vehicles. At least the ground, in contrast to the summit, wasn't a dead-end.

He turned the ignition. It shuddered, but didn't catch. He turned it again. And again. But it refused to catch.

Two armored vehicles slid around the last hairpin turn and came to a halt. Doors cracked open. Soldiers piled outside. A bunch of guns—including a bazooka—swung toward the van.

Chenoa Roberts emerged from a vehicle. The wind swept her hair back and rippled her long, red cloak. Undaunted, she stepped forward.

Caplan rolled down his window and stuck his head outside. The cold wind blistered his face. "Say, did you guys lose a wolf?" he called out. "Because I think we found it."

"Very funny. Now, take a look around. You're trapped. Step out of the van. Place your weapons on the ground, then kiss the gravel. Oh, and pray." Her lip curled at the edge. "Pray I let you live."

CHAPTER 25

Date: Nov. 26, 2017, 10:15 a.m.; Location: North Maine Woods, ME

For seventeen months, Caplan had protected his friends from the ongoing apocalypse. From the behemoths, the reborn megafauna, the Holocene extinction, and everything else. He'd deliberately kept a low profile, refusing to join up with Danter. He'd run from danger and hid in the shadows. In short, he'd done everything right. And yet, everything had gone horribly wrong. Perkins was dead. Morgan had been captured. Elliott had left. Now, he and the last remaining members of his group were cornered.

"You got us into this mess," Toland muttered under his breath. "So, get us out of it."

Caplan shifted his eyes from side to side. Armored vehicles littered every level of the mountainside. He saw no holes, no gaps. Running for it was a non-starter. "I can't fix the engine from here."

"What good are you then?"

"We don't have a choice." Leaving the key in the ignition, he cracked his door open. "I'll go first."

Climbing outside, he took a few steps away from the vehicle. The wind picked up speed, assailing him with tremendous force. He stared hard at Roberts' lean visage. Her hooded eyes stared back at him, watching his every movement.

He pulled out the twin axes and placed them on the ground. Then he turned in a slow circle, lifting his shirt, letting them know he didn't carry any hidden weapons.

"Good," Roberts said. "Now, the rest of you."

Toland and Mills climbed out of the van. Hands raised, they joined Caplan on the gravel road.

"If it isn't Bailey Mills, famous for being rich and utterly useless." Roberts eyed Mills with disdain. "We heard you were dead."

Mills forced a smile. "Those reports were greatly exaggerated."

Roberts cocked an eyebrow. "Where's Tricia?"

"Dead," Caplan said without missing a beat.

"You said the same thing about Bailey."

"Yeah, but I'm telling the truth this time."

"I bet." Roberts nodded at Mills and Toland. "On the ground. Now."

They dropped to their stomachs. A couple of soldiers shackled them, then hauled them to their knees.

"Very good." Roberts switched her attention to Caplan. "You met a man the other night. A guy with big muscles and a bright red face."

"Oh, I remember him. What was his name anyway? Steroid Sam?"

"Kevin. Kevin Pitt. We were lovers." Her lip trembled. "And you killed him."

Technically, that wasn't true. The deathblow had come from one of the Danter residents. But hey, he was willing to shoulder the blame. "You dated that creep?" He shook his head. "Truthfully, I did you a favor."

She let out a deep breath. "There's something you should know about me. I like to kill people. I really do. Especially cocky little pricks like you. There's something about it that's so ... fulfilling." She shivered with pleasure. "Know what I mean?"

"Not really. Then again, I'm not insane."

She regarded him for a few seconds. "Under different circumstances, you'd already be dead. But Mr. Corbotch wants you alive."

"I guess it's my lucky day."

"It depends on your point of view. You see, I might not get to kill you." A smile, sweet and full of venom, crossed her visage. "But I do get to break you."

He held her stare. He didn't see insanity in her eyes. But there was definitely an edge to them that set his nerves abuzz.

Quick as lightening, she unleashed a right jab in his direction. He saw the blow coming. There was no time to dodge it, so he decided to roll with the punch. But when her fist struck his cheek, excruciating pain exploded inside of his head. His legs wobbled and he slumped to the ground.

Dazed, he looked up. Roberts stood over him. Smiling, she rubbed her knuckles. *Her brass knuckles.*

"You're obviously used to ruling your own roost. Finding food, running from colossi. Helping your little friends, maybe even doing them if you catch my drift." She stared into Caplan's eyes. "All that ends today."

Kneeling down, she lashed out with her left fist. Caplan tried to roll away, but the last punch had left him sluggish. Her fist struck pay dirt and searing pain slashed up his side.

Another fist hammered into his right shoulder. Colors exploded in front of his eyes and it took everything he had to keep from passing out.

"I'm in charge now." She wiped grime and blood off her gleaming knuckles. "If I say jump, you jump. If I tell you to act like a dog, you'd better start barking. Do you catch my drift?"

He'd already lost the fight. That much was clear. But he had no intention of going down like a coward.

"Is that all you've got?" He spat out a mouthful of blood. "I've had tougher fights with the common cold."

Her fist cracked his jaw. His head snapped back, striking the gravel. He coughed, spitting up more blood.

He felt himself flipped over. A knee plunged into his back, driving the wind out of his lungs. His limbs turned spastic. But the knee kept him pinned down.

Hands grabbed his ankles, fitted them into restraints. Other hands cuffed his wrists. The knee lifted off his back and Caplan felt himself pulled to his feet.

Everything was blurry. He blinked a few times, clearing his vision. Mills stood nearby, her face twisted with fury. Despite her restraints, it still took three soldiers to hold her back. Meanwhile, Toland stood still and sullen. A single soldier guarded the grizzled old writer.

"Don't worry about your friends." Roberts snapped her fingers. A black hood slid over Caplan's face. The drawstring cinched tight. "Worry about me."

CHAPTER 26

Date: ?; Location: ?

The feminine screams, terrible and helpless, pierced Caplan's ears, driving him out of a deep, dreamless sleep. His eyes flew open and he stared at infinite blackness. Where was he? How had he gotten here? And who was screaming?

Heart pounding, he tried to sit up, to move. But leather straps, bulky and rough, kept him locked in place.

A squashing noise, flesh on flesh, sounded out. The screams turned into gurgles. Then into whimpers.

Then into silence.

His head swirled in the darkness. He couldn't see anything. He didn't know up from down, left from right. It was enough to drive him to the brink of insanity.

He closed his eyes. Took long, deep breaths. Then he focused on his other senses. He felt a soft, thin mattress beneath him. A cotton sheet stretched across it, covering his itchy, aching body. Leather restrained his ankles and wrists. Ah, he was lying in a bed, his limbs locked down with leather straps.

Faint footsteps struck a hard surface. Light metallic clatters, like forks striking plates, filled his ears. The air smelled of blood, excrement, and body odor, partially masked by a thick layer of disinfectant.

He decided he was in a hospital. The thought relaxed him until he recalled the leather straps. His heart raced again and memories poured into his skull with waterfall force.

He recalled the hood cinching tight over his head. He'd been hustled into one of the armored vehicles, then driven to a nearby helicopter. A needle had pricked his arm. His mind had grown foggy. Everything after that was a complete blank.

What had happened to Mills and Toland? Were they still alive? What about the van and its audio equipment?

A stinging ache erupted in his forehead. He clenched his teeth, biting off a yelp. The ache intensified and his muscles began to quiver. Colors exploded in front of his closed eyelids. A scream formed inside his throat. He fought to keep his jaw shut, desperate to avoid the uncertain fate of that other screamer.

The ache got worse and worse until it felt like his head might explode. Then, as quickly as it started, the pain eased. The colors faded. The scream died away. And then he felt fine again, as if nothing had happened.

He inhaled, exhaled. Then he opened his eyelids and stared into the darkness. Gradually, his vision adjusted to the dim light. Shifting his head, he noticed tiny beams moving throughout a vast area. It took him a few seconds to realize the lights came from headlamps. Who was wearing them? Doctors? Nurses?

He turned his head to the right and noticed a long row of beds and machines, stretching into the darkness. A woman with a bulging forehead and big hands lay on the closest bed, half-buried under a web of tubes and IVs. There were at least a dozen of them, sticking into her arms and shooting underneath the sheet to connect to other parts of her body.

Turning to the left, he saw the row of beds and machines continue into more darkness. Glancing forward and then over his shoulder, he saw more beds, more machines, more darkness. One thing was certain. This wasn't an ordinary medical facility. In fact, it looked a lot like a field hospital, albeit one with a ton of sophisticated machinery.

Looking to his side, he saw a single table. It was empty save for a clipboard. Squinting, he made out two lines. The first one read, *Savage Station Medical Chart,* in big bold letters.

Hey, look on the bright side, he thought with dark mirth. *You found Savage Station.*

But his mirth quickly melted away. According to what Mills had overheard, Savage Station held hundreds, if not thousands, of prisoners. Those prisoners were forced to endure vicious torture.

And apparently, he was now one of them.

The second line on the clipboard contained his name as well as the date, *November 26, 2017.* Ahh, that was a bit of good news. It meant he'd been unconscious for less than twenty-four hours.

He squinted harder, but was unable to read the rest of the chart. The ache reappeared in his forehead. Gritting his teeth, he fought it off in silence and continued to lay in the bed, restless and hyper-aware. Part of him wanted to call out to the strange people with the headlamps. To bombard them with questions. But he stayed quiet.

The strange woman to his right began to squirm. And then Caplan saw it. A surgical scar stretching along the back of her scalp. The stitched skin looked fairly normal, indicating the procedure had been done some time ago.

Looking left and right, he studied the other beds. The machines kept him from seeing much. But he glimpsed a few other heads. All of them sported identical scars.

His eyes narrowed. It wasn't a field hospital. Nor was it some kind of weird torture chamber. It was a research station. And that meant he and the others weren't really patients or even prisoners.

They were guinea pigs.

CHAPTER 27

Date: Nov. 26, 2017, 10:46 p.m.; Location: Savage Station, Vallerio Forest, NH

"Where …?" Caplan worked his tongue, trying to get moisture into his mouth. "Where are you taking me?"

The rolling bed halted. Footsteps scuffed the floor. Then a shadowy figure appeared overhead. The bright headlamp kept him from seeing the person's face. But he could see the syringe. A long, dripping needle positioned inches above his neck, just begging to put him to sleep.

He nodded. Fine. He'd be quiet. For now, anyway.

The bright light left his eyes. Footsteps scuffed the floor. The bed jolted forward.

Caplan lay still for the most part, conserving his strength. But every now and then, he'd shift his gaze. To the other beds, to the research subjects that lay upon them. He saw lots of men and lots of women. Many of them were burly with short limbs and large noses. All of them, as far as he could tell, sported identical surgical scars.

Did he have a scar, too? He rubbed the back of his head against a thin pillow, but didn't feel anything unusual.

He continued to roll forward, passing more beds and more people. He kept his eyes peeled for Morgan. For Mills and Toland, too. But he didn't see any of them.

He turned his gaze to the high ceiling. The room felt like it yawned on forever. But was it really that large? He couldn't tell, not with all the darkness.

The bed reached the end of the row and turned right. As it headed down a new row, he shot a glimpse to his left. He saw drywall, painted beige. Tables and chairs were pushed up against it. Corkboards hung on the wall. Notes, work schedules, and warning signs covered every inch of their surfaces. Oddball posters were pinned up between the corkboards. One particular poster caught his eye. It depicted a handsome man and a beautiful woman, happily clinking wine glasses in front of a mushroom cloud. The caption read, *These Are The End Times ... And It's About Time!*

And these people are going to operate on my head? he thought. *How comforting.*

He felt himself pushed to a pair of doors. They opened automatically. The bed rolled forward again and he entered a long hallway. He barely had time to look around before he was pushed into another room. In nearly all ways, it was different. Instead of beds in neat rows, he saw giant wheel-shaped objects standing on end. Bright lights from overhead fixtures cast a harsh glow on the wheels. Individuals roamed the room. They were clean-cut and dressed in white uniforms.

A kindly face appeared. It belonged to a bearded, elderly man. "Hello."

Caplan looked at him, but kept his mouth closed.

"Ahh, I see." The man cast a withering look at the person who'd been pushing the bed. "Your services are no longer required, Joel."

Footsteps scuffed the floor, growing fainter by the second. Meanwhile, the bearded man rolled the bed to one of the large wheels. He kicked the brake into place and cranked the mattress into a sitting position. "I'm sorry about that. The orderlies aren't known for their bedside manner."

Caplan didn't respond. Instead, he looked at the wheel. It measured about eight feet tall and was four feet thick. It was built from a tough, opaque material. Kind of like plastic, but definitely harder. He shuddered inwardly as he noticed a placard taped to the wheel. Block lettering read, *Zach Caplan*.

"My name is Dr. Luke Barden." The man glanced at the chart. "And it says here your name is Zach Caplan. Tell me something, Mr. Caplan. Are you famous?"

He ripped his eyes away from the wheel. "Well, I don't like to brag about it, but yes. It's me. Two-time winner of Warden High School's ping-pong tournament."

Dr. Barden hid a slight smile. "You see, I rarely work this late. But Mr. Corbotch sent word that I was to take personal care of you, Mr. Toland, and ..." He checked his notes. "... Ms. Bailey Mills."

"You work for James?"

He nodded.

"Then take a good look." He cast a glance at his restrained, sheeted body. "Because this is your future."

"Let's start with your vitals." He produced a blood pressure cuff and wrapped it around Caplan's arm. "In the meantime, I imagine you've got questions. I'll try to answer them if I can."

"Where are we? I know we're in the Vallerio Forest, but where in the Vallerio?"

"I'm afraid I don't know much about the surrounding geography." He finished taking Caplan's blood pressure and jotted it down on the chart. "But I can tell you that we're in an underground silo right now."

"We are?"

He nodded. "You know those silos from the Cold War? The ones used to house Atlas ICBMs? Well, Savage is kind of like that."

"Ahh, those were the days. When people just worried about an apocalypse rather than actually living in one."

"Yes, well …" He looked uncomfortable. "Anyway Savage predates the Cold War. The foundations were laid in the late 1800s by Miles Spencer Corbotch. From what I understand, he used this facility to conduct all sorts of strange experiments."

"So, nothing's changed, huh?"

Dr. Barden's face turned pink. Silently, he continued his examination.

Nearby, Caplan noticed a bank of computers and machines. Thick cables connected them to the wheel as well as to fifteen other wheels. The wheels, he realized, weren't placed randomly throughout the room. They were positioned in a circle. Something about the set-up nagged at him. "What exactly are you doing here?"

"Well, that's a complicated question." He stroked his beard. "Imagine a man with a terminal disease. Now, imagine that a cure exists for that disease, only the man isn't aware of it. He can't even fathom its existence and thus, would utterly refuse it if offered the choice. Someone should provide him with the cure, yes?"

"Not if he doesn't want it."

"Even if it could save his life?"

"It's his decision."

"Not if he's inclined to make the wrong one."

Bewildered, Caplan furrowed his brow. "If you're trying to say I've got a terminal disease, then you're right. But HA-78 doesn't affect me. I'm an asymptomatic carrier."

"It's not HA-78. And honestly, the exact nature of your affliction doesn't matter. What matters is that we can help you."

"Help me how?"

"As you know, the world has changed quite a bit these last seventeen months. It's become nearly unlivable for our species. We would like to help you adjust—to evolve, if you will—to this new world of ours."

Caplan's brain zoomed back to the clearing outside the cabin, to his face-to-face confrontation with Corbotch. *I don't look younger,* the man had said. *I am younger. Not all of my genetic engineering efforts went toward megafauna, you know.*

Did that explain Dr. Barden's cryptic remarks as well as the surgical scars? Was he reengineering people at a genetic level? Was he making them stronger and faster? Was he prepping them for the post-behemoth world? If so, why?

"Just what I always wanted," Caplan said. "Unnecessary brain surgery."

"Brain surgery? I don't …" His face brightened. "Ahh, I get it. You saw the scars back in the clinic. Well, you have nothing to fear. All of our patients underwent the same procedure. It's perfectly harmless."

"Then why don't you have a scar?"

"I'm Savage Station's only practicing surgeon, Mr. Caplan. And I can't very well operate on myself, can I?"

"I'd be happy to do it for you."

"No, thanks. But rest assured the procedure is quick and painless. I'll be implanting a small microchip under your skin." He nodded at the nearby wheel. "Among other things, it'll help you bond effectively with your module."

A microchip? The very thought made Caplan queasy. Corbotch had inserted microchips into the reborn megafauna and possibly the behemoths as well. Their exact purpose was unknown, but Morgan had speculated they were being used to fuel bloodlust. *Terrific,* he thought. *I always wanted to be a vampire.*

"I don't want to bond with it," Caplan said with a glance at the wheel. "It hasn't even bought me dinner yet."

The doctor's head rolled back and he laughed. "This really is for your own good, Mr. Caplan. Now, let's just get you loaded into this module and we'll—"

"Dr. Barden." The voice, loud and crisp, rang out over an intercom. "Mr. Corbotch would like a word with you."

"Excuse me." Smoothing down his beard, Dr. Barden rose to his feet. "I'll be back in a moment."

As the doctor walked to a telephone, Caplan turned toward the wheel-shaped modules. A long-dormant memory surged into his consciousness. He recalled sitting inside Corbotch's Rexto 419R3 helicopter. He recalled ascending from the Vallerio Forest, flying away into the great unknown. He recalled Mills talking about a barn-like building she'd seen in the Vallerio, about wheel-like objects inside that building.

They were in the basement, Mills had said. *Tricia and I went down there while Brian kept watch. She opened one and we saw this dead guy. At first, we thought the wheel was an isolation chamber. But the guy was plugged into it with wires and tubes. Tricia guessed it was some kind of life-support system and that the power failure had killed him. But who builds over a dozen life support systems in the middle of nowhere?"*

Caplan studied the modules. They definitely weren't life-support systems. In fact, he was pretty sure they'd been used to manipulate people on a genetic level. But how?

And why?

CHAPTER 28

Date: Nov. 27, 2017, 1:16 a.m.; Location: Savage Station, Vallerio Forest, NH

Cold water crested into Caplan's face. He shut his eyes and mouth. The steady spray ripped against his naked, bruised cheeks, then attacked the rest of his body.

"Turn around," Roberts commanded.

"If it's all the same to you, I think I'll—" The spray caught Caplan straight in the mouth. He coughed, sputtering for air. Instinctively, he twisted away, causing the chains that bound him to clank in the process.

The spray soaked the back of his head, his shoulders, his back, his rear, and his legs. Then the stream dried up. Drips of water struck the concrete floor.

He stood still, water slipping down his chest. His jaw ached. His ribs were sore, if not busted. His entire body felt like mashed hamburger meat.

Some two hours earlier, he'd been lying next to the modules, frantically brainstorming escape plans. Dr. Barden had returned to the bed, red-faced and quiet. He proceeded to sterilize and patch up Caplan's many wounds. But that was it. For whatever reason, the man stopped short of implanting the microchip.

Eventually, Roberts had arrived, flanked by soldiers. She'd taken him to a dimly-lit concrete room. He recalled every second of the subsequent thrashing, every brass-knuckled shot to his unprotected face and torso. It had been a vicious, ruthless attack. But he'd survived it.

Twisting around, he stared at Roberts and her lackeys. Their faces were impassive. One soldier held the end of a dripping hose.

"We call that the Savage Shower." She tossed his clothes, freshly laundered, to him. "How'd you like it?"

His head felt heavy, groggy. He could barely lift his exhausted arms. But despite it all, he still managed to crack a cocky grin. "Better than I like the company."

"Why do you have to answer everything with an insult?"

"Probably because it's so easy to insult you."

Her lips tightened.

As Caplan donned his clothes, he took in the rest of the space. Plain and sturdy, it reminded him of those safe rooms that were so popular in tornado-prone areas. The door was made of metal. The walls, floor, and ceiling were reinforced concrete. Light was provided by an overhead fixture.

He stared at the fixture for a few seconds, transfixed by its very existence. How long had it been since he'd seen working electricity outside of a car? He couldn't remember.

"You haven't asked about your friends yet," Roberts said, crossing her arms.

That was true. It was also deliberate. For now, he thought it best to act like they didn't matter to him. That way, she couldn't use them against him. But it wasn't easy. In fact, it had taken all of his willpower not to pepper her with questions.

"Oh, yeah," he replied. "How are they?"

"They're fine." She smirked. "By the way, which one are you screwing? Amanda? Bailey? Both? Just tell me you weren't doing that Tricia chick."

"A gentleman never tells."

Her smirk faded. "Anyway your friends are resting comfortably in our clinic. You remember the clinic, don't you? The room with all the beds?"

"It rings a bell."

"We use it to house and monitor our subjects between module sessions. Right now, Bailey and Brian are undergoing a battery of tests to determine their suitability. Amanda already passed her tests with flying colors. In fact, she experienced her first module session earlier today."

His face grew warm. What was a module session? Was Morgan okay?

"Just so you know, you won't be entering the modules," she continued. "In fact, you won't be staying here much longer. Mr. Corbotch is sending you on a little trip."

The news hit him like a sledgehammer. Savage Station creeped him out, but at least he was close to his friends. How was he going to save them now? "I hope it's someplace warm," he replied.

"It's not."

"Too bad." He turned his gaze to the walls. "I hear this place dates back to the 1800s," he said, changing the subject. "It must have quite a history."

"It was built by Mr. Corbotch's ancestor, Miles Spencer Corbotch. When Mr. Corbotch first found it, he discovered evidence of grisly activities, including human experimentation."

"James is related to a psychopath? Big surprise."

Her visage took on an annoyed look. "It took years of renovations, but Mr. Corbotch eventually transformed this space into a top-notch facility. In addition to the clinic and various labs, we've got ample quarters, a kitchen, a pool, a movie theater, and a library."

"If you're going to launch the apocalypse, might as well ride it out in style, right?"

"That's right." She arched an eyebrow. "By the way, I know what you're doing right now."

"Yeah? What's that?"

"You're fishing for information, hoping I'll give you something you can use to escape. You might as well forget it. This room is completely solid."

"Snug and cushy, too."

"It could be worse. You could be on Level X."

"What's on Level X?"

A scream, barely audible, filtered into his ears. A couple of bloodcurdling howls, even softer, followed suit.

Roberts smiled. "Them."

His blood chilled. These were clearly the sounds of torture. And yet, they weren't coming from the clinic two floors up. No, they were coming from somewhere beneath his feet. Evidently, Corbotch's torture program was separate from the clinic.

"Some say those sounds you just heard are the ghosts of Miles' victims," Roberts said.

"Stupidity knows no bounds, I guess."

"You've got a smart mouth."

"At least it's not a stupid one."

She glared at him. "It's time for me to go. But first, I want you to fully understand your situation. You're locked in a secure room. Dozens of my best soldiers monitor this floor. In other words, you're stuck. There's no escape, no way out. And that means playtime for me. Until Mr. Corbotch says otherwise, I'm going to make your life a living hell." She walked to the door, opened it, and stepped outside. "But don't feel too sorry for yourself. Your friends have it worse than you do. Much worse."

The door closed over. A lock clicked. The overhead fixture went dark.

And then Caplan was alone.

CHAPTER 29

Date: Nov. 29, 2017, 3:34 a.m.; Location: Savage Station, Vallerio Forest, NH

Screams and howls, soft and discordant, flooded Caplan's ears. His heart raced and his eyes shot open. Blinding light awaited him and he shied away from it. Where was he? What was going on?

He lay still, breathing heavily. Memories pushed their way into his sleep-deprived mind. He'd spent two days locked in the room, deep within Savage Station. Soldiers tortured him around-the-clock with bright lights, beatings, and electric shocks. Screams and howls, clearly human and yet not human at all, accosted his ears at all times.

He'd managed to nod off once or twice over the last forty-eight hours, but only for an hour or two at a time. How long had it been since his last real deep sleep? Would he ever sleep again?

He lay on the concrete floor a little longer, his ears awash in screams and howls. His brain felt like jelly. He wanted to curl his toes and clutch his ears. But he resisted the temptation. After all, Roberts was most likely watching him.

His thoughts turned to Mills, Morgan, and yes, even Toland. Where were they? Were they still alive? And where was Elliott? Was she still with Ross and the rest of the Danter colony?

The lock clicked.

Still squinting, he sat up. He'd quietly searched the room numerous times. He'd checked the floor for weaknesses. He'd scoured the walls for cracks. Unfortunately, Roberts hadn't been exaggerating. The room was escape-proof.

The door shifted open. Roberts appeared in the doorframe. "I see the ghosts are back," she said.

"Really? I didn't notice."

"Remember Kevin?" Taking her time, she donned her brass knuckles. "The man you killed back in Maine?"

"The musclebound freak? Sure, I remember him."

Her gaze tightened an iota. "We just buried his body."

"Did you bury Mike Ballard and the other people you killed in Danter, too?"

She ignored him. "I didn't cry at the funeral. Oh, I wanted to cry. But thinking of you—of what I was going to do to you—well, that was enough to keep me sane."

He stayed silent. Not because he had nothing to say, but because he didn't want to betray even a hint of his frazzled nerves.

She entered the room, followed by a couple of soldiers. Closing the door, she engaged the lock.

He shut his eyes and sealed off his mind. And then he was alone. Alone with the screams and howls. Alone with the bright lights. Alone with his darkest thoughts.

A couple of hands yanked him off the ground. They forced him into an upright position and immobilized him. Brass-knuckles slammed into his stomach and he screamed. He screamed out of pain and agony. He screamed out of concern for his friends. He screamed because he had no choice. But he didn't scream for mercy.

Forget thriving, he sang. *Just keep on surviving.*

CHAPTER 30

Date: Nov. 30, 2017, 2:04 a.m.; Location: Savage Station, Vallerio Forest, NH

He knew the date—November Thirtieth—but it held no specific meaning for him. He'd been locked up for … how long had it been? Three days? Four days?

His friend's faces ran through his mind on an endless loop. How many sessions had Morgan endured in those strange wheel-shaped modules? Were Mills and Toland now undergoing sessions as well?

His mind flitted to Stage Three. He still had no clue what it entailed. He only knew that it was scheduled to begin on the Third of December and would mean the end of humanity's last few population centers. With the exception of Savage Station, the *Homo sapiens* species would be all but finished. Not that he cared all that much. In fact, if it weren't for Elliott and the sizable Danter colony, he wouldn't have cared at all.

He flopped onto his stomach and tried to hide his head in his arms. But he couldn't block out the screams and howls. Meanwhile, bits of blinding light snuck through his crossed arms and stabbed into his eyeballs.

He shifted slightly. His body ached from the endless beatings and electric shocks. His mind, twisted into a pretzel from sleep deprivation, couldn't concentrate for more than a few seconds at a time.

The lock clicked. Metal scraped against concrete. He didn't groan, didn't budge. He didn't even care.

"You've got visitors," Roberts said.

Shielding his eyes, he glanced at the door. Roberts and her usual assortment of soldiers stood on the threshold. But they weren't alone.

"Bailey?" he said in a raspy tone. "Brian?"

Mills and Toland, weighed down by restraints and surrounded by soldiers, stood in the adjoining hallway. Their clothes, freshly laundered and pressed, looked almost new. The same, unfortunately, couldn't be said for their faces.

Mills' cheeks were red and splotchy. Big bags rested under Toland's eyes. They both appeared dazed and disoriented.

"Unfortunately, Dr. Barden declared them medically ineligible for module sessions," Roberts explained. "So, it looks like you'll be having company on your trip."

Relief washed over Caplan. "The more, the merrier."

"Just so you know, this is as merry as it's going to get. Amanda will be staying with us. She came along too late to make the first wave but—"

"The first wave?"

She smiled. Then she snapped her fingers. Two soldiers dragged Toland into the room. They removed his restraints and released him. His body sagged to the floor.

Roberts removed Mills' restraints. Then she shoved the woman. Mills stumbled into the room. She tripped over her feet and fell to the floor, smacking her head against the concrete in the process.

Caplan crawled to her side. "Bailey?" he asked, brushing damp hair away from her eyes. "Can you hear me?"

"This is your last night at Savage," Roberts said. "I suggest you make the most of it. Your next stop will be far less pleasant than this one."

Boots scuffed the floor. The door closed. The lock clicked. The overhead light, however, remained on.

Gently, Caplan rolled Mills onto her back. Ignoring the howls and screams, he placed his ear against her chest. Her heart sounded good. He checked her breathing and was relieved to find it was normal.

He stripped off his shirt. Wadding it up, he placed it beneath her head. Then he crawled to Toland.

"Uhh." Toland stirred. "My head ..."

Caplan gave the man a quick check. He saw numerous needle marks and accompanying bruises. But otherwise, Toland looked to be in good shape.

"What happened?" he asked.

"They poked us with needles, then stuck us into their wheels. They must've pumped me full of drugs because I don't remember much after that."

"But you do remember something?"

"This quack—he called himself Dr. Barden—was with us the entire time. He referred to the wheels as genome transplantation modules." Toland rubbed his head. "He said they were used to edit genes. To change people."

Caplan nodded. It was just as he figured. One of the modules had been used to edit Corbotch's genes, to bring the man to new levels of physicality. Now, the clinic's patients were undergoing similar treatment. "Change them into what?" he asked.

Renewed howls and screams floated up through the floor and pervaded every inch of the room.

Toland exhaled. "Into that."

CHAPTER 31

"It's hopeless." Toland sat down in the middle of the room. Lowering his palms to the floor, he stuck his legs out in front of him. "The only way we're getting out of here is with a battering ram."

Mills, now awake and partially recovered, paced alongside one of the walls. She studied it carefully, searching for any sign of weakness. "You're giving up?"

He shrugged. "What's the point?"

"If we don't escape, we're going on a one-way trip, courtesy of James Corbotch. Do you remember the last trip he took us on?" She arched an eyebrow. "The one to saber-tooth central?"

He considered that for a second. Then he rose up, limped across the floor, and began studying the walls anew.

Caplan ignored the cinching in his chest as he walked along one of the other walls. A part of him had suspected the screams and howls came from former clinic patients, now recovering from gene editing. Still, it was one thing to think it, another thing to know it.

Roberts had mentioned something about a first wave and how Morgan was too late to join it. Did that explain Corbotch's plan for Stage Three? Was he creating an army of genetically-engineered warriors to wipe out Earth's remaining population centers? Would this army swarm the planet in waves?

His fingers moved over the wall as he checked for crevices and cracks. He was pretty sure he'd gone over the area a thousand times already. But he'd do it a million more times if that's what it took to find a weakness.

He moved to the door. He jiggled the handle and checked the bolt. He ran his hands over the metallic surface and struggled to loosen the hinges. And all the while, he pondered his next move if—when—they secured an exit. Without weapons or back-up, their best bet was to disguise themselves, grab Morgan, and head for the surface.

But then what? Could they survive Stage Three? And even if they could, what about Elliott, Ross, and the rest of the Danter colony?

They worked for another fifteen minutes. Then Toland sat down again. "Calm down," he said when Mills gave him a dirty look. "I'm just grabbing some grub."

"Good idea." Caplan wiped his hands on his shirt and walked to the corner. His lunch—a hunk of stale bread, and a few thin slices of mystery meat—lay on a small paper plate. He sniffed the meat and nearly gagged.

Quickly, he wolfed down the stale bread. It didn't even begin to satiate his hunger. As such, he was tempted to try the meat. But ultimately, he thought better of it.

He grabbed one of three paper cups from the ground. Lifting it to his lips, he swallowed a bit of water. It burned as it slid down his parched throat.

"You know, this place almost makes me miss that cabin of yours." Toland took a bite of bread. "Almost."

Caplan crumpled up his paper cup and tossed it to the floor. As he walked to another wall, a soft howl drifted up from underneath the concrete floor. It made him think of his theory about Corbotch building an army of genetically-engineered warriors. Was he right about that?

And if so, how long before Morgan joined their ranks?

CHAPTER 32

Date: Nov. 30, 2017, 7:32 p.m.; Location: Savage Station, Vallerio Forest, NH

"I was right the first time." Toland scowled at one of the walls. "This is hopeless."

This time, Mills said nothing. Caplan remained quiet as well. The cold, hard truth was beginning to settle into his brain. There was no escape. Not for his friends, not for him.

The lock clicked. Metal scraped against concrete.

Twisting to the door, Caplan saw Roberts with her usual assortment of cronies. "Back so soon?"

"It's almost time to go," she replied.

"Good." Mills flipped her hair over her shoulder. "I was getting tired of this place."

"I said *almost time*. There are still two last things to do." She glanced at Caplan. "And they involve you."

He arched an eyebrow. "Do tell."

"We're going to pay someone a visit. Then Mr. Corbotch wants a word with you. Think of it as an exit interview."

Two soldiers entered the room. While they applied restraints to Caplan's wrists and ankles, he glanced at Mills. He saw the anger, the determination in her eyes. But he also saw the question marks, the uncertainty. If he gave her the go-ahead, he knew she'd launch an attack at that very second.

An attack that would, in all likelihood, get them killed. *I'll be fine*, he mouthed.

Her lips moved. *Good luck.*

He felt a soft nudge. Shuffling his feet, he moved to the door. He reached the hallway and two soldiers took the lead. Roberts and a third soldier sandwiched him on either side. Two more soldiers took up the rear.

They walked out into a large circular space. It was furnished like a fancy waiting room. Leather sofas and chairs, barely dented, provided plenty of seating. Small tables held paperback books and dog-eared magazines. Men and women, all dressed in long pants and lab coats, crisscrossed the floor, heading up and down connecting hallways.

Their small group entered a stairwell and climbed two flights. Then they walked out into another waiting room. From there, a short walk led them to the clinic.

The soldiers donned headlamps, their beams dancing across the enormous, dimly-lit space. They led Caplan to the side wall and across the room. Looking around, he saw tables and chairs and the wall-based corkboards. And he saw the oddball posters, still hailing the apocalypse.

They passed through double doors and entered a hallway. Then they slid through another pair of double doors.

Caplan's skin scrawled as he entered a brightly-lit room. It was the same room where he'd met Dr. Barden. Turning his head, he laid eyes on the wheels. What had Toland called them again? Oh, yes ... genome transplantation modules.

Roberts cleared her throat. "Hello, Dr. Barden."

The doctor swiveled around in his chair. "Hi, Chenoa. I wasn't expecting you for another hour."

"Mr. Corbotch made a few changes to our timetable." She glanced around at the modules. "Where's the subject?"

"Over there."

Standing up, the doctor led them to one of the modules. It hummed softly and Caplan could feel electricity all around it. He took a glance at the attached placard.

It read, *Amanda Morgan*.

"Open it," Roberts said.

"She hasn't finished this session yet," the doctor replied. "If we end it now, we'll have to start all over."

She glared at him.

"Which is just fine," he said hurriedly. "Hang on."

He hiked to the central computer bank. Sitting down, he began to peck away at a keyboard. The humming ceased and the electricity died down.

One side of the module popped open and lifted toward the ceiling. The interior was hollowed out, forming something similar to a cushioned dentist's chair. Morgan sat on top of the chair, looking like she was ready to have her teeth checked.

Caplan stared at her. A gray surgical gown rested gently upon her body. Wires and thin tubes connected her to the module's back wall. She looked the same and yet, there was something different about her.

"Amanda?" Roberts shook Morgan's shoulder. "I brought someone to see you."

Her head rolled toward the opening. Her eyes opened just a smidgeon. "Zach?" she whispered. "Is that you?"

"Yeah." He exhaled. "Are you okay?"

"It hurts." A look of pure agony crossed her visage. "Oh, my God, it hurts so ..." Her voice trailed off. Her eyes rolled to the back of her head and she fell still.

"Amanda?" He tried to step forward, but the soldiers held him back.

Dr. Barden hit more keys on the keyboard. The module closed over again.

"Do you know why I brought you here?" Roberts asked.

Caplan could barely breathe. "Why?"

"I wanted you to feel what I felt when I first laid eyes upon Kevin. We're killing her, Zach, one piece at a time." Sadistic venom filled her voice. "And when we're done, there'll be nothing left."

CHAPTER 33

Date: Nov. 30, 2017, 8:16 p.m.; Location: Savage Station, Vallerio Forest, NH

"Hello, Zach." Corbotch's voice boomed through the cavernous room. "Tell me, how has Ms. Roberts been treating you?"

"Terrible. But in her defense, she's deranged."

A fist, encased in brass knuckles, slammed into Caplan's unprotected side. It left him gasping and wheezing for air.

"Sit him over there," Corbotch said.

Soldiers directed Caplan through a pair of gigantic elephant doors and into an enormous wood-paneled room. Animal heads, some with horns and antlers, were mounted on the walls. Glass cabinets displayed a fine collection of antique pistols, muskets, and rifles. Old-fashioned chairs and couches, covered in red fabric, offered ample seating. Statues and figurines decorated nearby dark wood tables. The place looked like a hunting lodge, all the way down to the elaborate carpet covering the floor.

Overhead chandeliers, aided by lamps, cast soft light over part of the room. The other part was shrouded in darkness. Caplan squinted, but couldn't see through it. It was so dark he felt like he was staring into a black hole, one that would soon consume them all.

Two chairs, separated by a table, faced the darkness. The soldiers thrust him into one of the chairs. Then they applied a second set of restraints, binding him to the seat.

"That's fine," Corbotch said. "You can go now."

The soldiers exited the room. Meanwhile, howls and screams poured in through the open doors. They seemed to come from somewhere down the adjoining hallway.

Roberts cleared her throat. "Will you be coming along for the drop-off, Mr. Corbotch?"

"I wouldn't miss it for the world." He checked his wristwatch. "Come back around nine o'clock. We should be finished by then."

"Yes, sir." Twisting around, she left the room, closing the door after her. The howls and screams vanished. Silence came over the lodge.

Caplan looked at Corbotch. The man wore a tailored white shirt, topped off by a gray sport coat. He faced a large wall-mounted monitor bank. The monitors showed images of behemoths backed by cities, forests, suburbs, and more.

He turned his attention to the animal heads. They were similar to animals from the modern era. Similar, yet different. A wolf's head was larger and more swollen than that of any species he'd ever encountered. A bear's head, mounted above a faux fireplace, featured giant teeth and ... were those horns?

Corbotch left the monitor bank. He walked behind a long bar and picked up a bottle of Hamron's Horror. Producing a tumbler, he filled it with ice cubes. Then he tipped the bottle, pouring a healthy portion of copper-colored scotch into the glass.

He took a long draught from the tumbler. Then he followed Caplan's gaze to the animal heads. "Quite a collection, wouldn't you say?"

"They look old."

"They are old. Tell me, what do you know about the Dasnoe Expedition?"

Some kids obsessed over baseball statistics, others over celebrity gossip. But in his youth, Caplan had always gravitated toward monsters, myths, and legends. He'd spent many summer afternoons at Danter Library, poring over two shelves of books devoted to the Yeti, Atlantis, and the Lost Dutchman Mine. That was where he'd first read about the Vallerio Forest. Where he'd first learned of its many mysteries and strange horrors.

What would've happened if he'd never found those books? Would he have still applied for that job at the Vallerio's Hatcher Station? Would he have ever met Morgan or Mills? Would he have survived this long?

"It took place in 1904," he replied. "It was the last of three known expeditions to the Vallerio."

"Do you know how it ended?"

"In tragedy. A pack of wolves ambushed it, killing six people."

"I'm impressed." Glass in hand, he walked around the bar. "As you know, my family has owned the Vallerio for many years. One of my relatives, a man named Miles Spencer Corbotch, constructed at least two secret facilities within its boundaries during the late 1800s. The first, which he called the Cavern, is how I escaped death a year and a half ago. The second was code-named Savage City."

Caplan's brow furrowed. He worried about Morgan. He worried about Mills, Toland, and himself, too. Even so, he couldn't help but feel fascinated by the conversation. A secret city? Hidden in the already-mysterious Vallerio? How was that even possible? "I've never heard of it."

"Neither had I until I stumbled upon it in Miles' old papers. City is a bit of misnomer, by the way. It's more of a small town. This facility lies on the edge of Savage City, hence why we call it Savage Station. It was originally designed as some kind of research facility. We believe the town was built to give its technicians, scientists, and other employees a sense of normalcy." He cast a wistful eye around the room. "This place was a giant mess when I found it. Shattered equipment, strange skeletons, and trashed furniture littered the upper floors. The lower floors, including this one, were inaccessible. It took two months to stabilize everything and rebuild the staircases."

"Sounds like a lot of work."

"It was. But it was worth the effort. I found this room looking almost exactly like you see it today. The animal heads, the carpet, the statues ... they were all here." Corbotch took a sip of his drink. "And that brings me back to the Dasnoe Expedition. As you said, the media reported it came to a premature end because of a wolf attack. But Joseph Dasnoe went to his grave—an early one, I might add—claiming the creatures weren't wolves. What if the animals he saw that day were, in fact, the ones before you now?"

It was certainly a plausible theory. Scanning the heads, Caplan found himself wondering about the strange beasts. "How'd they get like that?"

"Most evidence points to a strange breeding program. But we can't be certain. There's no mention of these creatures anywhere in Miles' correspondence or notes." He shrugged. "But one thing is certain. When I walked into this room all those years ago, it changed my life. At the time, I was studying the potential of rewilding this forest via proxy animals. Elephants for mammoths, for instance. But when I saw these heads, I realized I might be able to create my own animals. This room, in many ways, was the birthplace of the Apex Predator project."

"Insanity breeds insanity, I guess."

Corbotch chuckled. "If you think that's insane, you're going to love this." He produced a small radio from his pocket and pressed a button. "We're ready for Lucy."

"Yes, sir," a voice crackled in response.

Corbotch walked to the wall and lifted a dimmer switch. A separate chandelier came to life. The room's darkness melted away, revealing a large cage. It was built into the far wall. A steel door provided access to whatever lay beyond the wall.

Silently, the door slid open, revealing a dark void. "That door connects the cage with another one directly behind the wall," Corbotch explained as he took the other seat.

A man, tall but stooped, stumbled out of the void. He reached the bars and wrapped his gnarled fingers around them. "Please," he said in a strangled voice. "Don't do this."

Corbotch took another sip of his drink.

A low howl rang out. The man's face fell. Spinning around, he faced the void.

The room was cool, but sweat dripped down Caplan's forehead anyway.

It happened so fast he almost missed it. A woman—presumably Lucy—raced out of the void. She slammed into the man, knocking him back against the thick bars. He collapsed in a heap and Lucy climbed on top of him. Lifting both fists, she pounded on the man's chest. He tried to push her off, but she was far too powerful.

Her blows intensified and he grew weak. Then her hands curled into claws. Viciously, she raked his face. Blood, first in trickles and then in gushes, splattered against the bars, the wall, and the carpet.

Horrible moans filled the lodge. Caplan tried to speak, but words escaped him. Meanwhile, Corbotch casually sipped his drink.

The man made one last attempt to fight back. But Lucy easily overwhelmed him and he fell still. She raked his bloodied skin for a little longer. Then she dipped toward his face. Slurping noises rang out.

Bile filled Caplan's throat. He'd seen reborn megafauna kill and feast on humans. He'd seen behemoths squash people underfoot. And yet, this was worse. Much worse.

Lucy lifted her head and stared directly at Caplan. Her lips curled back, revealing a set of blood-soaked teeth.

He stiffened up as he caught his first good look at her. He saw her relatively short limbs and her barrel-shaped chest. He saw her weak chin and her oversized nose. "What … what is she?"

"Her genes match those of a more primitive human species. *Homo neanderthalensis*, to be specific." Corbotch took another sip. "Or, if you prefer, Neanderthal."

CHAPTER 34

Date: Nov. 30, 2017, 8:33 p.m.; Location: Savage Station, Vallerio Forest, NH

Neanderthal. The word zigzagged like lightning through Caplan's skull. It was impossible. And yet, he knew it was true. He could hear it in Corbotch's voice. And he could see it in Lucy's powerful hands and sloping forehead. "You created Neanderthals?"

"Yes. And not just them. *Homo erectus. Homo rhodesiensis. Homo heidelbergensis.* Plus, other archaic human species, too."

Corbotch had used a specific process to recreate the reborn megafauna. To bring back the woolly mammoth, for example, he'd used ancient soft tissue samples to fully sequence its DNA. Then he'd extracted the cell egg from a female Asian elephant and replaced its nucleus with that of a woolly mammoth. He'd induced the cell into dividing and then inserted it into an artificial womb, known as an ectogenetic incubator. The incubator, in turn, carried the cell to term.

Corbotch must've used a similar process to create Lucy. Similar, yet different. Caplan thought hard, trying to figure out how the wheels, or genome transplantation modules, fit into the process. First, Corbotch must've fully sequenced Neanderthal DNA. Then he must've forced two prisoners—a male and a female—into the modules. He'd overwritten their genes in some fashion, which effectively replaced their eggs and sperm with those of ancient Neanderthals. Then he'd extracted these things from their bodies and used an ectogenetic incubator to do the rest.

But try as he might, Caplan couldn't quite fit the puzzle pieces together. Lucy looked to be about thirty years old. How had the creature aged so quickly?

Corbotch picked up his radio again. "Initiate clean-up."

The radio buzzed. "Yes, sir."

An animal control pole reached out of the dark doorway. It lassoed Lucy's neck and cinched tight. Howling, the archaic yanked and tore at the pole. When that failed, it tried to rush the pole's handler. But by that time, other poles had joined the first one. They swiftly lassoed the creature's neck and dragged it into the void.

Four workers entered the cage and divided into teams of two. One team gathered up the corpse and took it away. The other gave the cage a quick scrubbing.

Afterward, the second team filed through the open doorway. The door slid shut. For a long moment, Caplan stared at the now-empty cage. It was difficult to fathom what he'd just seen. And yet, he knew he'd never forget it.

"Why?" he asked.

"I felt a demonstration was in order before I sent you back into the outside world," Corbotch replied. "You had an inside track when I launched Apex Predator. Now, you have an inside track on its culmination as well."

"Culmination?"

"Just seven archaics—including Lucy—currently exist. At midnight on December Third, two hundred and fifty-six others will join their ranks. This will comprise the first archaic wave and it will be released into selected ecosystems, both here and abroad. Other waves, which currently comprise some three-thousand additional archaics, will follow."

Caplan shook his head. "So, how does this work anyway? Do you use the modules to edit sperm and eggs?"

"No. We don't give birth to archaic humans here."

Caplan arched an eyebrow.

"Most mammals, as you well know, go through an extremely short period of adolescence. They're ready to hunt and do other things at a very young age. But archaics—like *Homo Sapiens*—require a much longer childhood."

"You used a module to de-age your body. Can't you do the opposite with the archaics?"

"We can physically age them. But there are certain things—motor skills, for instance—that only come with experience." He paused. "Frankly, I would've preferred to take the route you're suggesting. But we don't have enough time to raise a whole new generation of archaic humans. We need them out in the wild as soon as possible, breeding and interacting with ecosystems."

"If you're not giving birth to them, then how ...?" A jolt of electricity shot through Caplan's heart. "You're creating them from people. You're transforming adult prisoners into adult archaics."

"That's correct." He leaned back in his chair. "Now, we're going to need lots of archaics to turn the tide. Far more than three thousand. Fortunately, plenty of survivor settlements, similar to Danter, still exist. We plan to, uh, recruit from their ranks."

The truth crystalized in Caplan's mind. Savage Station's clinic, although gigantic, could only fit so many people at a time. However, the releasing of each archaic wave would free up space. Roberts and her soldiers could then fill that space with new prisoners, kidnapped from the various survivor communities.

Another jolt of electricity stung Caplan's heart. "Amanda … is she an archaic?"

"Not yet. Archaic creation is more art than science. You see it's one thing to alter the genome of a human embryo and create an archaic baby. It's something else to alter the genome of a fully-formed adult human."

He swallowed. "How long?"

"Weeks. Maybe months." He swirled the ice in his glass. "We use the modules to, in effect, paste a complete set of genetic instructions over existing ones. Simple in theory, perhaps. But in practice, it takes a great deal of careful, personalized work. No transformation is the same and if we proceed too quickly, a pre-archaic could succumb from pain and shock."

The more Caplan thought about it, the more it boggled his mind. "How is it even possible? It's like …" His brain searched for a suitable analogy. "… like changing a pre-cooked meal by altering its recipe."

"It's more like changing a pre-cooked meal by altering the fabric of its ingredients." He paused. "Consider me, for instance. Seventeen months ago, I was a physical wreck. Dr.

Barden used a module to perform targeted edits to my DNA. The edits hardened my bones, increased my strength, and took a few physical years off my life. Now, take that concept and consider it on a much broader and deeper scale. That is, imagine similar editing on all of my genes. Then imagine that Dr. Barden used specialized germ-line engineering to ensure I passed those mutated genes on to future generations. And not just one or two generations. All generations. That is, in essence, what we're doing here."

"And it actually works?"

"Oh, yes. We've used modules to produce numerous test archaics at this and other facilities. The first few batches yielded horrific beasts. But with time, we've perfected our procedures." He paused. "You see, nothing about the human body is set in stone. Nothing. Bones, for example, stop growing upon the fusing of their growth plates. But Dr. Barden and his assistants are able to dissolve that fusing and, with time, coax bones into growth again."

Caplan arched an eyebrow. "It sounds painful."

"It is. Fortunately, we've found ways to help our pre-archaics manage the pain. Recovery time between module sessions is, of course, essential."

"Manage their pain?" Caplan's ears nearly popped out of his head. "For the last few days, I've heard nothing but howls and screams coming from this floor."

"Some pain is unavoidable." He shrugged. "When a patient nears the end of genome transplantation, they're brought down here. The final module sessions, for reasons we don't fully understand, are the hardest to endure. Even the Wipe, unfortunately, offers no relief."

"The Wipe?"

"In a physical sense, the pre-archaics become archaics after completing the genome transplantation. Neanderthal archaics, for instance, tend to gain strength as well as more robust builds. From a mental perspective, they're largely archaic as well. But there's still a human component that must ultimately be erased to complete the transformation."

"You're talking about their memories, their emotions." Caplan exhaled. "Their sense of self."

He nodded. "The entire first wave has undergone genome transplantation as well as the Wipe. Right now, they're undergoing a period of painful rest, designed to cement the transformation. But they are, in every conceivable manner, archaics."

"Yeah?" He turned his gaze to the far end of the room. A splotch of blood on the carpet outside the cage caught his eye. "Because I find it hard to believe the original archaics had that kind of bloodlust."

"That bloodlust, as you call it, is a temporary condition. We deliberately don't program it into the genomes. Instead, we artificially induce it via implanted microchips. I won't bore you with the details. But in essence, we have the ability to plague our archaics with a horrible ringing noise that only subsides with the consumption of blood."

"I don't get it." Caplan shook his head. "Why would you pit them against humanity? I thought you needed people to make more archaics."

"We do. That's why we're releasing archaics into non-populated areas first." He stroked his jaw. "The bloodlust is really more for the archaics' protection than anything else. Once Stage Three is complete, we'll simply stop issuing instructions to their microchips."

"But in the meantime, they'll kill any person they cross?"

"Not just people. They'll attempt to kill any animal they meet out in the wild."

"So, you're turning people into archaics against their will. And you're turning archaics into bloodthirsty monsters." He shook his head. "How do you live with yourself?"

"Quite easily, actually." He shrugged. "If I had done nothing, the Holocene extinction would've wiped out humanity along with practically every other species on Earth. This way, many of those species—including ours, I might add—may yet survive."

Perhaps Corbotch's heart was in the right place. But his methodology bothered Caplan. Surely, there must've been a way to end the extinction without so much death and misery.

"So, what's the point of Stage Three?" he asked. "Filling the world with archaics? Or removing every single person not fortunate enough to live inside this station?"

"Both," Corbotch replied. "As you know, animals similar to our colossi—or behemoths, as you call them—should've evolved millions of years ago. Our work shows they would've kept the *Homo* genus from evolving past the archaic stage. To recreate the world as it should exist, we need to replace ordinary humans with archaics."

"Except for yourselves, right?"

"Correct." He swirled the alcohol in his glass, then downed it. "Savage Station will remain in operation for the foreseeable future. Even after we reverse the Holocene extinction, we'll need to keep a watchful eye on things."

Caplan's thoughts turned to Morgan. Then to Elliott, now living with the Danter colony. Could he save them from becoming archaics? And what about Mills and Toland? What did Corbotch plan to do with them?

Painfully, he swallowed his pride. "We can help you."

Corbotch arched an eyebrow. "I don't think so. Even if I was desperate for help, which I'm not, I could never trust you or your friends."

A strange sort of hatred boiled up within Caplan's soul. Corbotch had murdered billions of lives over the last seventeen months. Now, he was transforming the last dregs of humanity into bloodthirsty archaics. It was horrible and sickening.

And yet, Corbotch wasn't doing it out of malevolence. Instead, he was trying to stop a mass extinction event. An event that would, if left unchecked, kill anything and everything in its path. From that perspective, couldn't his actions be considered, well, righteous?

Regardless, the stakes were now clear. And Caplan wasn't about to abandon Morgan to her fate. Very soon, he, Mills, and Toland would be taken to an unknown destination. Somehow they needed to return to Savage Station. They needed to rescue Morgan before she could be transformed into a full-fledged archaic.

And then what? he wondered.

Perhaps he could take his little group to some ultra-remote location. A place even more remote than the cabin. They could stay out of sight, live off the land. They could eke out a meager existence. But was that enough?

His old battle cry—*forget thriving ... just keep on surviving*—came to mind. Did he really want to keep looking over his shoulder? Did he really want to deal with behemoths, reborn megafauna, and bloodthirsty archaics for the rest of his life?

An audacious plan came to mind. A crazy, impossible plan. A plan with near zero odds of success. And yet, the very thought of it made a thin smile curl across his lips.

He'd return to Savage Station. He'd rescue Morgan. And then he'd take Savage for himself.

That's right. He'd conquer the station. Then he and his friends could ride out the rest of the apocalypse in relative safety and comfort. No more worrying, no more running.

Conquering Savage wouldn't be easy, of course. He'd have to survive whatever Corbotch had planned for him.

He'd have to fight his way back to the station. He'd have to deal with reborn megafauna, behemoths, and soldiers.

A realization crystalized in his head. The odds were too great to face alone, even with Mills and Toland at his side. Which meant just one thing.

He was going to need help.

CHAPTER 35

Date: Nov. 30, 2017, 9:04 p.m.; Location: Savage Station, Vallerio Forest, NH

A fist pounded on one of the elephant doors.

Corbotch stood up. "Come in."

The door opened and Roberts stepped into the frame. "It's a few minutes past nine o'clock."

"Yes, I suppose it's time."

"Time for what?" Caplan asked.

"For your little trip." She snapped her fingers. Two soldiers strode into the room and began freeing Caplan from the chair. "Don't worry about your friends," she added. "They're waiting for us upstairs."

He inhaled through his nostrils. There was no use arguing. He had no bargaining chips, nothing to offer. "Where are we going?"

"Did your friends ever tell you how they arrived in the Vallerio?" Corbotch asked.

"They said you dumped them into a clearing full of beasts. They called it your killing ground."

"The place you're going is kind of like that." He smiled. "Except on a much larger scale, of course."

CHAPTER 36

Date: Nov. 30, 2017, 9:28 p.m.; Location: Savage Station, Vallerio Forest, NH

Another killing ground? The very idea unnerved Caplan. He'd heard plenty of stories about the previous one. Mills, Toland, and Elliott had been taken there in a small group. They'd barely escaped with their lives. Not everyone had been so lucky.

At the top of the stairwell, he passed through an open door and into a giant space, illuminated by numerous wall-mounted lights. High above, an enormous metal hatch slid open. Moonlight, partially obscured by a light snow, flooded his eyes.

"Zach?" Mills called out.

A couple of soldiers dragged her and Toland across the floor at gunpoint. He wanted to rush forward, to hold her tight. But the restraints arrested his movement. "Are you okay?" he asked.

"We're fine." She glanced at Corbotch. "So, where are we going?"

"You'll find out soon enough."

A numbers of helicopters, heavily armed, sat on the concrete floor. One of the choppers started up, its rotors whipping in circles.

Corbotch walked to the rotorcraft. He wrenched the cabin door open and climbed into the interior.

A couple of soldiers waved their guns in menacing fashion. Grumbling under his breath, Toland shuffled to the helicopter. Two soldiers tossed him unceremoniously into the cabin. Two others then positioned Toland onto a metal bench and buckled his seatbelt.

"It's your turn." Roberts said.

Caplan hiked to the helicopter. The two soldiers heaved him through the open doorway. He landed hard on his side. Normally, he wouldn't have felt it. But after the damage Roberts had done to his body, pretty much any impact came with agonizing pain.

The other two soldiers helped Caplan to the bench. Mills was last to arrive. The soldiers were a bit gentler with her, placing her into the interior rather than merely throwing her through the doorway.

Once all three of them were seated and belted, Roberts climbed into the cabin. She shut the door and sat down next to Corbotch.

As her fellow soldiers filled the remaining seats, Caplan turned his head. Thick wires and cables hung from the walls. Tool kits and bags were stored under the benches. A metal container, welded to the floor between the cockpit and the cabin, held parachutes and other gear.

In a netted sack next to the door, he spotted something that raised his eyebrows. It was Morgan's duffel bag. Evidently, they were in the exact same helicopter that had flown them to Savage Station in the first place. Roberts' soldiers must've forgotten to take the bag out after landing. What was inside it? Food? Water? Weapons?

Vibrating softly, the helicopter jerked upward. The rotors picked up speed, drowning out all other noise. The result was almost hypnotic.

Caplan glanced out his window. He watched the hatch close over, blocking off all access to Savage Station. Old buildings and a long road, covered with dead and dying vegetation, rested near the hatch. *That must be Savage City*, he thought.

They gained altitude. The details melted away and he started to notice giant swathes of crushed trees and flattened soil. It looked like bulldozers had run amok, forming curved trails through the dense forest.

He'd seen similar trails in the past. They'd been formed by behemoths venturing out of the Vallerio and into the world. Once upon a time, nature would've reclaimed these behemoth trails. But the continuing extinction had kept that from happening.

They gained more altitude and he started to notice familiar landmarks. He'd studied numerous maps of the Vallerio, both before and while working there. So, he was able to pinpoint Savage Station's location as being within the remote Sector 214.

The helicopter flew south over the Vallerio. Seconds turned into minutes. The minutes started to add up and eventually, Caplan lost track of time.

He continued to stare out his window. The snowfall had stopped. The sky was free of clouds and the moon and stars shone brightly in the night. But Earth, free of artificial light, remained dark. What was it like down there? Were there any survivor communities in the vicinity, eking out an existence in the ice and rubble? If so, did they have any idea what was coming their way?

Caplan noticed Mills looking at him. Their eyes locked together and he found himself doing somersaults into that beautiful ocean-blue color. He ached for her and he could sense how much she ached for him. Even now, even after all that had happened. The world was indeed a nightmare and the sheer amount of death staggered him every time he thought about it. But the apocalypse had brought them together and for that, he was eternally thankful.

Maybe when this was over, when they had conquered Savage, they could be together. They could relive those few wonderful hours at the campground over and over again. The thought made him smile, a rare occurrence these days.

They flew over a large body of water that Caplan took to be the Atlantic Ocean. It sparkled in the moonlight and he could see every wave, every ripple. He wondered about the water, about the creatures that lived within it. Back in the old days, it had held a wide variety of life. Striped bass, bluefish, mackerel, blue and mako sharks, rock crabs, lobsters, sea urchins, whales. Had any of them survived the Holocene extinction?

The question intrigued him. After all, the blue whale was the largest animal of all time. It was even longer and heavier than prehistoric giants like the *megalodon*. It was, in short, a behemoth. So maybe the oceans hadn't needed Corbotch's monsters. Maybe they were surviving the extinction just fine.

"We're getting close," Corbotch said.

Toland stared outside. Then he stiffened. He didn't say so much as a single word. No flippant remarks, no smug insults, nothing. He was completely still, utterly silent.

"Oh, my God," Mills said.

Caplan shifted his gaze. The city of Boston, smoldering and in ruins, lay before him. Apartment buildings and offices, once strong and tall, had been reduced to rubble. Cars and trucks, many of them pulverized, were scattered about the uprooted and snow-covered streets. Broken billboards, crumbled statues, and loads of windswept litter were everywhere.

They flew over the Back Bay neighborhood. Small fires raged in various places, adding light to the otherwise dark streets and buildings. Caplan's eyes lingered on the city's tallest structure, the 790-foot tall building once known as the John Hancock Tower. A massive *Megalonyx jeffersonii*, also known as a giant ground sloth, clung to the building's once-smooth glass façade. It was almost one hundred feet from end to end and its heavy build made it look even larger. Its forelimbs featured three humongous claws apiece. They'd pierced the building's glass panes and now clutched onto the steel frame.

They flew over the Financial District. A couple of boats, partially submerged, filled Boston Harbor. Inland, Caplan saw clusters of skyscrapers and high-rises, all over 400-feet tall. Fires raged in a few buildings, casting a thin smokescreen that obscured his view of the street. It was beautiful in a way, like staring down at a fantastical cloud city. A cloud city, unfortunately, that was populated by monsters.

Dozens of behemoths stalked the smoke-filled streets. A flat-headed peccary, some thirty-feet long, stabbed its tusks into the lower levels of an apartment building. A scimitar-toothed cat plunged its massive incisors into a section of sidewalk, reducing it to dust and rubble. A giant beaver, which could grow to a height of some seven feet back in the Pleistocene epoch, crushed a car beneath its seventy-foot tall frame. He saw other behemoths, too. A Harrington's mountain goat, a saiga antelope, mastodons and mammoths, an American lion, an American cheetah, and many more.

His brow furrowed. He'd fought and killed some of these animals, or rather their smaller counterparts, over the last seventeen months. But it was one thing to go up against reborn megafauna. It was something else to face behemoths.

Shifting his gaze, he noticed some new species. New, at least, to him. He wondered if they'd been harvested from the Pleistocene epoch or if they'd come from even earlier times. After all, the groundwork for the Holocene extinction had been laid some thirty-five million years ago during the

Mammalian Plateau. Chances were good that Corbotch had taken that into account when creating his animals.

A giant armadillo-like behemoth waddled down a snow-covered street, its large shell slicing through glass and crashing against metal poles. On its back right foot, Caplan glimpsed a gooey red blob. His stomach churned. *Was that a person?* he wondered.

His gaze fell upon corpses, covered by a razor-thin layer of snow and illuminated by roaring flames. Thousands of people had been smashed into pulp and now lay amongst the smoke and rubble. He couldn't make out individual faces and the bodies were squished beyond recognition. But he could see their clothes. Some, presumably soldiers, had died in battle gear. Others had worn everyday attire. Skirts and blouses, dresses and slacks. T-shirts and polo shirts, jeans and cargo shorts.

"They're dead." Mills exhaled. "They're all dead."

Roberts unbuckled her belt. Standing up, she walked to the metal container and rummaged through it. She returned with three objects, which she tossed at Caplan's feet.

He gave them a quick glance. *Well, you always wanted to take a sightseeing tour of Boston,* he thought. *Now's your chance.*

"Obviously, those are parachutes. We're going to release you from your restraints and send you on your way." Smiling lightly, Roberts studied their faces. "Any questions?"

"Forget it." Toland's face turned ashen. "There's no way I'm putting one of those things on."

"You can always jump without it."

He swallowed.

"How do they work?" Mills asked.

"You reach in here, pull out the pilot chute," Roberts said, mimicking the act. "It'll catch air and drag out the deployment bag. If that fails, pull the ripcord to deploy the reserve parachute."

Toland shook his head. "Knowing my luck, I'll land right in a behemoth's jaws."

"That's up to you. There are two steering lines. Pull the left one and you'll turn left. Pull right and you'll go right. It's simple." She paused. "We're going to push you out over the Financial District. Now, before you get any ideas, we're not going to give you much space to maneuver. You won't be able to leave the city or even the district. The best you can hope for is a clean landing. Now, who wants to go first?"

"Me," Mills said quietly.

Caplan arched an eyebrow. "Are you sure?"

She nodded. "First one out is first one done, right?"

Soldiers rose from the benches. They strapped on monkey harnesses and clipped the harnesses to the floor. Hoisting their weapons, they took careful aim at the trio.

A soldier unlocked Mills' restraints. Then he helped her into the parachute and hauled her to the door.

"What about jackets and gloves?" Mills asked. "It's cold out there."

"I'm afraid you won't last long enough to make good use of them," Roberts replied.

The soldier unlocked Toland's restraints. He waited for the writer to secure his glasses in a pocket. Then he helped him put on a parachute. After directing Toland to the door, the soldier turned toward Caplan.

"Oh, no," Roberts said. "This one's all mine."

She unlocked Caplan's ankles. She waited for him to stand up before unlocking his wrist restraints. He took the parachute from her outstretched hand and strapped it over his sore shoulders.

She donned a monkey harness and clipped it down. Icy air rushed into the cabin as she slid the door open.

Caplan stood still, utterly helpless and furious about it. He saw no way to overcome Roberts or her many soldiers.

His only option, like it or not, was to make the jump and hope for the best.

The helicopter jolted to a halt. Blades whirring, it hovered above the Financial District. A rudimentary plan began to form inside his head. Once they landed, they'd stick to the rubble. Make their way to Boston Harbor and commandeer a boat. They'd sail north, well clear of the city. Then they'd find a car and start to look for other survivor communities. It was the ultimate long-shot plan. But it was a whole lot better than nothing.

Roberts pulled Mills to the open door. Without further ado, she shoved the woman into open space.

Caplan held his breath. Released it when he saw Mills' dark green parachute fly open. Held it again as she slowly descended into the smoky abyss.

"Your turn." Roberts pushed Toland toward the door. He grabbed at the edges of the doorframe, but she just pushed him harder. He pitched outside without so much as a shriek. He tumbled through open air once, then twice. His parachute flew open. It jerked him out of a spinning somersault and he started to drift toward the Financial District.

"Your turn." Roberts glided behind Caplan. Her fingers touched his back and he felt himself propelled toward the door. At the last second, he reached down. Wrapped his fingers around the duffel bag's strap.

Corbotch's eyes widened. "What the …?"

Caplan yanked the strap, pulling Morgan's bag free from the netted sack. Then he dove headfirst into the waiting sky. As he plummeted toward Boston, an electric charge shot through his body. He was about to enter Corbotch's killing ground.

But at least he wasn't going there empty-handed.

CHAPTER 37

Date: Nov. 30, 2017, 11:11 p.m.; Location: Airspace, Boston, MA

Rushing wind, whirring rotors, and angry screams filled Caplan's ears. Bone-chilling cold accosted his face.

The air thickened and started to vibrate. Shooting a quick glimpse upward, he saw the helicopter angling across the sky. *Oh, you want this back?* he thought, wrangling the duffel bag over his left shoulder. *You'll have to catch me first.*

Wind screamed in his ears and the ground came up fast. He saw behemoths, ravaged streets, and crumbling skyscrapers. But he didn't pull his parachute.

The helicopter descended toward him. Roberts leaned outside, supported by her monkey harness. She stared at him, face flushed, unblinking.

He could see the fury in her eyes. She didn't care about the duffel bag. She just cared he'd gotten one over on her.

He gave her an oily smile. Her face twisted with rage and she shouted something he couldn't hear.

The rotors shifted direction. The helicopter angled to the north. Cold air blasted against Caplan's face.

Then the chopper flew away.

Searching the sky, he saw Mills descending toward Boston Harbor. The water glinted in the moonlight and he noticed a boat. A luxury yacht, from the looks of it. A pleased smile crossed his visage. If they had to travel by sea, better to do it in style.

Looking straight down, he spotted Toland. The man's parachute was swirling through the air, a slave to the currents.

Face tightening, he shifted his gaze to street level. Toland was heading toward a smoke-choked intersection. Five or six cars filled it. They were flattened and smashed up together, making it almost impossible to distinguish one from another.

He looked up and down the snow-covered cross streets. They were crawling with behemoths. He saw a moose with a long snout and giant antlers. A horse with zebra-like stripes and a long blonde mane. A grotesque pig-like animal with plenty of bulk and a mouthful of powerful, sharp teeth. *This really is a killing ground*, he thought. *Come on, Brian ... steer away from here. Go east. East!*

But Toland continued to descend unchecked toward the intersection. And as much as Caplan wanted to join Mills on the yacht at that very moment, he couldn't just abandon one of their own.

Tightening his grip on the duffel bag, he yanked his pilot chute. It billowed out followed by the main chute. His body jerked. And then he was floating in mid-air, high above the cracked, snow-ridden pavement.

Despite all of the smoke, he could see the behemoths quite clearly. He could see their height, their drooling jaws. At the moment, they stared at buildings, at the street. But if even one of them glanced up, well, Caplan knew he and Toland wouldn't make morning.

The smoke thickened and he checked over both shoulders. The tall buildings locked them into the general area. But there was still time to steer away from the intersection. If Toland could land on one of the still-intact smaller buildings, Caplan could join him. From there, they could sneak out onto the street and make their way to Boston Harbor.

But Toland continued to drop with very little movement. He hit the street with a soft thud and his parachute deflated. Rolling onto his back, he tried to sit up. But a gust of wind caught hold of his parachute. It reinflated and started to drift southward, dragging a cursing Toland along with it.

The pig-like behemoth rotated toward the intersection. Its lava-orange eyes scanned the parachute and the now-shouting Toland. Cocking its head, it scraped its cloven hooves at the snow.

Fierce winds slashed into Caplan's face, forcing him to squint. A loud bellow rang out and he saw the pig-like behemoth take a step toward Toland.

He maneuvered the steering lines and drifted into the middle of the street. The wind blew faster, pushing him closer to Toland.

The road rose up to greet him. Right before striking the pavement, he turned his head. He stared at the behemoth, stared at its blazing lava-orange eyes. *Let's do this,* he thought.

CHAPTER 38

Date: Nov. 30, 2017, 11:25 p.m.; Location: Downtown, Boston, MA

His feet struck snowy rubble and Caplan fell sideways, distributing the shock along multiple points of contact. He rolled to a standing position and pulled the kill-line, collapsing the pilot chute. Then he unbuckled the container and shrugged it off. In one swift move, he replaced it with Morgan's duffel bag, donning it like a backpack.

The pig-like behemoth towered before him, its coarse hair bristling in the chilly wind. Then its nostrils flared and its head dipped to the street. It didn't grunt or bellow or squeal. Instead, it inhaled and exhaled, inhaled and exhaled.

Caplan's knees weakened as a sense of horrid awe and strange unease came over him. It felt like evil spirits were invading him, dipping in and out of his body. His mind unhinged itself from time, traveling back to that market in the North Maine Woods. Back to that odd feeling he'd experienced just before spotting Dire. *It's emitting infrasound*, he thought. *Which means ...*

Other behemoths spun in Caplan's direction. Their eyes widened. Their faces grew taut. Their lips peeled backward, revealing dirty, bloodstained teeth.

... it's communicating, he thought with a groan.

Staring through the dense smoke, he took in the behemoths and their heaving, rippling flesh. Adrenaline pumped through his body. His breaths, visible in the cold air, came faster and faster. He could feel the massive creatures. Their raw power, their unrelenting energy. He could smell their fur, their feces, their rancid breath.

His senses, fueled by adrenaline, expanded past their normal range. He heard wind slashing against the metallic wrecks in the intersection. He tasted snowflakes, smoke, and brick dust on his tongue. He felt shifts in the air flow as it passed by gaps—alleys, open doorways, the ruins of former buildings—on either side of the street.

He took a step backward, his foot leaving a slight imprint in the thin snow. Then another step. And then another one.

The behemoths continued to stare at him. Their facial expressions hinted at deep, conflicting emotions. Furious anger offset by intense curiosity. Hunger offset by strange disgust.

Tiny shards of glass crunched under his feet. Then his boots pressed into a squashed metal door. Keeping his gaze locked on the behemoths, he continued backward, passing over the smashed and burnt-out hulk of a car wreck.

"Get this stupid thing off of me," Toland shouted.

Caplan stepped back a few more feet and passed onto a second car wreck. Out of the corner of his eye, he saw Toland pinned against a wreck, his parachute whipping in the wind.

Approaching Toland, he knelt down. His icy fingers fumbled with the man's parachute container. He found the kill line and pulled it, collapsing the pilot chute.

Snow kicked up as Toland fell to the street. Moaning, he shrugged off the parachute container. Then he reached into his pocket, pulled out his now-bent glasses, and wrangled them back into the proper shape. "What took you so long?"

"I was making friends." Caplan nodded at the behemoths. "A whole bunch of them."

Donning his glasses, Toland turned his head. He groaned softly. "What are the chances they'll let us walk away from here?"

"Only one way to find out."

He stood up and took a practice step. His knee nearly buckled under his weight. "I must've twisted it."

Caplan shot a quick glance to his left, then to his right. He saw more behemoths on either side of the cross street. Some were farther back, a couple of hundred feet away. Others were much closer. They hadn't seen him yet, but it was just a matter of time.

Looking forward again, he saw the behemoths begin to shift back and forth. He could see the hunger, the impatience in their eyes. Not that he was complaining, but why hadn't they attacked yet? Were they waiting for something?

He saw Toland out of the corner of his eye. He saw the man take another step and wince. *They're waiting to see if anyone helps us,* he realized. *They're hoping for a bigger meal.*

Of course, it was just him and Toland. But the behemoths didn't know that. That was the trick, he decided. Pretend you're looking for people. Maneuver into a good position. And then disappear.

Wind whistled as he shifted his eyeballs. He studied the rubble of fallen buildings. The missing doors and broken windows of still-intact structures. The sidewalks, the ravaged cars. The dark alleys.

"Over there." He gave a slight nod toward a thin alley. It was situated between an old Chinese food restaurant and an apartment building. "Walk slowly. Keep your eyes moving. Act like you're looking for people."

Toland inhaled a deep breath. Then he hoisted himself over one of the wrecks and hobbled toward the alley. Caplan, still staring at the behemoths, tightened his grip on the duffel bag's straps. Carefully, he weaved his way between a trio of wrecked vehicles.

The pig-like behemoth grunted. It scraped its cloven hooves on the pavement for a second time. Then it sprang forward.

Planting his hand on a flattened roof, Caplan vaulted over it. "Run," he shouted.

Toland, still limping, picked up speed and hustled into the waiting alley. Caplan's gaze shot from the behemoth to the alley. His lip curled in irritation.

He wasn't going to make it.

The pig-like behemoth galloped down the street, followed closely by the others. Cackles and deep-throated grunts rang out. Thick snorts and ear-piercing bellows. Vicious roars. Eerie howls.

Caplan veered away from the alley. His boots pounded against the snow as he sprinted toward the massive creatures.

The pig-like behemoth closed the distance in a matter of seconds. Grunting, it lowered its head to the ground. Its jaws opened wide.

He dodged to the left and rolled. A hot breeze struck his side as the creature's teeth, long and thick, shot past him. They struck pavement, stabbing deep into the street and unleashing a thunderous quake. The behemoth jolted to a halt. Other behemoths crashed into it. Losing their balance, they fell into a pile of hissing, thrashing flesh.

Shifting course, Caplan sprinted toward the alley. He saw Toland on the far end. The man leaned against a brick wall, breathing heavily and grinding his teeth. His eyes were locked on a spot just behind Caplan. His face showed intense concentration.

The air shifted. Caplan sensed something—a giant hoof?—swing toward his head. Legs churning, he ran into the alley.

Debris, snow, and smoke exploded as the swinging object collided with the apartment building. A shockwave knocked him to the ground. A discordant ringing noise flooded his ears.

Dazed, he turned his head. Behemoths were stacked up at the mouth of the alley, forming a bottleneck of terrifying proportions. Jaws clamped onto the adjoining buildings, crunching glass, biting through concrete. Clawed feet scraped the pavement.

The ringing noise faded away. Coughing and gasping, he climbed to his feet. Then he staggered to the end of the alley.

Toland stared at the frenzied pile of behemoths. "They look hungry."

"Agreed." Caplan studied the buildings on either side of him. The eastern building looked tougher, sturdier. He turned toward a metal door and tried the knob. It didn't open. He gave it a kick. The door flew open, revealing a dark, cold interior. "So, let's make sure they don't get fed."

CHAPTER 39

Date: Nov. 30, 2017, 11:33 p.m.; Location: Downtown, Boston, MA

The cackles, growls, and shrieks didn't go away when Caplan closed the door. But at least they weren't as loud. At least he could hear himself think.

Shivering, he rubbed his shoulders. A bit of fiery light filtered through the dingy windows and the thin space beneath the door. They illuminated an industrial kitchen with metallic walls. Pans and pots lay upon multiple stoves. A thick layer of dust covered the long counters. The stench of rotten meat hung heavy in the chilly air.

Out of habit, he flicked the light switch. He wasn't surprised when nothing happened.

"Nice work, Zach." Wincing, Toland took a few halting steps. "You managed to trap us in behemoth central."

"Me?" He shrugged off Morgan's duffel bag. Kneeling down, he unzipped it. "You're the one who couldn't figure out how to use your steering lines."

"I didn't need them. In fact, I was doing just fine until you arrived."

He quickly searched the bag. Inside, he found the Apex Predator logbook along with some food and a few bottles of water. The logbook was heavy and he considered throwing it away. But at the last second, he decided to hold on to it.

"Yeah, you were doing great." He tossed a bottle to Toland. Then he opened one for himself and took a long swig. The cold water tasted like plastic. But he choked it down anyway. "Pinned up against that wreck, screaming like a fool."

"Regardless, they didn't notice me. And they wouldn't have noticed me either. In case you forgot, they didn't turn our way until you showed up." Toland opened his bottle and swallowed down some water. "You got Derek killed back in Maine. I'm not going to let you do that to me."

An image of Perkins, of the man's torn-up body, shot through Caplan's mind. It seemed so long ago, almost like it had happened in a past lifetime. And yet, only a week had passed since the attack. Since the emergency cauterization. Since the man's death.

"I did everything I could to save him," Caplan retorted.

"And yet, he still died." Toland crossed his arms. "So, what now, Mr. Survival? How are you going to risk our lives this time?"

Caplan sighed. He didn't like ending the argument on that note. But from experience, he knew there was no point in continuing on with it. Toland saw the world through a very unique—and irritating—set of lenses and that wasn't about to change anytime soon.

"We're not," he replied. "For now, we wait."

"And let those behemoths bring this building down on top of us?" Toland shook his head. "I don't think so."

"Then leave. Nobody's keeping you here."

Toland frowned. But he didn't go anywhere.

"That's what I thought." Caplan searched the rest of the duffel bag. He discovered Mills' collapsible bow and quiver at the bottom. His axes, meanwhile, were stuffed into a side pocket.

He withdrew the axes and gave them a long look. They wouldn't help much against those behemoths. But he felt incomplete without them. So, he stuck them into his belt.

He ate a little food and offered the rest to Toland. Then he zipped up the duffel bag and rose to his feet. Crossing his arms, he tried to fight off the chill. When that didn't work, he began to pace back and forth across the room.

The clamor died off. He could still hear behemoths, could still feel their ground tremors. But their shrieks and growls had grown faint. Their tremors had lost ferocity.

"I think they're gone." He shrugged the bag over his shoulders. "Ready to get out of here?"

Toland took a few practice steps. "Not really, but I'll manage. Just don't get us killed."

Caplan opened the door. A sharp breeze stung his face as he looked for behemoths. They were gone so he stepped outside and made his way to the mouth of the alleyway.

A weird shriek rang out. His eyes lifted skyward and he saw a massive bird soar across the dark sky. It carried a wingspan of over two hundred feet. Its head was peach-colored. Its feathers were black with white streaks.

"A bird behemoth?" Toland grunted. "Now, I've seen everything."

"Don't be too sure about that."

"What's that supposed to mean?"

"If James made bird behemoths, he probably made other types of behemoths, too." He arched an eyebrow. "Maybe even insect behemoths."

"That's not funny."

"Who's laughing?"

Toland exhaled. "So, where are we going, Mr. Survival?"

"Boston Harbor."

"Yet another dumb idea. We need to go north and get out of this city as fast as possible."

Caplan stared east, the telltale sounds of distant behemoths ringing in his ears. "You're forgetting Bailey. She went down near the harbor."

"I'm not forgetting her. I just don't care. And neither should you if you want to survive."

"We're not going to die." His jaw steeled up. "But we're not leaving her behind either."

CHAPTER 40

Date: Dec. 1, 2017, 1:10 a.m.; Location: Downtown, Boston, MA

Not much to see around here. But hey, look on the bright side, Caplan thought with a dark chuckle as he snuck down the chipped and battered sidewalk. *At least you don't have to deal with tourists.*

The moon and surrounding fires shone brightly, but much of the light was gobbled up by the thick smoke and growing cloud cover. The result was an unsettling combination of dark light and light darkness.

Ahead, he saw Faneuil Hall. Or rather, what was left of it. The brick walls, drenched with snow, stood tall. But they sagged a bit and many of their windows were broken. The roof and bell tower were gone, presumably obliterated by a passing behemoth. As for the giant bell, it lay embedded in the sidewalk.

A loud wail rang out. Looking up, he saw yet another behemoth bird.

Toland eyed the creature with a mixture of apprehension and disdain. "This is a terrible idea. Boston Harbor is probably the most dangerous spot in this city right now."

"What makes you say that?"

"Haven't you ever seen birds swooping down into water, plucking up fish in their jaws? Now imagine that, just with us instead of some stupid fish."

"That bird doesn't need water to get us. It could snatch us right off the sidewalk at any moment."

Before Toland could respond, the ground tremors intensified. Looking around, Caplan spotted an old building. He led Toland to it and they hunched down in its shadow.

Two behemoths, scuffling and biting and kicking up snow, rolled into the intersection. One looked like a cross between a llama and a camel. The other was part pig, part hippopotamus.

Growling in unison, they lunged at each other. The first behemoth got its teeth around the second one's shoulder. But it bit gently. The second behemoth shook it off and emitted an exaggerated snarl. Still rolling, still scuffling, they passed through the intersection. The noises soon died off. The tremors normalized.

Caplan found the behavior curious. What he'd just seen wasn't a real fight. It was a play-fight, waged with puppy-like enthusiasm.

The reborn megafauna fought anything that moved, including members of their own species. They killed each other with astonishing frequency. The behemoths, on the other hand, seemed to act differently. Why was that?

He examined the area around Faneuil Hall. "It's clear," he said. "Come on."

They hurried east, sticking to the shadows. Caplan saw ice cream shops, clothing stores, hotels, salons. Some had been reduced to dust and rubble. Others had merely been abandoned to the elements. He also noticed cars, trucks, vans, ambulances, motorcycles, large potted plants, lampposts, and cash registers. Many of these things, these remnants of the old world, had been smashed underfoot. But not everything. Indeed, the more he looked, the more he realized just how much had survived the onslaught.

Lots of stuff, he thought. *But unfortunately, not many people.*

They hiked past dozens of corpses, all covered with thin veils of snow. Some showed symptoms of the HA-78 virus. Others had been stabbed or shot. Still others had been squished into now-dry bloody pulp.

As they walked, he kept his head on a swivel. He checked their rear, their flanks. But his search turned up nothing. No behemoths, no reborn megafauna. Oddly enough, the harbor was quiet and many buildings were in pretty decent shape. Looking ahead, he caught a glimpse of sparkling water. *Don't say it's too easy*, he thought. Which, of course, was immediately followed by another thought. *It's too easy.*

He raced onto Long Wharf. He ran past a long building, parked cars, and numerous dying trees. Up ahead, he saw Boston Harbor. The rippling water was navy blue with just a foot or so of visibility. Most of the docks were damaged or submerged. But a few were still in good shape.

He hurried to the viewing plaza. Passenger ferries, Cape Islanders, sailboats, yachts, and sightseeing boats filled the harbor. Some ships were attached to still-intact docks. Others were offshore. Regardless, almost all of them were partially submerged in the dark water.

A light splash caught his attention. Turning south, he saw a boat cutting through the water. The object grew larger and larger until he recognized it as the luxury yacht he'd seen from above. Shifting his gaze to the helm, he saw Mills. She stood straight and tall, her blonde hair rustling in the wind.

A tired smile creased his face. He didn't dare call out to her, lest he attract a behemoth. But he did raise his arms above his head and wave them in the air.

The yacht swerved north and then back to the west. Mills adjusted the wheel, aiming the bow at the wharf. The yacht, which was listing starboard just a bit, picked up speed.

His smile vanished. He could see details now. Her clenched jaw, the stress lines on her face. On top of that, she was coming in way too fast.

"And this is why women shouldn't be allowed to drive." Toland adopted his most superior look. "If she doesn't slow down soon, she'll blow that boat all to hell."

Caplan shifted his gaze to the wake. "She can't slow down." His jaw tightened. "Something's chasing her."

CHAPTER 41

Date: Dec. 1, 2017, 1:36 a.m.; Location: Downtown, Boston, MA

A dark shadow, ancient and mysterious, materialized in the navy blue water. At sixty to seventy feet in length, it was the size of a mature sperm whale. But Caplan knew this was no whale. It was another creature from the past, reborn and blown up to a monstrous size by Corbotch's scientists.

Toland's superior look vanished. Tentatively, he took a step backward.

The giant shadow launched itself out of the water. Its salmon-like body, sleek and scaly, surged forward. Its mouth opened wide, revealing a pair of giant fanged teeth.

The teeth snapped wildly at the yacht. They came up a few feet short and the behemoth fish splashed back into the harbor. But the impact roiled the water, sending a large wave screaming into the boat. Water rained down on Mills, soaking her from head to foot. Undeterred, she continued to direct the boat forward, distancing herself from the sea monster.

Toland retreated to the far end of the viewing plaza. Caplan, meanwhile, stood his ground. *Faster*, he urged. *Faster!*

The yacht ripped through the water. Even so, the behemoth had little trouble catching up to it. With another gigantic surge, it flew out of the water.

Mills looked at the creature. Then she released the wheel and ran to the edge of the boat. Extending her arms, she dove into the dark water.

The behemoth's fangs crashed into the yacht, puncturing the fiberglass. It bit down hard as it smashed back into the harbor, ripping the boat in half and sending out another gigantic wave.

Caplan raced toward a set of sturdy docks. He couldn't see the behemoth or even its shadow. But he could see Mills in the rippling, choppy water. She was swimming hard and with good form. Unfortunately, she looked exhausted. Exhausted and freezing.

Digging into his energy reserves, he thundered across the wood planks. Mills swam up to the docks. Shivering, she tried to climb out of the water. But fatigue caught up to her and she slipped back into the icy liquid.

He grabbed her hand. With one quick movement, he yanked her out of the water. The momentum drove him backward and they crashed onto the wood planks.

She rolled off onto her back, sputtering water and gasping for air. He rose to a knee and leaned over to help her.

Then he saw the dark shadow, saw it moving through the navy blue water.

Saw it moving toward them.

CHAPTER 42

Date: Dec. 1, 2017, 1:42 a.m.; Location: Downtown, Boston, MA

This is the day from hell, he thought. *And it just keeps getting worse.*

He helped Mills to her feet. She started to sag so he tossed her over his shoulder. Then he sprinted for the wharf.

Wood planks splintered, shattered. Glancing back, he saw a giant swell of water crashing into the docks. It chopped them up with ease.

He tried to run faster, but his legs felt rubbery. His saliva dried up. His lungs ran short of air.

Water roared in his ears. The splintering and shattering wood gained volume. Then fiberglass and metal began to groan, to crunch.

He snuck another glance and saw the behemoth tear through a submerged catamaran. In a matter of seconds, it would come into range. It would surge out of the water. Even if they managed to dodge its fangs, it would still come crashing down on top of them.

The behemoth slammed into a submerged passenger ferry. Then into another one. Boats began to pile up and the massive creature lost some speed.

Caplan ran out onto the viewing plaza. He kept running and didn't stop until he'd reached Toland. Then he spun around and stared at the harbor.

The behemoth, blocked by ravaged boats, floated just beneath the surface. It stayed still for a couple of seconds. Then it started to retreat. At a leisurely pace, it made its way back into the middle of the harbor.

Caplan placed Mills on some dead grass, then collapsed next to her. His shoulders felt like they'd been stabbed multiple times. His limbs felt like spaghetti. He lay still for a minute or so, watching his breath form little clouds in front of his face. Meanwhile, shrieks, roars, howls and splashes accosted his eardrums.

He regained a little strength, then crawled to Mills. Her lips were blue and her skin felt cold to the touch. She needed fire and she needed it fast.

"Howdy, folks."

The voice caught Caplan by surprise. Blinking, he looked up. "What …?" His teeth chattered and he rubbed his shoulders for warmth. "What are you doing here?"

"A little bit of this, a little bit of that." Ross shot him a wily grin. "Need a hand?"

He nodded. "Definitely."

CHAPTER 43

Date: Dec. 1, 2017, 10:06 a.m.; Location: Downtown, Boston, MA

"There." With a heave, Caplan tossed a stack of empty wood drawers into the makeshift fire pit. Sparks flew. A trail of smoke shot through the open window as the dying flames sizzled back to life. "That should keep it burning for a little longer."

Ross, sitting comfortably in an easy chair, kicked his feet up on an old coffee table. "I can't remember the last time I enjoyed a fire. I've run from a few and I have to tell you, I prefer this by a long shot."

"You and me both." He eased himself into a soft chair and instantly regretted it. Not because it was uncomfortable, but for the exact opposite reason. It was so nice he didn't know how he'd ever get up again.

He shot a sideways glimpse at Mills. She sat on a sofa directly in front of the fire pit, cloaked in thick blankets. Her hands clutched a mug of steaming instant coffee, made from melted snow.

"Where's Brian?" Ross asked.

"Still sleeping, I imagine."

"You should consider doing the same."

"I got four hours." He took a moment to smooth out his shirt. Like the rest of his clothes, it had been harvested from one of the building's many apartments. Then he draped a blanket over his legs, picked up his mug, and took a long sip of coffee. He couldn't remember the last time he'd tasted something so hot, so delicious. "I owe you one. If you hadn't showed up …"

"Don't mention it. I'm just sorry we didn't catch up to you sooner." Ross took a draught from his mug. "A couple of days ago, we intercepted some radio traffic. The speaker said you'd been spotted with a dire wolf behemoth. But when we got there, you were gone. All that was left was your van."

An image of the rickety, old vehicle passed through Caplan's brain. If truth be told, he kind of missed the old clunker. It reminded him of simpler, better days. Days spent with Perkins, with Morgan. He would've given anything to get those days back. But alas, that could never happen.

Ross took another drink. "Anyway there wasn't much we could do at that point. We waited for Sydney to fix it up. Then we added it to our fleet and continued along our way."

"You've still got the van?"

"Tricia and Sydney insisted. They said it contained some real valuable audio equipment, stuff that could ward off behemoths. I wasn't about to turn that down." He grinned. "Best decision I ever made. That van is the closest thing we've got to a behemoth wrecking machine."

"It is?"

He nodded. "As soon as we turn on the infrasound weapon, they head for the hills. It's amazing to see."

"I bet." Caplan added another blanket to his lap. "How'd you know we were here? More radio traffic?"

He nodded. "We were hanging around up north, waffling about where to go next. George broke off to check the traffic. He heard you were being dropped off in Boston. Literally."

Caplan chuckled.

"Tricia insisted on helping you guys and the rest of us agreed. We drove to the outskirts and waited until we saw your parachutes. The harbor was closer so we figured we'd head there first."

Mills set down her mug and stretched out on the sofa. Her breathing softened. Faint snores filled the room.

Caplan stared at the crackling fire for a few minutes, drinking in its warmth. There hadn't been a lot of quiet moments since the behemoths arrived and he was enjoying this particular one.

But like all good things, it would soon end. He needed to get back to the Vallerio. He needed to rescue Morgan. And he needed to conquer Savage Station. But before he could do any of those things, he needed to recruit some help.

"You didn't have to come here," he said.

"Stop."

"I mean it. I gave you—all of you—the cold shoulder for a long time."

Ross shrugged. "You were doing what you thought best. And honestly, you had a point. If we hadn't been so populous, those soldiers would've never found us."

"You're still pretty populous from what I can tell."

The trace of a grin creased Ross' lips. "What can I say? I'm a slow learner." Then he exhaled. His gaze turned toward the flames. "Don't get me wrong. I thought long and hard about it. Ultimately, I decided it was better to stick together. They're pretty much my family at this point. Plus, we're kind of it, you know? The last people. We're a dying resource and once we're gone, we're gone for good."

Caplan nodded silently.

"So, how'd you end up in this hellhole?"

"It's a long story."

"And we're stuck here until nighttime."

"Fair enough." So, Caplan told him everything. He described the Vallerio Forest and Savage Station. He discussed the beatings, the sleep-deprivation. He talked about Morgan, the clinic, and Lucy. And he revealed Corbotch's plans for Stage Three.

Through it all, Ross listened quietly. He asked the occasional question, but offered no comment of his own. Afterward, he leaned back and lifted his gaze to the ceiling. "That's quite a story."

"Yes, it is."

"So, what's the next chapter?"

"Escape Boston, then head back to Savage Station."

"To rescue Morgan?"

"Yes. But also because Savage is our best shot. At survival. At normal lives."

"This is the part where I tell you I want to help." Ross finished off his mug and set it on a side table. "And then you tell me you don't want it."

"You're right. I don't want it." Caplan looked him square in the eye. "I need it."

CHAPTER 44

Date: Dec. 1, 2017, 6:47 p.m.; Location: Downtown, Boston, MA

"Hang on." Mills' legs started to sag. Reluctantly, she leaned on the wall for support. "Just … give me a second."

Caplan paused next to the door. He adjusted the duffel bag, then gave her a quick once over. Her clothes were dry. Her lips were no longer blue. She was past the worst of it, but had yet to fully recover. "You sure you're up for this?"

She nodded. "Just as long as I don't have to drive."

"That won't be a problem." He opened the door and peeked outside. The sun had set for the evening. Darkness, illuminated by firelight, slowly crept over the area. Turning his head to both sides, he caught glimpses of distant behemoths, wrapped up in dense fog and smoke.

"We're late, aren't we?"

"I prefer to call it, 'making an entrance.'"

Smiling faintly, she released the wall and stood straight. "And we're absolutely sure the infrasound weapon works?"

"Like a charm, according to Noel."

"That's good." She took a few wobbly practice steps. "We're lucky he tracked us down."

"Tell me about it." He turned his gaze to the opposite side of the street and zeroed in on a dark parking garage. "Are you ready?"

She nodded. Keeping low, they hurried outside and sprinted across the street. They ducked into the parking garage. Then they walked down a series of ramps to the bottom level.

A number of vehicles, surrounded by torches, were clustered in a corner. Caplan saw dented and soot-covered armored vehicles, complete with gun turrets. He also noticed other trucks and cars, plated with all kinds of makeshift armor. And of course, he caught sight of the old van, looking almost exactly like he'd left it.

Danter residents milled about the strange fleet of vehicles, looking anxious and nervous. Amongst the crowd, he spotted a bunch of familiar faces. But one stuck out above all the rest.

"Tricia." Mills wrapped Elliott into a tight hug. "It's so good to see you."

Elliott, as might be expected, winced at the touch. But she smiled a bit as well. "You too."

"Thanks for coming after us," Caplan said.

"Of course." Her face flushed bright pink. Turning away, she nodded at the woman behind her. "You know Sydney, right?"

"You could say that." Caplan wrapped his childhood friend into a bear hug. She returned the hug in kind. "I hear you turned our little van into every behemoth's worst nightmare."

"It packs a wallop, alright," Teo replied.

"I can't wait to see it in action." Turning on his heels, he studied the crowd. "So, what's the plan?"

"Last I checked, Ross was still hemming and hawing over it. Don't get me wrong. I love the guy. But he's not exactly the decisive type."

Caplan spotted Ross next to an armored car. The man's attention was focused on a map spread out over the hood. Five people surrounded him, pointing and talking over one another.

Excusing himself, he walked to the armored car. By that time, the conversation had turned heated and Ross looked like he wanted a place to hide.

He glanced around at the gathered faces. He saw Mike Tuffel, owner of Danter Hardware. George Pylor, Danter's most renowned hunter. His wife, Dr. Sandy Pylor. Luann Cordell, Head Librarian at Danter Library. And of course, Connie Aquila, wilderness guide extraordinaire.

"Hey, everyone," Caplan said.

George and Tuffel offered him hearty handshakes. Cordell offered him a limp, icy one. Dr. Sandy and Aquila, meanwhile, gave him warm hugs.

"I need to talk to Noel," Caplan said. "Alone."

"Sure thing." George glanced at Ross. "Let us know when you're done and we'll iron this out."

"Of course." Ross waited for them to file away. Then he lowered his voice. "Thanks."

"Don't mention it. So, what's the plan?"

"We were just trying to figure that out. We could retrace our steps, but there are a lot of behemoths that way. Of course, behemoths are everywhere, right? So, maybe I'm just overthinking it. Or maybe I'm not and it's better to head north along the quickest route. But what if—?"

"How were the roads on the way in here?"

"Not the greatest."

"But they were drivable?"

"Well, sure."

"Then that's our route."

CHAPTER 45

Date: Dec. 1, 2017, 9:32 p.m.; Location: Downtown, Boston, MA

"Hey everyone, this is Mike." Tuffel's voice, tense and clipped, screeched out of the radio's speakers. "We've got a behemoth at Washington Street, right where State turns into Court."

After fleeing Roberts and her soldiers, the Danter Colony had come across a number of abandoned vehicles, military or otherwise. They'd fixed some up and left others behind. In the process, they'd located a number of old CB radios. Teo had installed these radios in their vehicles and added amplifiers to boot. It was a far cry from the networks of the old world. But it did the trick.

Caplan, situated in the van's driver's seat, waited for Ross' response. "It looks like we've lost Noel."

"Maybe," Mills said. "Or maybe he's waiting for you."

He exhaled through his nostrils. Was he the leader of this group now? He didn't want that. But he grabbed up the CB radio anyway. "What kind of behemoth, Mike?"

"An ox. A real nasty-looking one, too."

"Can we go around it?"

"That's a negative. The streets are ravaged. Only way forward is through this thing."

"Hang on." Shielding the radio, he glanced over his shoulder. The audio equipment had been anchored to the rear of the cargo space. A large speaker, added by Teo, faced outward. "Are you ready?"

She studied the equipment, then offered him a nod.

He glanced at Mills. "Landscape?"

She consulted a detailed map, marked up by Ross and his cohorts. "Ross' route goes past a few side roads. Then we take Broad to State Street. That'll put us about two hundred and fifty yards east of the behemoth."

"From what I can tell, the weapon really starts to hurt them at one hundred yards," Teo added.

"We need two locations," Caplan said. "One for the initial attack and one for the trap."

"Congress Street is probably our best bet for the trap." She showed him the map. "It's about eighty yards away from the behemoth. Group One can set up on the south end of the intersection. As for the initial attack, we can launch it from Kilby Street."

"Sounds good." After much debate, Ross and his five advisors had settled on a pretty simple strategy to bypass a behemoth. Caplan saw no reason to change that now. "Listen up everyone," he said into the radio. "We're going to blast this sucker with the infrasound weapon at the corner of Kilby and State. Group One, I need you one street west of Kilby, on the south side of Congress. Move out."

Caplan handed the radio to Mills. Using the map, she directed him past the side streets. They drove onto Broad Street, then turned left onto State Street.

"Wow." Mills' gaze drifted upward. "That's a big behemoth."

Big was an understatement. The road twisted a bit, but Caplan still caught glimpses of the ox behemoth. It stood over forty feet tall, making it considerably larger than Dire.

He halted alongside Tuffel's scout vehicle at the corner of Kilby Street. He could see the behemoth more clearly now.

He saw its horns, its ferocious teeth. Its powerful legs, its heavy hooves. The creature was awe-inspiring, even for a behemoth.

A powerful wind blew embers across the street. Snowflakes and smoke swirled around the behemoth's hooves, trailed up its body, and gathered around its massive head. The ox snorted gently, puffing air through its gigantic nostrils. Smoke and snow swirled away.

He eyed the neighboring buildings. An old brick building, probably some kind of landmark, lay in ruins. Other buildings sagged at the seams, looking ready to fall at any moment. If that happened, no amount of fancy maneuvering would save them.

Mills pointed at the windshield. "We've got company."

A small surveillance drone hovered one hundred feet in the air. It looked exactly like the one that had spotted them back in Maine. *James is watching us*, Caplan realized.

Four armored cars—Group One—slipped past the van. Dirt, grime, and rust covered the battered vehicles. Weaving through a maze of smashed crates, uprooted asphalt, and rusted bicycles, they drove to Congress Street. Then they hung a left and vanished behind a medium-sized building.

Two more armored cars—Group Two—pulled up, one on either side of the van. Ross' voice came pouring out over the radio. "We've got eyes on a drone."

"We see it, too," Caplan replied.

"I'm a pretty good shot. Want me to take it out?"

They couldn't let the drone follow them. But they didn't have to destroy it at that exact second either. "Not yet. James wants a show. Let's give him one."

"Sounds good."

In the rearview mirror, Caplan saw the rest of the caravan. Toland sat in one of the vehicles, jawing at local busybody, Dana Vallon.

For years, Vallon had prowled the streets of Danter, seeking to extinguish any and all signs of fun. She'd even sought out Caplan's parents on a few occasions, reporting him for such indiscretions as chewing with his mouth open, loitering in Danter Square, and uttering so-called curse words such as the dreaded "crap."

I'm glad I'm not riding in that car, he thought. *Give me the behemoth any day!*

He turned to the rest of the caravan. Each vehicle sported makeshift armor, like something out of a post-apocalyptic movie. It wasn't going to stop any behemoths. But hey, at least it looked snazzy.

He shifted his gaze back to the ox behemoth. The plan was to lure it to Congress Street and knock it off-balance with gunfire. Then they'd hit it with the infrasound weapon, driving it north. The caravan would cross the intersection. After that, rinse and repeat until they exited Boston.

"Everyone in position?" Caplan asked.

"Group One is ready to go," George replied.

"Same with Group Two," Ross added.

Caplan directed the van forward and spun the wheel. The vehicle turned in a half circle so the cargo doors faced the behemoth. "Power up the infrasound weapon," he called out.

Teo flicked a few switches. "Powered."

"Open the doors."

Elliott unlatched the doors and pushed them open. "Open," she said.

"The infrasound weapon is locked and loaded," Caplan said into the radio. "Let's get this party started. Group Two, open fire."

Turrets shifted into place on either side of the van. Gunfire rang out. Streaking across the sky, it crashed into the ox behemoth's tough hide. Twisting their guns, the shooters stitched the creature's enormous legs.

Quivers ran through the behemoth's enormous body. Shifting its gaze, it looked straight at the caravan.

"It spotted us," Caplan said into the radio. "Group One, fire at first sight."

The creature's hooves scraped the pavement, leaving long marks in their wake. When it reached Congress Street, Group One opened fire from the south. Gunfire spat at the behemoth, striking its legs and belly. It bellowed. But this bellow was soft, hesitant. Like it wasn't quite sure what to do next.

"Activate infrasound," he called out.

"Infrasound activated." Teo paused to check a screen. "The frequency looks good and we've got a nice, strong signal."

Muscles tensed, Caplan stared out the rear doors. Although he'd heard about the infrasound weapon, he still found it hard to believe. The behemoth was simply gigantic. It was hard to imagine anything—especially an invisible force like sound—hurting it in the least bit.

The ox behemoth snorted through its nostrils. It didn't come any closer. But it didn't retreat either.

"Man the speaker," he said.

Elliott sat down behind the speaker. "Speaker manned."

He backed the van across the icy road, angling it gently toward the north. Meanwhile, Elliott swiveled the speaker, keeping it aimed directly at the target.

A strange look came over the behemoth's face. Twisting its body, it backpedaled to the north. The ground roiled as its hooves crashed onto the six lanes making up Congress Street.

Caplan blinked, shocked to the core. Was this really happening? Was the behemoth really retreating?

Still angling the wheel, he backed the van to the edge of the intersection. Group One and Group Two, no longer spitting gunfire, slid to its sides.

Meanwhile, the ox behemoth continued to withdraw. One hoof stomped down on the ruins of a small building. Another one sent a garbage truck skittering across the pavement.

It kept backing up, distancing itself some two hundred yards from the infrasound weapon. Bellowing with fury, it focused its lava-orange eyes on the van. Then it turned around. And walked away.

"And stay out," Ross shouted over the radio.

Elliott snickered. Teo guffawed. Their laughter was contagious and Mills began to chortle. Caplan emitted a deep breath and soon found himself laughing as well.

Wiping her eyes, Mills glanced at the sky. "Well, I'd say we gave him a pretty good show."

"No doubt." Caplan laid eyes on the drone, still hovering overhead. Confidence and defiance surged within his heart. But caution reared its head as well. "Hey, Noel," he said into the radio. "I think the show's over, don't you?"

"I sure do." One of Group Two's turrets turned skyward. Gunfire rattled. The drone exploded in mid-air. "Connection terminated."

CHAPTER 46

Date: Dec. 2, 2017, 3:55 a.m.; Location: Longfellow Bridge, Boston, MA

"I know I've said this already but I still can't believe how well that infrasound weapon works." Caplan glanced in the rearview mirror. "What do we need to make more of them?"

"A miracle," Teo replied.

He frowned. "Why is that?"

"This is hyper-specialized ornithology equipment. Even in the old world, you couldn't just pick it up at your local electronics store. You would've had to special-order it."

He'd spent the last few hours envisioning the caravan's vehicles, all armed with sonic weaponry. Abruptly, those visions began to melt before his eyes.

"It's Mike again." Tuffel's voice screeched out of the radio's speakers. "We've got a behemoth just off the bridge at the corner of Third and Broadway."

Caplan grabbed hold of the radio. "What kind is it?"

"Another ox. Similar but different to that other one from a few hours back."

"Different how?"

"It's a little shorter. The coat is a bit shaggier. Just cosmetic stuff, really."

Caplan directed the van through a web of car wrecks occupying Longfellow Bridge. Squinting into darkness, he saw a few shadowy buildings but no behemoth. He wasn't worried though. They'd driven away plenty of behemoths since leaving the parking garage. What was one more?

He yawned. He'd driven for several hours with no breaks, all by moon- and starlight. It had been a tense, exhausting trip. Fortunately, it was coming to an end. They'd left Boston and were about to drive into neighboring Cambridge. The behemoths, which were everywhere just a little while ago, were now few and far between.

"Can we bypass it?"

"That's a negative," Tuffel replied. "Main Street is drivable, but only for a hundred yards or so."

"Then I guess it's time for another round of Break the Behemoth." He muted the radio and glanced at Mills. "Where's the best place to lay our trap?"

"Right here." She showed him the map. "The geography works in our favor for once. We don't even need the guns. We can just sneak onto the drivable portion of Main and launch our sonic attack from the south. That should drive it northeast onto Third Street."

"Sounds good." He glanced over his shoulder. Elliott held a toolbox in her lap. Teo, screwdriver in hand, knelt before the audio equipment. "Ready for another round?"

"Yes," Teo replied. "But once we're clear, I need to do a little maintenance work."

"I think we can arrange that." He unmuted the radio and lifted it to his mouth. "Group One, we don't need you this time. Pull up after we drive off the bridge and protect the caravan. Group Two, follow our lead. We're going to leave Broadway and circle around to the behemoth's left."

The two groups confirmed the strategy. Meanwhile, Caplan inched the van farther down the bridge. To his left, he saw old train tracks, protected by metal fencing and covered with dead weeds. To his right, he noticed the icy waters of the Charles River, blocked off by an ornate metal barricade.

He drove past the river and over a dark, snowy street. On his right, he saw a stone tower shaped like a pepper shaker. Old graffiti carried a variety of depressing messages: *Don't Repent, God is Dead,* and *We Deserved It.*

Ahh, graffiti. The voice of the rebels, the vandals, and the disenchanted. It had a long history, dating back at least as far as ancient Rome. How long would this particular graffiti last? Would it outlive the human race? What would the archaics make of it?

He turned his attention back to the road. He still saw the shadowy buildings. But he also noticed a new shadow, one that was shifting and vibrating.

Group One pulled to a halt and the caravan stopped behind them. Caplan drove over some rubble and entered the far left lane. Like all the others, this new behemoth towered above him. But he didn't feel much fear toward it. It was just another obstacle between him and Savage.

Main Street veered off to his left. Ignoring a *Do Not Enter* sign, he drove onto the road. A little park rested on his right, complete with a crushed fountain, dilapidated benches, and moss-ridden trees. The ox behemoth stood on the opposite side of the park, its gaze focused on some point to the north.

Quietly, he backed the van over the curb and onto a brick walkway abutting the park. Group Two split up and drove to either side of the van. Their gun turrets swung into position.

Caplan placed his lips close to the radio. "Is everyone ready?"

"Group One is with the caravan," George replied.

"Group Two is good to go," Ross said.

"Power up the infrasound weapon," Caplan said.

Teo's fingers flicked a variety of switches. "Powered."

"Open the doors."

Elliott unlatched the doors. Silently, she shoved them open. "Open."

"We should be able to do this without gunfire," Caplan said into the radio. "So, keep your turrets in check, Group Two. Don't open up unless the behemoth advances on us."

"Understood," Ross replied.

Caplan glanced at Teo. "Activate infrasound."

Her hands flew over the audio equipment. "Infrasound activated." She gave a cursory look at her screen. "Frequency and signal are both good."

The ox behemoth stiffened up at once and offered a soft bellow to the sky. Facing northeast, it took a few steps down Third Street.

Caplan edged the van in reverse over some pulverized benches and then onto a snowy road. He maneuvered around a dead tree, between two sagging fences, and onto a chipped sidewalk. Moments later, the van bumped into the intersection of Broadway and Third.

As Group Two took up flanking positions, he watched the ox behemoth retreat down Third Street. It covered a distance of about one hundred yards before coming to a halt. Its head twisted toward the van. Despite the dim light, Caplan could still see its lava-orange eyes.

"Okay," he said into the radio. "The coast is clear. Group One, take the caravan and—"

The sound of whirring rotors stopped him cold. Sudden bursts of noise pierced the dark sky. Moments later, bullets sliced through the roof.

Mills ducked her head. Teo and Elliott threw themselves to the floor.

The gunfire swept past the van and lit into one of Group Two's armored cars. The driver twisted the wheel and stomped on the gas pedal. The vehicle smashed up against the van, pinning it against Ross' vehicle in the process.

Caplan slammed into his seatbelt. Shaking off the cobwebs, he watched the helicopter disappear behind an office building. "It's Chenoa," he said, his fingers tightening around the wheel. "She must've sent another drone to track us."

"We need to find cover," Mills said.

He glanced at the office building. One corner was recessed and supported by thick columns. There was enough space to hold the van and a few other vehicles, too. "Group Two, take cover under the office building," he called into the radio. "Group One, head for the bridge. There's space beneath it."

No one responded. He tried again. Again, no response. "The radio's broken," he said.

Teo exhaled. "That's not the only thing that's broken."

He whirled around. Icy tentacles slipped down his spine. "The infrasound weapon?"

"It took two bullets. I can fix it, but it'll take time."

Time, unfortunately, was a luxury they didn't possess. With the van still in reverse, he pressed on the gas pedal. Metal squealed as the van scraped past the two armored vehicles.

The behemoth turned its entire body around. It squared its shoulders. Another bellow rose out into the night.

Caplan shifted gears. Driving onto the sidewalk, he slipped between a pair of columns.

The ground rumbled. Apprehension filled his chest and he cast a tentative look at the ox behemoth. Sure enough, it had taken a tiny step forward. It snorted through its nostrils. Then it took a second step. A third step. A fourth step.

More gunfire filtered down from above. Engines roared in response.

"The chopper's targeting the caravan," Mills cried.

The engine noises gained volume. Meanwhile, the helicopter passed over the office building again. Its cannons opened fire, riddling Group Two with bullets. Fortunately, the armor repelled the attack.

Tires screeched as the armored cars reversed into the intersection. They arrived at the same time as the caravan. Deafening bangs rang out as four or five armor-plated sedans crashed into the armored vehicles. Tires popped and vehicles skidded across the icy road.

Doors flew open. People, bruised and bloodied, lurched outside into the snow and ice. The helicopter shot overhead, stitching the area with brutal gunfire. It came to a halt about one hundred feet west along Broadway.

"What now?" Mills wondered.

The helicopter descended to the street, stopping about six feet above the pavement. The cabin door slid open. Seven figures spilt out onto the ice.

The chopper rose up into the sky. Seconds later, it flew off to the north. Meanwhile, the seven figures picked themselves off the ground. They broke into a run, heading straight for the tangled mess of vehicles.

Shifting his gaze, Caplan saw dozens of people, dazed and hurt, milling about the street. He needed to help them.

As he reached for his seatbelt, he caught a closer look at one of the seven approaching figures. His eyes popped. He'd seen her before. And she was no ordinary person. In fact, she wasn't a person at all.

It was Lucy, the archaic.

CHAPTER 47

Date: Dec. 2, 2017, 4:12 a.m.; Location: Kendall Square, Cambridge, MA

Lucy led the six other archaics into the intersection. They pounced on people and threw them to the pavement. Then they began pounding their chests and clawing their faces. A dozen Danter residents scrambled to help their friends. They were thrown back but more came to join them. In seconds, a full-blown war erupted between the two species.

Caplan's mind rewound to his conversation with Corbotch. *Just seven archaics—including Lucy—currently exist,* the man had said. *At midnight on December Third, two hundred and fifty-six others will join their ranks.*

That was, of course, just the first wave. Other waves would soon follow. They'd splash across Earth, engulfing the last of humanity. Only those holed up in Savage Station would survive.

Tearing his eyes from the carnage, he looked down Third Street. The ox behemoth stared back at him. It had halted for the moment, perhaps apprehensive about another infrasound attack. But it wouldn't hold back forever.

"Try to fix the infrasound weapon," he told Teo. "I'm going to help the others."

Caplan raced outside. Mills grabbed her bow and quiver and joined him. A chilly wind assaulted their skin as they darted toward the intersection.

Up ahead, Caplan saw Toland roll out from behind a sedan, locked in a death grip with a male archaic. Meanwhile, another archaic climbed on top of Devon Staton, manager of Danter Federal Credit Union. The creature pounded Staton's chest. Staton struggled to defend himself without much luck.

A wild scream filled Caplan's ears. Whirling in a quarter-circle, he saw a female archaic bearing down on him. He grabbed an axe from his belt. But before he could swing it, the archaic bowled him over.

His back crashed into the icy pavement and he lost the axe. The archaic mounted him and slammed a fist at his chest. He gasped in agony.

The archaic raised another fist. But before it could strike, its eyes bulged and it slumped to the ground.

Mills yanked her arrow out of the archaic's skull and popped it back into her bowstring. Her face was tight. Her eyes were unreadable.

He grabbed his axe from the ground and rose to his feet. "Nice shot."

"I aim to please."

It was a lousy pun but it still brought the tiniest of smiles to his lips. However, that smile died the instant he glanced at the dead female archaic. A lump formed in his throat. Once upon a time, it—she—had been a woman. A woman with a family, friends, desires, and hobbies. But that woman was now gone, replaced by this horrid, bloodthirsty creation. Was this to be Morgan's fate as well?

Looking around, he saw the tide had turned. Four archaics, including the one at his feet, had fallen. The other three, including Lucy, were on the defensive. But the damage had been done.

His gaze focused in on the many corpses. Randy Dewar, the elderly pharmacist who'd once slipped a free candy bar his way. Raji Kharel, the grumpy owner of Raji's Diner. And Erin Vosseller, housewife and part-time writer on the joys of rustic living. There were others too, over a dozen in total.

The ox behemoth shook its head back and forth. Its horns ripped through the glass exterior of a tall building and tore away large chunks of the façade. With thumping footsteps, it started toward the intersection.

Caplan looked down Broadway. He saw a gaping hole in a red brick building. There was no sign, but from his vantage point, it looked like a parking garage.

"Take everyone there." He pointed at the garage. "Once you're inside, get out of sight."

"What about you?" Mills asked.

"I'm going to get Tricia and Sydney."

As Mills spread the word, Caplan ran back to the van. "Well?" he asked.

"I need more time," Teo said.

"We're out of time. Come on."

While he grabbed the duffel bag, Teo scrambled out of the van. Elliott tried to follow her, but her knees buckled when she touched the ground.

"I got you." Teo slid under Elliott's arm.

Shockwaves struck the street. Hunching down, Caplan led his friends to one of the many gray columns helping to prop up the office building.

Debris and dust exploded into the air. Caplan pushed Teo and Elliott ahead of him and ran out into the intersection. Taking cover behind one of the sedans, he looked back and saw the ox behemoth ramming its horns into the office building. The building wavered for a moment.

Then it collapsed.

It came down all at once, burying the van—and the broken infrasound weapon—beneath tons of steel, concrete, and glass.

His lips tightened. Their greatest weapon was now gone. And unless they reached the garage soon, he and his friends would surely share its fate.

CHAPTER 48

Date: Dec. 2, 2017, 4:12 a.m.; Location: Rockford, NH

Saber kicked its front paws into the air. Seconds later, they came smashing back to the snow. Shockwaves ripped through the soil, all the way over to *it*. ArcSim. Otherwise known as *Arctodus simus*, or short-faced bear.

ArcSim stood still and silent as an icy breeze crested through its wiry, black fur. Saber had doubled in size since escaping the Vallerio Forest seventeen months ago. Now, its shoulders rose some sixty feet into the air, making it roughly equivalent to the massive bear.

ArcSim rose up on its hind legs. Its body slowly unfolded until it stood over one hundred feet tall. Its lips curled back, exposing its bloodstained teeth. A mighty growl erupted from the depths of its being.

Saber locked eyes with ArcSim. It knew the creature. Not by sight or sound, but from a much deeper place. A place buried within its very soul.

The two behemoths had exchanged signals a long time ago, back in that vast, dense forest. Recognizing ArcSim's enormous strength, Saber had set out to destroy it. But tremendous heat and blinding light had gotten in its way. Disoriented, it had stumbled upon that little flying object in the clearing. It had seen—and smelled—the prey within it. And then the scent was gone. The infernal ringing noise had started shortly afterward. The two things, it figured, were tied together somehow. Stop the scent, stop the ringing. Ahh, that scent … where was it now?

ArcSim fell back to the snow-covered soil. A second shockwave, bigger than the one caused by Saber, swept through the ground.

Saber bared its teeth. While it had battled behemoths in the past, none of those fights had lasted for more than a few minutes. Once those creatures had tested its strength, they'd turned tail. Saber, of course, had chased them down and killed them. Always. Not because it wanted to feast on their remains, but because nothing could be allowed to stand in its way.

But ArcSim was different than those other behemoths. It was bigger, stronger, more aggressive. Its hostility was off the charts and Saber knew it wouldn't back down from a fight.

Plagued by that infernal ringing noise, it strode forward. Just ahead, it spotted several of those little structures preferred by prey. Oh, how it ached for prey. For their pungent red blood and the relief that came with it.

ArcSim trotted out to meet it. The two behemoths circled each other for a few moments, their eyes sizing up one another's enormous bodies. Then ArcSim dipped its head. Saber lunged at it with both front paws. ArcSim shook off the blows and plowed forward, knocking Saber back twenty feet.

Sliding to a stop, Saber coiled up its rear legs. Leaping into the air, it sank its teeth into ArcSim's skull. Growling, the enormous bear gave its head a couple of violent shakes. Saber held on for a few seconds, but was ultimately thrown to the ground.

It was an awe-inspiring show of strength. And yet, Saber felt no fear, no apprehension. Simply put, ArcSim was just another obstacle to its ultimate goal. Nothing more, nothing less.

ArcSim growled. Blood began to pour from a deep gouge on its face.

Saber's adrenaline surged. Rising up again, it went into attack mode, swinging a series of paws at the gouge.

ArcSim batted away most of the blows, but a few deepened the gouge and one caught its eye. Emitting a deep bellow, it backed up a few steps, crushing a tiny structure in the process.

Saber circled ArcSim once, then twice. It moved quickly, forcing the gigantic bear to keep up. In response, ArcSim rose up on its hind legs. Saber feinted low. ArcSim took the bait and dropped back to the ground. And that was when Saber made its move.

Leaping up, it crunched its teeth into the soft spot between the creature's neck and right shoulder. ArcSim slumped and let out a mighty wail.

Saber slammed its body into the behemoth. With a soft crash, the short-faced bear fell onto its side. Before it could get up, Saber tore into its belly, slicing through thick hide and piercing organs and entrails.

ArcSim struggled for another few minutes. Then it exhaled a soft gasp and fell still. Saber paused just long enough to make sure the creature was dead. Then it stepped over the corpse, triumphant in victory. Quickly, it checked the surviving little structures for prey. Then it continued onward, in search of the scent.

Always in search of the scent.

CHAPTER 49

Date: Dec. 2, 2017, 4:19 a.m.; Location: Kendall Square, Cambridge, MA

Hooves struck pavement as the ox behemoth passed into the intersection. Lowering its head to the ground, it began feasting on Randy Dewar's dead body.

Caplan winced at the sound of crunching bone and flesh. Hunching behind a gray sedan, he cast a glance at Teo and Elliott.

Elliott sat on the pavement, fighting off shivers. A bullet had grazed her right thigh. Teo knelt behind Elliott, rubbing the woman's shoulders in a vain attempt to warm her up.

"How's your leg?" Caplan whispered.

Gently, Elliott touched the wound. Her mouth twitched. "I'm fine."

"You're not fine." Teo looked at Caplan. "She's going to need our help."

The behemoth crossed to another corpse. In the process, it stepped on Lucy's writhing form. A slight gasp rang out, along with a gross, squishing noise.

The fastest way to the parking garage was to travel in a straight line. But that meant staying out in the open for a long stretch of time. Peering around the sedan, Caplan saw a large parking lot situated across from the garage. It ran all the way up to the demolished office building. Bushes, thin and sickly, gave it a bit of cover. "I'll take one side, you take the other," he told Teo. "Head for the parking lot. Stay low and watch your step. We need to make as little noise as possible."

She nodded.

He waited for the behemoth to find another corpse. Then he slipped under Elliott's right arm and helped her stand up. Teo slid under the woman's left arm and together, they helped her around the sedan. Picking up speed, they hurried out of the intersection and slipped through the bushes.

Crouching down behind the thin vegetation, they waited for the behemoth to find another corpse. Then they snuck into the snowy parking lot. They weaved between abandoned vehicles, passing old bodies, broken suitcases, and a variety of busted gadgets and phones.

They stopped across from the dark parking garage. Six lanes, two of them intended for bicycles, were all that stood between them and temporary refuge.

"How's your leg?" Caplan whispered.

Elliott gritted her teeth. "Fine."

"Let's go," Teo said.

They slid past the bushes and hiked into the street. Looking past Elliott and Teo, Caplan saw the ox behemoth lift its back right leg. Its hoof came crashing down on top of a car. A horn blared weakly into the night.

The behemoth's head spun toward the sound. In the process, it caught sight of them.

Its lava-orange eyes swirled. Its thick hair bristled in the cold wind as its body twisted around. Bellowing, it raced down Broadway.

Awe and horrid unease filled Caplan's gut. Steeling his emotions, he helped Teo haul Elliott to the garage. Darkness fell over them them as they slid between two lines of abandoned cars and hurried down a steep ramp.

The behemoth shoved its nose into the garage. The walls shook and dust shot into the darkness. A sudden gust of wind slammed into Caplan's group, knocking them over. As they coughed and hacked, a fierce bellow filled the air.

Mills ran out to help Teo. The Pylors grabbed hold of Elliott. Meanwhile, Ross pulled Caplan to his feet. Assaulted by bellows and snorts, they made their way down the ramp.

They hung a right and hurried down more ramps. Cars were everywhere. Most were neatly parked in spaces. Others had been abandoned in the driving lanes.

The ox behemoth's wails and bellows grew faint. The building fell still and the dust settled to the ground. Slowly, Caplan's awe and unease melted away.

Stepping off the last ramp, he saw dozens of people perched on car hoods or sitting on the ground. A few cried. The rest wore dazed, vacant expressions.

He counted heads and came up with just seventy-seven people. That meant seventeen members of their little group were dead or missing. And out of the known survivors, at least half had sustained fairly serious wounds.

The Pylors took Elliott to a makeshift clinic set up by Dr. Sandy. Teo cleared her lungs, then joined her. Meanwhile, Caplan and Mills joined Toland in an empty parking space. Leaning against the back wall, Caplan exhaled, watching his breath form little clouds in front of his face.

Noses sniffled. More people began to sob. Rotating his head, Caplan saw a couple of Danter residents gather around the pale, still form of Luann Cordell.

Cordell had once ruled Danter Library with an iron fist. He could still recall the time he'd returned his copy of

Atonement two days late. She'd glared at him through those thin, lightweight spectacles of hers. Then she'd given him the tongue-lashing of a lifetime.

He'd never cared for her. She was a mean-spirited woman, the sort who'd sneer at a little kid for no good reason. But he still got choked up when Ross stooped down to shut her eyelids for the last time.

"That's eighteen." George exhaled. "Eighteen dead men, women, and children."

Ross stood up. His face was splotchy and sweaty. "They're missing. But they might not be dead."

"Where's Mike?" Aquila asked.

"Mike Tuffel?" George looked around. "I don't see him. He must be one of the dead. Oh, excuse me. I mean missing."

Dr. Sandy cleaned Elliott's wound. Then she wrapped it in a gauze bandage. "Those things …" She glanced at Caplan. "Were those the archaics you told us about?"

He nodded.

She fought to control her voice. "And you say there are more of them where we're going?"

He nodded again. "Two-hundred and fifty-six are being released at midnight. Another three thousand or so are waiting in the wings."

"I think I've had my fill of archaics." Aquila glanced at Ross. "No offense, but I'm skipping this little trip of yours."

A few people nodded. Murmurs of assent rang out.

"Hang on, Connie," Ross replied. "We need to calm down, think rationally. We've got to keep our heads."

George snarled. "It's pretty hard to keep our heads when archaics are trying to rip them off."

Ross raised his palms in a conciliatory gesture. "I know emotions are running high right now. But if we can just sit down and—"

"And what? Talk about our feelings? Say a prayer?" He shook his head. "We lost eighteen people to just seven archaics. That doesn't bode well for our future."

More people nodded. The murmurs gained volume.

"Listen to me," Ross said.

But no one listened.

"I say we go with Connie." George gave his wife a look." "What do you think?"

"I agree," she replied. "We can take one of these cars and head south. At least we'll be warm."

"Maybe for now." Caplan cleared his throat. "But what happens when Chenoa comes for you?"

"I like you, Zach," George said. "Always have. I'm trying real hard not to blame you for all of this. So, do me a favor and keep your nose out of our business."

"I'll tell you what'll happen," he said. "If you resist, she'll capture you. One way or another, you'll be carted back to Savage Station. You'll be turned into an archaic and all traces of your identity will be removed. You'll spend the rest of your life thirsting after blood, with no memory of Sandy or anyone else."

George's face twisted with uncertainty.

Caplan turned toward the crowd. "I know you're scared. And I know you're pissed-off. But you can't hide from this. Sooner or later, James is going to find you."

The nods stopped. The murmurs ceased.

"Our only hope is to take the fight to him," he continued. "To conquer Savage Station."

Dr. Sandy shook her head. "We don't have the manpower or guns to beat Chenoa's soldiers."

"Then we'll use our brains." Caplan scanned the many faces before him. He knew them all so well. "The first wave of archaics is currently resting. Come midnight, they'll be taken to various non-populated areas. Chenoa's soldiers will most likely handle the transport. And their absence will leave Savage vulnerable to attack."

"What if Chenoa sees us coming?"

"Hopefully, she thinks we're dead. Regardless, we'll stick to side roads whenever possible." He paused. "I know this seems like a long shot. But it's got a big payoff. If we capture Savage, we won't have to worry about behemoths anymore. We won't have to worry about anything."

A few heads started to nod again. The murmurs began to support Caplan's side.

"What if we have to fight behemoths on our way there?" Aquila asked. "The infrasound weapon could be destroyed for all we know."

"It was destroyed." Gasps rang out, but Caplan pushed right through them. "And we won't be able to replace it anytime soon. Fortunately, there should be fewer behemoths now that we're out of Boston."

A full minute passed. Then Dr. Sandy glanced at her husband. "What do you think?"

"I think he's right," George said. "About everything."

Aquila sighed. "So, when do we leave?"

"Soon. We need to get to Savage by midnight." Caplan looked around at the crowd. "But for now, I need half of you to stay here. Help the wounded. Then check out the cars and see if any of them still work. Search for gas and other supplies, too. The rest of you come with me. We're going to look for survivors."

The crowd split into two groups as he strode toward the ramp. Ross joined him and together, they ascended the incline. Shoes and boots scuffed against wet concrete as people followed after them.

"That was one hell of a speech," Ross said quietly.

Caplan gave him a pointed look. "It should've come from their leader."

"I think it did."

CHAPTER 50

Date: Dec. 2, 2017, 4:51 a.m.; Location: Kendall Square, Cambridge, MA

The pavement trembled and Caplan froze, ready to sprint back to the garage. Another tremble, just a bit softer, streaked through the ground one second later. He took a deep breath. His body relaxed. Clearly, the behemoth was still heading away from the garage.

His head on a swivel, he crept past Third and continued down Broadway. He passed a bank and then walked through a maze of broken picnic tables, all chained together.

Soft moans filled his ears and he stopped outside a small shop. A stiff awning above the doorway indicated it had once been called Jeel's Coffee Bar, Home of the Incredi-Latte.

Back in the old world, a tough sheet of tempered glass, along with a tempered glass door, had blocked off the interior. But rioters had broken the glass long ago, most likely in an effort to reach the cash register.

Rubbing his hands for warmth, Caplan thought back to the early days of the apocalypse. At first, looters had focused on the usual assortment of luxury goods. Televisions, video game consoles, designer shoes, and the like. But as the true scope of the situation became apparent, they'd switched their attention to more basic necessities. Food, water, fuel, camping gear, and sturdy boots, among other things.

He'd kept his friends alive for four solid months without looting. But when things got tough, he'd been forced to check his morals at the door. Of course, it helped that he saw it more as salvaging than looting. After all, he was stealing from the dead. And could the dead really own anything?

Withdrawing his axes, he poked his head into the open doorway. "Who's there?"

"Zach?" The voice was faint, halting.

"The one and only." He stepped nimbly over ice and glass and walked behind the countertop. Tuffel lay stretched out on the ground in a pool of dry blood. Although pale, he looked awake and alert.

Caplan performed a quick physical and found some deep scrapes on the man's legs as well as a bullet hole in his left shoulder.

"Just my luck," Tuffel groused. "Another few inches to the left and I'd be fine."

"True. But another few inches to the right and you'd be dead."

"Your bedside manor stinks."

"So, does your wound." He clamped his nostrils shut. "Can you walk?"

Tuffel shook his head. Caplan helped him up and took him back to the garage. He turned the man over to Dr. Sandy, then strode back out to the street.

The sun had yet to rise, but its rays were starting to streak across the landscape. He looked for the ox behemoth, but all he saw were buildings. The tremors, meanwhile, grew fainter.

Mills rounded the corner with Victoria Fisher propped up on her shoulder. Caplan ran out to help her and together, they hauled the yoga instructor to the garage.

Ross greeted them just inside the entranceway. "Hey Victoria," he said. "How are you feeling?"

She gave him a pained smile. "Alive."

"You're one of the lucky three."

"How many more are still question marks?" Caplan asked.

"None." Ross sighed. "We found them all. Fourteen dead bodies. Three survivors."

Mills grimaced. "That's it?"

"Yeah." Ross' face twisted with a mixture of sadness and relief. "Still, it's more than we had an hour ago."

CHAPTER 51

Date: Dec. 2, 2017, 1:27 p.m.; Location: Nashua, NH

Energy surged within Caplan as he directed the battered, old SUV over the Massachusetts border. "Welcome to New Hampshire," he said.

"Already?" Stifling a yawn, Toland pushed his glasses farther up his nose. "But it's only been five hours."

Caplan ignored his sarcasm. Indeed, it had taken them five hours to travel just over forty miles. On the other hand, *they'd traveled forty miles.* Forty miles away from behemoth-infested Boston. Forty miles closer to the Vallerio. And of course, forty miles closer to Savage Station.

All in all, things were looking up. They numbered almost eighty people. They'd procured two-dozen vehicles and plenty of fuel from the garage. And they'd located a decent amount of water along with plenty of canned and packaged food, too.

To top it off, it had been a fairly smooth ride. They'd been forced to clear a couple of obstacles as well as circle around three or four behemoths. But they had yet to experience any real trouble.

Even so, a thick layer of tension hung over the SUV. Caplan could see it in Mills' eyes, in Toland's fidgeting. He saw it in Elliott's drowsiness and in Teo's bitten fingernails. They knew what he knew. Namely, that this corridor between Boston and Savage was merely the eye of the hurricane. Very soon, they'd leave the eye behind and reenter the storm. And this time, the storm might very well kill them.

He glanced in the rearview mirror. Teo sat in the left-side seat, her back at an angle. Elliott, currently napping, was draped over her like a blanket. He wondered about them, if they were just friends or something more. He'd spotted a few stolen glimpses that suggested the latter. On the other hand, his stress was off the charts and he was running on very little sleep. So, maybe it was just his imagination.

"Noel must really hate you," Toland said.

Slowing the SUV, Caplan drove around a fallen highway sign. "What makes you say that?"

"He was in charge of this motley bunch. Then you came along and stole that away from him."

"I didn't ask to be leader."

"No, you didn't. You just did your whole boss-everyone-around-until-they-become-sheep routine."

Mills rolled her eyes. "Here we go."

He spun around to face her. "I'm just telling it like it is."

"No, you're just trying to stir up trouble."

"I just want to rescue Amanda and take over Savage Station," Caplan said. "Once those things are done, someone else can take the reins."

He snorted. "You really expect me to believe that?"

"Whoever's in charge is going to face a tough decision. Do we continue kidnapping people and forcing them to become archaics? Or do we let the Holocene extinction run rampant?" He gave Toland a sideways glance. "Do you want to make that choice?"

Toland muttered something under his breath and turned away. Meanwhile, Mills shot Caplan a shocked look in the rearview mirror. Her lips moved silently. *You did it*, she mouthed. *You actually shut him up*.

He grinned.

Yes. Things were definitely looking up, alright.

CHAPTER 52

Date: Dec. 2, 2017, 4:03 p.m.; Location: Ashland, NH

Mighty forests had once bound this particular section of I-93 for as far as the eye could see. But now, the trees lay dead and dying, their withered branches covered in ice. It hurt Caplan just to look at them, to see nature in this awful state of despair.

Exhaling, he turned his gaze to the sky. He looked for drones or helicopters or any other type of aircraft. Anything that might indicate Corbotch's presence. Fortunately, the skies remained clear.

Mills pointed at the windshield. "There's something in the road."

A fierce gust of wind sent broken branches and snow into his field of vision. He squinted at the road. A yawn escaped his mouth. Unfortunately, his earlier surge of energy was long gone. Sheer exhaustion had taken its place.

Up ahead, he noticed a couple of long objects—trees—sitting across the road. His cheeks burned with annoyance. *Oh, goodie*, he thought. *Another obstacle.*

He parked the SUV about ten feet from the trees. Opening his door, he stepped outside. A bitter wind quickly iced down his burning cheeks.

He walked around to the back and lifted the cargo door. Inside, he saw Morgan's duffel bag along with a number of supplies salvaged from the parking garage.

He rooted through the items, eventually locating a long-sleeve knit shirt and a pair of work gloves. He pulled the shirt over his other shirt and donned the gloves. The extra clothing helped a bit. But he still shivered as he shut the cargo door.

The fleet of vehicles pulled to a halt. People piled outside. They donned jackets and gloves and then joined Caplan at the fallen trees.

"I wish I had an axe." Tuffel kicked the skinniest of the three trees, a forty-foot long quaking aspen measuring about a foot in diameter.

Caplan fingered the axes hanging from his belt. Unfortunately, they were far too small for a job like this one.

"We don't need axes." Ross came forward with a handful of chains. "This is a tow job, pure and simple."

Caplan studied the chains, then nodded. "Set it up."

Ross started to untangle the links. Meanwhile, Mills walked to the side of the road. Kneeling down, she studied one of the trunks. "It's all chewed up down here," she observed.

"That looks like beaver work." Caplan's face turned puzzled as he peered over her shoulder. "Which doesn't make a lot of sense."

"Why not?"

"Beavers usually fell trees near water. They use them to build dams."

"There's not a lot to eat these days. So, maybe this beaver was just hungry." She frowned. "Beavers eat trees, right?"

"Sometimes. But not mature, dead ones. They prefer to snack on young, small trees." Brow furrowed, he studied the landscape. "We're missing something. It's almost as if …"

"As if what?"

A steep hill, dotted with trees, lay on the side of the road. Four masses of fur strode up its snow-covered side. They weren't behemoths. But they were still quite big.

His gaze tightened. "As if this was a trap."

CHAPTER 53

Date: Dec. 2, 2017, 4:18 p.m.; Location: Ashland, NH

He'd seen this form of reborn megafauna before, back in the early days. Morgan had called them *Castoroides*, or giant beavers. And indeed, the name fit the bill. The giant beavers were six to seven feet long and looked like they weighed over two hundred pounds apiece. Their incisors were six inches in length and far sharper than those found in the jaws of more modern beavers.

He grabbed hold of his axes. "How are you doing with those chains?" he called out.

"Just a few more minutes," Ross replied. "Why?"

"Because we're about to have a meet-and-greet with four very nasty-looking giant beavers."

Chains fell to the pavement. Ross and others ran over to join Caplan and Mills. At that moment, one of the beavers lifted its head and gave them a crazed, tense look. Its eyes were bloodshot and it appeared to be hyperventilating.

"Well, there's no way around these trees," Ross said, his gaze shooting to the safety barricades on both sides of the road. "What do you want to do?"

"Fight," Caplan decided. "If you want to help, grab a weapon. Otherwise, hunker down in the cars."

Feet scuffled as people raced to the vehicles. They reemerged within seconds, their hands filled with tire irons, daggers, baseball bats, and yes, even swords, all of which had been scrounged up from the Cambridge parking garage.

The beavers stepped over the metal barricade. Spitting and drooling, they raced toward their prey. Mills struck first, sinking two arrows into a beaver's face. Screeching in pain, it tripped and rolled head over heels. Caplan was on it quickly, slicing its throat with an axe.

Aquila sidestepped a charging beaver and swung her sword at its back. The creature flopped onto its face. Six others surrounded it, using a variety of blades to finish it off.

George knocked the third beaver for a loop with his baseball bat. Dr. Sandy attacked its skull with a metal folding chair. Others joined in to subdue the creature.

The fourth beaver, seeing all of this, tried to run away. But Ross threw his chain around its neck, cutting off its escape. People leapt onto the creature's limbs, holding them down. The beaver extended its jaws, snapping viciously. But before it could bite anyone, people dispatched it with blades and heavy tools.

The battle was over quickly. Afterward, Ross unraveled his chain from the giant beaver's neck and wrapped it around the trees. Mills and the Pylors took up lookout duty alongside the road. Meanwhile, Dr. Sandy walked amongst the crowd, looking for wounds and injuries. Outside of a few scratches and scrapes, everyone was okay.

Caplan helped Ross secure the chains to a truck. Meanwhile, others rolled the beaver carcasses off the road. Still others walked around with food and water, offering the items to anyone who needed them.

After the logs had been moved, Ross turned to Caplan. "Beavers are dead and the road is clear. We're getting pretty good at this survival stuff, huh?"

"Don't get cocky." Caplan looked around. Still no helicopters, still no soldiers. But for how much longer? "It only gets tougher from here."

CHAPTER 54

Date: Dec. 2, 2017, 6:07 p.m.; Location: Rockford, NH

"That's ArcSim. I'm sure of it." Caplan's voice was hushed as he leaned forward, his gaze focused on the windshield. "I think … yes, it's dead."

Toland arched an eyebrow. "How can you be sure?"

The sun had set and the sky had grown dark. On a normal night, Caplan would've driven by moon- and starlight in order to avoid attracting attention. But with time running short, he'd switched on his headlights. Now, those headlights illuminated a giant mass of black, wiry fur.

"Its chest is still," Caplan pointed out. "And look at all that dried blood. It must be dead."

"Or merely unconscious. I say we go around it."

He checked the dashboard clock. Just six hours remained until the first wave of archaics would enter the world. "There's no time," he replied.

He released the brake and eased down on the gas pedal. As the SUV rumbled forward, he kept his gaze locked on the textured black fur. ArcSim wasn't an ordinary behemoth. In Caplan's eyes, it was *the* behemoth. The undisputed king of all it surveyed.

He'd first crossed paths with ArcSim seventeen months ago in an underground laboratory. At the time, it had stood twelve feet on its hind legs, making it two feet taller than even the most massive grizzlies. After venturing outdoors, it had expanded in size, eventually reaching a full behemoth length of over one hundred feet.

He recalled escaping the Vallerio in Corbotch's Rexto 419R3 helicopter. Looking down, he'd seen the massive ArcSim slice through the forest with ease, leaving a bulldozer-like path in its wake. Its sheer raw power had stunned him.

He pulled to a stop just shy of the creature. Leaving the headlights on, he stepped out of the car and took a good long look at the behemoth. It lay on its side, its head resting on its right shoulder. Long scratches marked its face. Its head was cocked at a weird angle. Strips of flesh had been torn away from its torso, causing organs and copious amounts of blood to spill out onto the snow.

Mills climbed out of the backseat. "Those look like claw marks," she said, pointing at its face and torso.

He nodded. "Another behemoth did this."

"Behemoths are killing behemoths? That's new."

She was right. He'd seen behemoths nipping and biting each other in the past. But he'd never seen them battle each other to the death.

"James spent a lot of time and resources making the behemoths," he remarked. "I wonder how he'd feel about them hurting each other."

"Not good, I bet. He didn't build them just so they'd bump each other off."

"Then we must be dealing with a rogue behemoth." He gazed at the whale-sized ArcSim. "A really big rogue behemoth."

CHAPTER 55

Date: Dec. 2, 2017, 6:53 p.m.; Location: Outskirts of Vallerio Forest, NH

The dead trees looked like dark, icy columns. The spaces between them, blacker than night, resembled long-forgotten corridors and alleys. Caplan's skin tingled. Even now, even after all that had happened, the Vallerio still reminded him of an ancient city. An ancient, wicked city brimming with lost ruins. Still, the forest had changed over the last seventeen months. It no longer pulsed with evil, mystical life. The seething fury that had once inhabited its dark corridors had been snuffed out as well. Indeed, the Vallerio felt disturbingly calm, disturbingly dead.

"Tell me something, Zach." Toland arched an eyebrow in superior fashion. "Did you ever stop to think about how we'd actually drive through the forest?"

Shifting his gaze, Caplan stared at the sagging remains of a giant electric fence. In the old days, it had stood proud and tall, cutting off the Vallerio from the outside world. But the rampaging behemoths had taken their toll on the barrier. As such, it was no longer an obstacle. No, the real obstacle was the forest itself.

The Vallerio was undergoing a process of rapid disintegration. Hundreds of ancient tree trunks, once unbreakable columns, had cracked open and toppled over. Now, they crisscrossed the dark corridors and alleys, blocking off all access to the interior.

"You used to work here," Mills said. "How'd you get in and out of the forest?"

"By helicopter," he replied. "We used a ground vehicle for short expeditions. But that was all off-roading."

Teo's brow hardened into a ridge. "Maybe we could move the trees."

"Be my guest," Toland replied. "There must be only about, oh, a million of them between here and Savage."

Teo arched an eyebrow at Elliott. Elliott, in turn, gave her a look as if to say, *See? I told you he was a jerk.*

Caplan propped his elbow up on the windowsill. He continued to study the forest, to search its lifeless corridors for answers. His mind slipped back to forty-eight hours earlier. He recalled sitting in the helicopter, held captive by Roberts' soldiers. He recalled ascending into the air. He recalled seeing the exterior of Savage Station along with the ruins of Savage City. They'd continued to rise and …

A sly smile crept over his face. He twisted the steering wheel and stepped on the gas. The SUV jolted and vibrated as it drove over uneven ground.

"You're wasting your time." Toland spoke slowly, enunciating each word. "I don't care if you do find an entry point. This entire forest is clogged with dead trees."

"Don't be too sure about that." He drove a little farther, leading the rest of the caravan east along the Vallerio's outskirts.

He turned left and pressed the brake. A dark corridor stood before him. No, not a corridor. A street … a multi-lane street consisting of crushed, sunken trees and flat soil, all covered with a thin sheen of snow.

Mills cocked her head. "Is that a behemoth trail?"

"It sure is," Caplan replied.

Seventeen months ago, the behemoths had stomped out into the world, carving out enormous swathes of forest in the process. Thanks to the ongoing Holocene extinction, the vegetation had never regrown.

"This is crazy," Toland said. "We don't even know where this trail goes."

"Maybe not," Mills said. "But it probably intersects with other trails. And those trails will intersect with still other trails. It's like a vast system of roads."

"Yes. An *unmapped* system of roads."

"Oh, I don't know. I got a pretty good look at them when we flew out of here two days ago. A few cut pretty close to Savage. With a little luck, we just might find them." Caplan released the brake and gunned the engine. Then he directed the SUV over a section of ruined fence.

And into the Vallerio.

CHAPTER 56

Date: Dec. 2, 2017, 11:46 p.m.; Location: Sector 214, Vallerio Forest, NH

"I see something." Mills stabbed a finger at her window. "A glint of light. It could be nothing, but …"

Caplan eased down on the brake, bringing the van to a slow stop. The other vehicles, which trailed him in a line, halted as well.

It had taken them several hours to navigate the curving, twisting behemoth trails. But at long last, they'd forged a path to Sector 214.

The mysterious Savage City lay within that sector. Savage Station existed on the edge of that ancient, forgotten place. Thus, find the ruins, find the station. It seemed simple enough. Unfortunately, the darkness, coupled with the dense and dying forest, played tricks on their eyes. They thought they'd seen the ruins over a dozen times. But they had yet to find anything other than fallen trees and boulders.

He checked the clock. Less than fifteen minutes left until the commencement of Stage Three. Then two-hundred and fifty-six archaics would emerge from Level X. Shortly afterward, they'd be taken to their new homes, most likely by helicopter.

He needed to reach Savage before that point. He needed to be sure Chenoa's soldiers had left the station. Then he could launch his attack.

"I see what you mean," Teo said. "You know, I think that's water. And a bridge. A broken bridge."

His ears perked. Switching off his headlights, he looked out the side window. He saw a faint glimmer of light, shrouded in darkness. Gradually, the darkness faded and he noticed a dry creek-bed, filled with the remnants of a stone bridge.

Sweeping his gaze to either side of the bridge, he noticed old brick and cement structures. They were dilapidated and covered with withered vines and dead vegetation.

"Nice work. This is definitely it." He shut off the engine and climbed outside. The other drivers turned off their engines as well. The headlights vanished and the buzz of electricity died off. People piled out of their cars. Grabbing their weapons, they gathered together.

Axes at the ready, Caplan walked toward the broken bridge. He crossed over the dry creek bed and kept walking. His boots passed onto a hard surface. Scraping away snow and dead plants, he saw the cracked remains of an old asphalt road.

He walked down the road, seeing the charred, burnt remains of a small post office, houses, stables, a school, and a general store. He even saw the burnt-out hulk of a bank, complete with a very large concrete vault. Between the buildings, he caught sight of rusty machines, well-rotted wooden carts, and other odds and ends.

The forest was dead but the ancient town felt very much alive to Caplan. He sensed its evil, its pent-up fury. Something had happened here long ago. Something bad.

He walked farther. His gaze narrowed as he laid eyes upon a giant metal hatch.

There it is, he thought. *Savage Station*.

Savage Station was certainly a refuge. But as he stared at the hatch, he couldn't help but think about how it was so much more than a mere sanctuary. Indeed, the last hopes of a dying world rested upon its metal and concrete shoulders.

An uneasy feeling filled his gut. Corbotch had made it clear that archaics needed to replace people. That was the only way to end the Holocene extinction. Simple enough. And yet, as he'd indicated to Toland, not so simple at all.

If Caplan's group took over Savage, they'd also take over responsibility for managing the Holocene extinction. If they abandoned the archaic program, they'd doom Mother Nature to certain death. But continuing the program meant transforming more innocent people into archaics. Could he and his friends bring themselves to do that? To knowingly hurt people for the greater good?

"That's the hatch," Mills said, whispering loud enough so everyone could hear her. "Savage Station is below it."

"Wonderful." Toland pulled up next to Caplan. "Just one question. Once Chenoa's soldiers take the archaics away, how are we supposed to get in there? Because I'm pretty sure chanting 'open sesame' won't do the trick."

The ground rumbled. Metal scraped gently against metal as the hatch slid out of the way. A gaping hole, filled with bright light, appeared.

"I can get it open," Teo whispered.

Toland gave her a withering look. "With what? A bunch of feminist nonsense?"

"No." She met his gaze. "With tools."

"Oh really? I bet you don't know a hacksaw from a—"

Caplan raised his voice to a sharp whisper. "Everyone down."

Collectively, the group flung themselves to the soil. Other than the passing wind, the air remained silent. There were no rotors, no clanking restraints, no voices.

"What's taking so long?" Ross whispered.

"There are two-hundred and fifty-six archaics," Caplan reminded him. "It'll take time to load them into the helicopters."

"I suppose that's true. Still … hang on …" He furrowed his brow. "Something's happening."

Caplan turned back to the hatch. He saw a dark figure emerge from the brightness. The figure scrambled over the lip of the hatch, then rose up to its full height.

"Is that a soldier?" Aquila wondered.

"I don't see a rifle." Teo looked thoughtful. "I bet it's a mechanic, performing maintenance on the hatch."

Other dark figures emerged from the brightness. They came from all sides, scaling ladders. Gliding onto solid ground, they joined the first figure in front of the hatch.

Aquila arched an eyebrow. "A team of mechanics?"

A collective howl rose up into the night sky.

"Those aren't mechanics." Mills shook her bow open and reached for an arrow. "They're archaics."

CHAPTER 57

Date: Dec. 3, 2017, 12:04 a.m.; Location: Sector 214, Vallerio Forest, NH

They knew we were coming, Caplan realized. *They were watching us the entire time.*

His plan to seize Savage Station at a moment of vulnerability was now defunct. Even worse, retreat was out of the question. Corbotch and Roberts clearly knew of their presence and could easily follow them. No, the only way out of this mess was to just suck it up and fight.

He scanned the archaics, counting thirty-three in total. They were barefoot and wore light gowns. A close look revealed their prominent brow ridges, weak chins, and barrel-shaped torsos.

His face screwed up in distaste. These archaics had been housed on Level X during his previous visit. As such, he'd never laid eyes upon them. But he'd spent several days listening to their howls and screams while locked in Roberts' torture chamber. So, in a way, he still felt like he knew them.

They hadn't asked for this. It had been done to them, against their will. But that didn't make them any less dangerous. Like it or not, it was kill or be killed.

The small archaic army, moving as one, advanced into the ruins of Savage City. Snarls and howls filled the air.

"They know we're here," Caplan said, his face hardening into rock. "Everyone on your feet. Stay close and watch each other's backs. And whatever you do, don't panic."

His friends, almost eighty strong, pushed themselves off the ground. Quickly, they sorted themselves into little groups. Bravado laced their voices, but their pale cheeks and trembling fingers spoke of a deep, instinctual fear. People had fought archaics long ago and the memories of those battles ran deep within the human genome.

Laying eyes on Caplan's group, the archaic army bellowed as one. Waving their arms, they hurtled forward, driven by confusion, pain, and microchip-inspired bloodlust.

A tiny vibration streaked through the snow-covered soil. Caplan's brow tightened. *A behemoth*, he thought. *Probably the same one that took out ArcSim. Well, that ought to kick this party up a notch.*

The little groups formed into circles, their backs facing inward. They held their weapons—chairs, knives, hammers, trashcan lids—in white-knuckled grips.

Caplan backed up against Mills. She held her bow like a staff and an arrow like a dagger. Toland, clutching a crowbar, joined them. So did Teo and Elliott, both armed with bats. Ross was the last to join their circle. He'd wrapped chains around his fists and traded in his boisterous personality for one of quiet venom.

Raising his axes, Caplan uttered a guttural scream at the stars. One last plea to the Heavenly Father above. One last attempt to forgo violence.

The archaic army smashed into the circles. Their momentum and power caused them to burst right through them, tearing them apart. People twisted, turned, fought to stay upright on the slippery snow. Some fell, but quickly rose up again, eager to avoid the violent fate that had befallen their friends back in Cambridge.

Four archaics rushed Caplan's circle. Their eyes were wide and bulging. They ran full-tilt, moving at incredible, almost reckless speed. It gave him an idea.

"Split apart," he shouted. "Now."

The circle broke up. The four archaics tried to adjust their gaits. But their bare feet slid on the icy soil and they fell to the ground.

Axes in hand, Caplan pounced on an archaic man. But the creature threw him off like he was nothing. Scrambling across the snow, it bit his left arm.

Cloth and flesh tore as he yanked the limb out of the archaic's jaws. Grimacing in pain, he rolled away. The creature snarled and came at him again. But this time, he was ready.

His left axe slammed into its shoulder. His right one sliced deep into its side. The archaic's face twisted in horrible fashion as it sank to the ground.

He yanked his axes out of the corpse. Scanning the battlefield, he saw Elliott swinging her bat at a female archaic. Flesh and bone crunched. Curling up in agony, the archaic rolled to the side. Teo, bloodied but alive, slid out from underneath it.

A male archaic shoved Toland. The man fell hard and his glasses flew off onto the snow. Twisting around, he began feeling for the lenses.

The archaic moved in for the kill, but Mills bowled it over. Her hand shot downward and she stabbed an arrow into the creature's head.

Toland grabbed hold of his glasses. Donning them, he spun around. His gaze flitted between Mills and the dead archaic. "I hope you're not expecting a thank you," he said.

"Don't worry." She yanked the arrow out of the first archaic's skull. Fitting it into her bowstring, she let it fly. It whistled through the air and split a second archaic's forehead. The archaic died in mid-stride, collapsing just inches from Toland's prone form. "I'm not."

Shifting his gaze, Caplan watched George roll around the snow, locked in a deadly struggle with an archaic. Dr. Sandy, chair in hand, rushed over to help him. Meanwhile, Tuffel and another man had pushed an archaic up against a tree. Taking turns, they stabbed it with sharp knives.

His gaze turned toward Ross. The man lay on his side, chains unraveling from his knuckles. A shrieking female archaic pounded his head and shoulder with both fists.

Raising his axes, Caplan prepared to help his friend. But at that instant, he caught sight of the archaic's face. His heart wrenched. His jaw slowly unhinged from his face.

No. No, it wasn't possible. Corbotch had said so. And yet, how could he deny what he saw before him?

His lips moved. A single silent word left his mouth.

"Amanda?"

CHAPTER 58

Date: Dec. 3, 2017, 12:12 a.m.; Location: Sector 214, Vallerio Forest, NH

Amanda Morgan paused in mid-attack. Her eyes lifted up from Ross's body and stared straight at Caplan. Her face was different now. Different, yet still undeniably hers. Her eyes were still blue, although not quite as sharp as he remembered. Her forehead was sloped and her nose had grown a bit. Her cheeks, once rounded at the top and angular all the way down to her pointy jaw, had lost their shape. They were wider now. Wider and softer.

"It's me." He lowered his axes. "Zach."

Her head cocked to one side. She observed him with quiet intensity.

Another tremor rocked the ground, but Caplan barely noticed it. How could this have happened? Corbotch had told him a proper archaic transformation took weeks, maybe even months. Otherwise, the archaic could expire from shock.

He knew she'd die. Caplan squeezed his eyes shut. *But he sped up the transformation anyway.*

Corbotch had watched them leave the Boston area, likely via drones. He'd seen them head north, knowing they were on their way to Savage Station. And so, he'd told Dr. Barden to expedite Morgan's transformation. Not because he needed an extra archaic. No, he just wanted to hurt Caplan.

Unfortunately, that was hardly atypical for the man. Corbotch's moral code defied easy explanation. He protected his friends and allies while killing his enemies in the most horrible ways possible. He fought to stave off mass extinction. But he had zero qualms about hurting innocent people to do so.

Caplan's eyes teared up as he stared at Morgan. Was any bit of her still inside that body? Or had the Wipe removed her personality forever? How much longer did she have before the shock killed her? A minute? An hour? A day?

"Your name is Amanda." He sensed vicious fighting all around him. But at that moment, it was just him and her. Like old times. "We're friends. Good friends."

She lunged at him. One hand hit his chest. The other cracked his right fist. Fingers unfurling, he fell. His back hit the snow and he lost his axe.

Morgan grabbed it up. She turned back to Ross. Her right hand, clenching the deadly weapon, lifted into the sky.

Caplan's back shot off the snow. His left hand, still wielding the second axe, swung forward. The axe hurtled through the night air and slammed into Morgan's shoulder.

Shrieking, she dropped the axe. Her hand flew to her shoulder. She found the handle and yanked it. The blade slipped out of her flesh and blood began to pour onto the snow. Dropping the second axe, she gave him a furious look. Then she fled into the dead forest.

Ross sat up, dazed but alive. Caplan grabbed both of his axes, then helped the man to his feet. He took one last look at the forest, searching for Morgan.

But Morgan, at least the Morgan he knew, was gone.

Forever.

CHAPTER 59

Date: Dec. 3, 2017, 12:16 a.m.; Location: Sector 214, Vallerio Forest, NH

Screeches and howls rang out as a fresh batch of archaics pulled themselves onto the snow-covered soil. More archaics—a seemingly endless amount—streamed out after them. Metal squealed as the hatch slid back into place. The bright light vanished.

Caplan stared out at the force arrayed before him. The sheer size of it caused his breath to quicken. There were dozens of archaics. No, hundreds.

It's all of them, he realized. *James just released his entire first wave upon us.*

He scanned the battlefield. Fourteen members of his group had perished in the initial skirmish. That left just sixty-five people to face over two-hundred archaics. Overwhelming odds, to be sure.

The ground rumbled again, more fiercely this time.

Overwhelming, indeed.

"Run," he shouted.

Twisting around, he ran down the cracked road, retracing his footsteps through the charred, ancient ruins. Along the way, he saw old friends, now dead. Matt Palermo, local accountant and notorious tightwad, lay in a pool of blood and melted snow. The stunning Virginia Cukic, who Caplan had dated one glorious summer long ago, had been literally torn to pieces.

Flesh smacked into flesh. Screeches and howls, human ones this time, filled his ears. Casting a look over his shoulder, he saw the archaic army galloping toward his people. They lunged at the slowest runners, their gnarled fingers clawing at air. When they caught a fistful of clothing, they'd drag the runner to the ground and immediately go on the attack. Other archaics would join in and within seconds, the runner was a bloody corpse.

Caplan gauged the distance to the vehicles. He and a few others might make it. But the vast majority of his group would almost certainly perish under the onslaught.

He sprinted past roofless houses, claw-footed bathtubs, and a gigantic stack of ancient, weathered firewood. Up ahead, he spotted the building he'd pegged as a bank. Scraggily vegetation, all dead, ran up and down its charred walls. A concrete vault, way too big for a town of this size, sat on one end of the bank. A thick metal door, partially open, served as the sole entry point.

"Head for the vault," he shouted, veering toward the building.

He left the road and his feet pounded across the earth. A thin layer of snow partially covered a variety of strange artifacts from another age. The soggy remains of a dime novel. A broken jar of Clayer's Cathartic Tonic. A busted electrical telegraph, partially buried in the soil.

He stopped next to the vault and began waving people through the door. Toland, Aquila, Teo, Elliott, and Tuffel sprinted past him into the dark void. Ross, Mills, and others followed them in at high speed. But not everyone was so fortunate. He saw Kay Abbey fall. Same with Pablo Sandford. Local busybody Dana Vallon fell too, her screams swallowed up by surging archaics.

The Pylors, their faces twisted with terror, hurried out of the night. Dr. Sandy was limping. George helped her, but at a cost to his own speed.

Caplan's gaze turned to a pair of sprinting archaics. If left untouched, they'd intercept the Pylors long before the couple could reach the vault. "Bailey," he shouted.

Mills darted out of the vault and took stock of the situation. Bow in hand, she let loose a couple of arrows, striking the two archaics in rapid succession. The archaics fell, rolling and bouncing over the snow. Other archaics tripped over them and hit the ground as well.

Mills slid back into the vault. Following her inside, Caplan took up position next to the door. He stuffed one axe into his belt and grabbed hold of a large metal handle. Still wielding the other axe, he watched the Pylors with bated breath.

Archaics grabbed at Dr. Sandy's clothing. George swatted their hands. Shrieks rang out.

Moments later, the Pylors dove into the vault. Caplan yanked the handle, but archaics filled the gap before he could close the door. He swung his axe, drawing blood. Wounded archaics howled and tried to back up. But other archaics surged toward the vault at the same time, pushing them back toward the door.

Mills drew a pair of arrows from her quiver. Clutching them tightly, she stabbed at an archaic. It backed up just a bit and Caplan was able to close the door over a few more inches. Ross, Aquila, and others waded into the fight. Using bats, a sword, and other weapons, they forced the archaics out of the gap.

Caplan slammed the door. His fingers fumbled over a series of locks. Some were too rusty to move. But he was able to slide three bolts into place.

Flesh slammed into metal. But the thick door didn't budge. Squeezing his eyes shut, Caplan took a deep breath. Morgan was gone. Bloodthirsty archaics surrounded him and his friends. And that behemoth, possibly the same one that had killed ArcSim, was still out there as well. *No one ever said this would be easy,* he thought.

A couple of flashlights came to life, casting dim light through the vault. Turning around, Caplan saw it was far larger than the exterior would suggest. He stood on a sizable landing. A desk occupied one side of it. A steep concrete staircase descended twenty feet into the earth.

Most of his group was gathered on the lower level. Their clothes were covered with mud and blood splatter. Their eyes looked devoid of light.

"So, this is how it ends." Exhaling, Mills put away one of her arrows. "Holed up in a house of horrors."

His gaze turned to the walls. He saw weird skeletons— some human, some not—mounted on the concrete. Shelves were positioned between the skeletons. They held arrowheads, fossilized bones, and ancient dishware with strange depictions of unearthly animals. The room was definitely a vault. But a bank vault? Not so much.

"These are artifacts," he said slowly. "From a dig site."

"So, Savage City was built to study an ancient civilization?"

"Yes. Plus, the creatures that lived amongst it. It must've been a joint archaeology-paleontology dig." He wandered down the steps and grabbed a small metal chest from one of the shelves. Peeking inside, he saw finely granulated dirt. He picked up a handful of it and let it slip through this fingers.

Small creaks rang out and quickly gained volume. The door began to tremble.

Aquila bit her cheeks. "That door won't hold forever."

Another vibration shot through the earth. Dirt and dust kicked into people's faces. They started to hack, to choke.

Stifling a cough, Caplan closed the metal chest and searched the other shelves. He passed over a section of carved stone tablets and broken pottery and focused in on bundles of old cloth and tattered rope.

"Does anyone have a lighter?" he asked.

George fished one out of his pocket. "Yup."

Dr. Sandy, taking a break from bandaging up her own leg, arched an eyebrow.

"I know, I know." He shrugged. "But what's a few more cigarettes if I'm going to die anyway?"

Caplan took the lighter. He flicked the spark wheel and a bright flame appeared. "That'll do," he said. "Now, we need to make torches. Use your weapons as the base. There's some old cloth around here that should burn nicely. But we're going to need more. If you can afford to shed a layer, do it."

"Torches?" Toland rolled his eyes. "Do you really think those archaics are afraid of a little fire?"

"Everything's afraid of fire," Ross said.

"Not behemoths," Mills replied. "In fact, they might even be drawn to it. We saw Dire try to put out a fire on the night we lost Derek."

"Wait, I don't understand." Aquila's face looked pensive. "Are we trying to bring a behemoth here?"

Caplan shook his head. "That's the last thing we need. Hopefully, the torches will keep the archaics at bay. If we stick together, we might be able to forge a path to Savage Station."

"What if we forget about Savage?" George waved particulate out of his face. "And shoot for the cars instead."

"That's a longer hike," Caplan pointed out. "And besides, we need to get into Savage as soon as possible."

"Easier said than done," Toland said, his voice smacking of condescension. "They closed up the hatch, remember?"

"And I promised to get it open." Teo gave him him a withering look. "Remember?"

"Okay, let's assume this works," Ross said. "Let's say we get into Savage. Obviously, Roberts and her soldiers aren't going to be dropping off archaics tonight. They're going to be waiting for us. That's at least one hundred soldiers, all armed to the teeth. How are we supposed to beat them?"

Caplan racked his brain, but no answer emerged. "I'm not sure," he admitted. "We'll just have to figure it out along the way."

CHAPTER 60

Date: Dec. 3, 2017, 1:01 a.m.; Location: Sector 214, Vallerio Forest, NH

Horrible sounds—shrieks, screams, and cries—grew louder and louder. The vault's door continued to shake and tremble. The locks, subjected to tremendous pressure, started to groan and buckle.

"Okay," Caplan called out. "Light your torches."

He held up a baseball bat. It was swathed in layers of clothing, held together by tattered rope. Flicking the lighter, he doused the cloth with flame. It lit quickly and black smoke lifted to the ceiling.

He lit Mills' torch with his own. Then he moved on to Ross. Meanwhile, Mills touched her torch to George's torch and his burst to life as well.

After all ten torches were lit, Caplan hiked up the steps. "As soon as I open this door, shove your torches at the crack. Once the archaics back up, filter outside. Form a ring around the door. Got it?"

Heads bobbed.

"Make sure to stay tight with the group. Don't let the archaics goad you out of position. And whatever you do, don't lose your torch."

Again, heads bobbed.

The door continued to tremble and creak. Gripping one lock, he released the bolt. Then he undid the second lock. He readied his torch and took a deep breath. Then he unlocked the third bolt.

The door crashed against his foot. Long fingers wrapped around the edges. Hands stabbed into open space, stretching, reaching for victims.

Bracing himself against the wall, Caplan kept the door from swinging all the way open. Mills and Ross jabbed their torches at the hands. The sound of sizzling flesh filled the vault and the fingers withdrew.

Elliott, George, and other people added their torches to the mix. The front row of archaics backed up a few feet.

Caplan threw open the door and looked outside. The archaic army filled his field of vision. It was enormous, the stuff of nightmares. Archaics pushed against each other, grabbing and struggling. Many of them gnashed their teeth.

The torchbearers filtered outside. They formed a tight ring around the door. The archaics wanted no part of the flames. But that didn't stop them from trying to snatch the torches away.

A male archaic rushed Caplan. He jabbed his torch at it. The archaic reversed direction and started to backpedal. Stretching a bit, Caplan tagged the creature's back. The archaic screamed. Throwing itself to the ground, it rolled through the snow.

A cold wind pressed up against Caplan's face. Snow, big and heavy, fell at a fast clip. He looked toward the hatch. But it was difficult to see much of anything.

He waited for everyone to ascend the steps and exit the vault. Then he cupped a hand to his mouth. "Circle up," he shouted. "And head for the station."

The small group, which had been reduced to just fifty people, slid away from the vault. Torchbearers circled around to protect the backside. Then the group started to move through the ruins.

The archaics quickly encircled the humans. Howling and screaming, they rushed forward time and time again. Only the quick reflexes of the torchbearers kept them from breaking through the line.

The torches gave off a little heat. Even so, Caplan's teeth chattered as he strode past heaps of dead trees and the remains of ancient vegetable gardens. "How are we looking?" he called out.

"Not good." George jabbed a torch at a particularly-aggressive archaic. "They're getting bolder."

The archaics weren't exact replicas of original archaics. Thanks to Corbotch's microchips, they desired blood. Not because they enjoyed drinking it, but because doing so provided relief from a horrible ringing noise. Would desire for relief eventually overwhelm their instinctual fear of fire?

"Then let's pick up the pace." Caplan's slow walk turned into a brisk one. A moment of confusion arose as the group adjusted its speed. A few archaics tried to take advantage, but the torchbearers made them pay for it.

The ground quaked yet again. A deep-throated snarl shot through the darkness. To his left, Caplan saw the faint outline of a hulking, vibrating shadow.

"Get back here, George," Dr. Sandy said.

"Don't worry." Stepping outward, he stabbed his torch at the aggressive archaic. "They're idiots. They wouldn't know how to—"

Two archaics swept in on his blindside. One hit his knees while the other delivered a devastating shoulder block. Dropping his torch, George crumpled to the snow.

The aggressive archaic snatched up the torch and heaved it into the forest. It landed amongst a mass of cracked and splintered tree trunks. Withered branches and dead leaves started to burn.

"George, get inside the circle," Caplan shouted. "Torchbearers, give him cover."

George socked an archaic in the face, then scrambled over the snow. Other archaics rushed forward but Sandy and Ross waved torches at them. Reluctantly, they stopped and George was able to slip into the center of the circle.

Caplan swung his head in both directions, checking the other torchbearers. "Keep going," he called out.

Shuffling his feet, he moved closer to the hatch. The wind ripped into his cheeks. The snowflakes felt like tiny icicles jabbing at his skin.

The archaics, shrieking and snarling, doubled up their attacks. The torchbearers managed to fight them off, but it wasn't easy.

Metal groaned. The hatch slid open again and bright light pierced the darkness.

"They're reopening the hatch," Tuffel said, grinding to a halt. "Get ready for more archaics."

Caplan frowned. By his count, the entire first wave of archaics had already been released. Of course, Savage still held plenty of pre-archaics. Had Corbotch rushed their transformations like he'd done with Morgan?

New figures emerged from the depths of Savage. Scaling over a dozen ladders, they scrambled out onto the soil.

"They're not archaics. They're soldiers." Ross' lip curled in anger. "The ones who blackmailed us. The ones who killed Mike."

Caplan watched the soldiers pour out into the night. There were at least a hundred of them, all armed for battle. The last figure to emerge from Savage wore jeans and a gray shirt, topped off by a dark red cloak. His gaze focused in on the cloak. He'd recognize it—and its owner—anywhere.

Hello, Chenoa, he thought.

The hatch slid shut. The soldiers took up position around Roberts. Acting as one, they aimed their rifles skyward.

And gunfire blazed out into the night.

CHAPTER 61

Date: Dec. 3, 2017, 1:21 a.m.; Location: Sector 214, Vallerio Forest, NH

"Scatter," Caplan shouted.

Chaos erupted. Turning tail, Caplan sprinted back into the heart of Savage City. Meanwhile, his friends ran toward the ruins of small houses, toward the vault, toward the dying forest. Toward anywhere that offered cover. The archaic army, startled by the gunfire, fled as well. But they showed little interest in finding places to hide. Instead, they seemed most interested in getting as far away as possible.

A second burst of gunfire filled the dark night. Ducking down, Caplan ran in a zigzag pattern, hoping to throw off any pursuers. Then he dodged behind the ruins of a small store. He plastered his back against a wall. The concrete, covered with snow and ice, felt cold to the touch. A stiff breeze made his teeth chatter. Breathing deeply, he refilled his lungs.

What are you doing out here, Chenoa? he wondered.

Yes, his group had won a few minor victories. They'd temporarily repelled the archaic army. They'd even started to forge a path back to the hatch. But he couldn't imagine Roberts viewing them as much of a threat. Why would she come out to kill them now? Why not give the archaic army more time to finish the job?

His bat-based torch dimmed, then died. Tossing it away, he sidled to the edge of the wall and took a peek at the landscape. He saw many people. They hunkered down behind brick buildings and dilapidated carriages. They hid behind fallen outhouses as well as old sidewalk signs advertising Prickly Ash Bitters and other odd products.

Frowning, he scanned the street and open ground. Not that he was complaining, but where were all the dead bodies? He didn't see a single new corpse, human or otherwise. Could Roberts' soldiers really have missed every single shot?

A brave—or perhaps foolhardy—archaic ran out to challenge the soldiers. One of them fired a few rounds into the sky and the archaic scampered away.

Ahh. His eyes widened. *The gunfire's just a scare tactic.*

Clearly, the soldiers had orders not to hurt the archaics. So, they'd deliberately fired into the air instead, causing everyone to scatter. Now, they could march through the ruins with ease, picking off Caplan's group in the process.

Roberts barked another order. Maintaining a tight formation, the soldiers left the hatch. But they didn't hike into the town. Instead, they headed toward the forest. Following their path, Caplan saw their intended destination.

They didn't come out here to kill us, he realized. *They came to stop the fire.*

A mid-sized fire had sprouted up around George's torch. It burnt rapidly, eating up the dead wood of numerous tree trunks. Smoke, thick and gray, wafted into the dark sky. Anything within a couple of miles would be able to see it. Other survivors. Modern animals. Reborn megafauna.

And behemoths.

A sharp tremor passed through the earth. The behemoth was already close and getting closer by the second. If it was anything like Dire, it would hone in on the blaze.

Savage Station was, Caplan decided, in no real danger. Corbotch would've made certain the hatch could withstand the weight of even the biggest behemoth. But the archaics were another matter altogether. Out in the open, they had no real protection from the behemoth. And Corbotch probably wouldn't be too thrilled if the entire first wave of archaics ended up as gum on a behemoth's shoe.

The soldiers stopped near the fire. Producing a bunch of red extinguishers, they doused the flames. The blaze winked out and soldiers shoveled snow onto the embers. The smoke thinned, then vanished.

Archaics gathered together and approached the soldiers. At first, errant gunfire was enough to drive them back. But with each deliberate miss, the creatures grew bolder.

An archaic grabbed for a soldier's gun. The man shoved it away and fired a bullet into the sky. The archaic didn't flinch. Instead, it slammed its shoulder into the man's gut. He grunted and fell to the snow. Lunging and clawing, the creature gouged his eyes and tore up his neck.

Soldiers turned to help their fallen comrade. Then a bloodcurdling howl rang out. A dozen archaics raced out of the forest. Rushing across the slippery soil, they crashed into Roberts' soldiers. A few soldiers crumpled under the brutal attack. Others fought back, using their guns as clubs.

More archaics raced out of the forest. They charged into Savage City. Looking around, Caplan realized his torch wasn't the only one that had died.

They were all dead.

An archaic, hunchbacked and screaming, chased after Tuffel. Another one, sporting a long beard, slammed into Ross, knocking him to the ground. Two more archaics, twins from the looks of it, backed Mills up against the ruins of a ravaged jail.

Heart racing, Caplan stepped away from the wall. He saw other people spring up from their various hiding spots. Some began to fight, others ran. Regardless, he knew none of them would last long, not when faced with so many archaics. He needed to help them. All of them and all at once.

A snarl slid into his ears.

He spun around. But before he could swing his axe, an archaic dove at him. His back slammed against the concrete wall and he lost both axes. The impact drove the air right out of his lungs. Before he could refill them, a forearm struck his throat. It pushed his windpipe hard, blocking off all oxygen.

Keep fighting, Zach. His lungs started to ache. His eyes bulged and his vision dimmed. *You've got to …*

CHAPTER 62

As his consciousness faded, the old wall started to sag. Then a small section of concrete burst into dust and rubble and Caplan felt himself propelled through a hole. One second later, he collapsed onto a concrete floor, gasping and wheezing.

The archaic leapt at the hole. Its fingers clawed at Caplan's feet, then his legs. He tried to back away, but his body didn't respond to his commands.

"I've got its legs." Aquila's yell stabbed through clouds surrounding his brain. "Kill it."

He choked down some air and his body started to function again. He slid away from the snarling, spitting archaic. He rose to his knees, then his feet.

His head swooned and his vision dimmed all over again. Acting more on instinct than anything else, he jumped up and grabbed the top of the fractured wall.

Frantically, the archaic scraped the floor. Its nails broke and blood seeped out of its fingertips.

"Hurry," Aquila said. "I can't hold it much longer."

Caplan yanked at the wall. It refused to budge. Kicking his feet up, he braced them against the concrete. Then he pulled with all of his might. Sharp cracks rang out. Chips broke away. Ancient dust shot into the air. Then the wall came crashing down.

It fell in a heap of broken concrete and mounds of dust. The archaic uttered a strangled scream, then fell silent. Its bloodied fingers curled tightly, then relaxed.

Caplan crashed back to the floor. He took a few deep breaths, inhaling about a pound of dust in the process. Coughs racked his body as he picked himself up.

Aquila stood on the other side of the broken wall. Her hair was matted to her forehead and a thin trickle of blood ran down her right arm.

"Nice performance." Caplan hacked a few more times. "We really brought the house down on him."

"Very funny." She released the archaic's legs. Her lips curled into a tired, but genuine, smile. "Need anything?"

He shook his head.

As she ran off to help someone else, he climbed over the rubble. He retrieved his axes from the ground, then turned toward the rest of Savage City. Tuffel had filled his arms with chunks of brick and concrete. Now, he was chucking them at the hunchbacked archaic. Ross was wrestling the bearded archaic. Mills, meanwhile, was no longer backed up against the jail. Somehow she'd managed to find her way to the top of a stone column. From there, she poured arrows into the twin archaics.

He looked for Roberts and saw her hiking back to the hatch with her soldiers. Dozens of archaics continued to attack them, but the soldiers managed to club them away. In a matter of minutes, she'd slip back into Savage Station. The hatch would swing shut and the dozens of archaics would turn their attentions elsewhere.

Namely, toward Caplan's group.

He couldn't let that happen. He had to find a way to keep Roberts outside. No, he needed to do more than that. He needed to turn the tables on her. To catch her off-guard, to throw her off-balance.

You've got one move left, he thought. *It'll probably kill us all. But hey, at least you'll go out with a bang, right?*

He ran into the forest. Using an axe, he felled a dead spruce tree and sectioned the trunk. He piled up most of the logs. Then he split open the remaining ones, exposing the heartwood. He further split this dry, interior wood into thin sticks.

He darted to a dead juniper tree and stripped off large chunks of bark, revealing a fibrous underside. He scraped away a bunch of fine fibers and gathered them into a loose tinder bundle. Turning his back to the wind, he used George's lighter to ignite the tinder. A bit of smoke lifted into the sky.

Hustling back to the wood pile, he touched the tinder to the dry, thin sticks of wood. They started to burn. While they caught steam, he chopped off a bunch of withered, dead branches from surrounding trees. He fed the branches to the growing blaze and a new column of gray smoke rose into the sky.

Here, little behemoth, he thought. *Come see the nice fire I made for you.*

The soldiers stopped short of the hatch. Ignoring the attacking archaics, Roberts pushed her way to the front. Her face twisted with obvious displeasure.

He grabbed a long branch from the fire and darted through the forest. As he passed the ruins of an old barn, he caught sight of George Pylor. Two archaics circled the man, staying just out of reach of his baseball bat.

Pulling out one of his axes, Caplan slipped into the barn. Quietly, he jabbed his burning branch at an archaic. The creature howled and curled its back in pain. Spinning around, it laid red-rimmed eyes on Caplan.

Caplan swung his axe. It sank deep into the archaic's stomach. Blood gushed forth. A dying howl escaped the creature's throat as it sagged to the floor.

Gnashing its teeth, the other archaic rushed Caplan. He saw its angry eyes, it drooling lips. It smelled of dirt, body odor, and blood.

Dropping his bat, George tackled the archaic to the floor. Desperately, he tried to pin the creature. But the archaic powered out of the maneuver and bit the man's arm. George screamed as teeth punctured his skin.

Eyes aglow, the archaic released George's arm. Its jaws lunged at the man's face.

Caplan yanked his axe out of the first archaic's stomach. Rearing back, he threw the bladed weapon. It hurtled through the icy air and slammed into the second archaic's skull. The creature fell still.

George pushed away the dead archaic. Clutching his injured arm, he sat up.

Caplan retrieved his axe. "Are you okay?"

"Nothing a bath and a good bottle of rum won't cure."

"You and me both." Another tremor roiled the ground. It was the fiercest one yet and Caplan felt his fingers tighten around the still-burning branch. "I need you to do me a favor. Get everyone back to the vault. Don't wait for me. Just secure the locks and take everyone to the lower floor."

George gathered up his bat and rose to his feet. "I'm not leaving you alone with these monsters."

"I'll be fine." The ground roiled again. "And the monster I'm worried about isn't an archaic."

George's eyes widened with understanding. "That's a behemoth, isn't it?"

He nodded. "We need everyone underground before it gets here."

His gaze hardened and he shot Caplan a quick salute. Spinning around, he darted out of the barn.

Exiting the ruins, Caplan peered into the forest. He saw Roberts and her soldiers, fire extinguishers at the ready, hiking to the new blaze. But in the meantime, it continued to burn brightly, ejecting tons of gray smoke into the air.

He hurried back into the forest and drove the burning branch into the ground. Finding another spruce tree, he quickly felled it. As he sectioned the trunk, an icy wind swept across the landscape, freezing his cheeks.

Am I really doing this? he wondered. *Am I really bringing a behemoth here?*

It wasn't the greatest plan in the world. It wasn't even a good plan. If the behemoth stepped on the vault, its paw would crush the concrete exterior to smithereens. Ensconced in the basement, his friends might survive the destruction. But they'd also be buried under tons of heavy rubble.

Still, what else could he do? The status quo was untenable. Bringing the behemoth to the party, as dangerous as it was, represented his last chance to shake things up.

The ground tremors turned into light quakes. Quickly, Caplan built a new pile of kindling. He used the burning branch to ignite it. Another fire appeared.

He chopped off more dead branches and slid them into the fire. A second column of gray smoke shot skyward.

Loud bursts rang out. Bullets whizzed by Caplan's head. As they slammed into trees, he flung himself to the ground.

"Are you crazy?" Roberts shouted. "You're going to—"

The quakes turned ferocious. An ear-splitting snarl cut through the night.

Heart pounding, he lifted his head. To the north, he saw dense, dying forest. The snow fell thick and hard, obscuring his vision. But he could still see *it*. A hulking mass of shifting, thumping blackness.

A deafening roar filled the night. Then the hulking mass surged forward.

Archaics and soldiers backed away, stumbling over the roiling ground. Trees cracked and splintered, falling before the hulking mass. Then Caplan glimpsed something he'd hoped to never see again. Something that belonged to this new world and yet, didn't belong to it at all.

The behemoth … it was Saber. But not the Saber he'd faced seventeen months earlier. No, this Saber was different. It was taller, longer. A behemoth of such proportions that it couldn't even be called a behemoth.

It was a mega behemoth.

CHAPTER 63

Date: Dec. 3, 2017, 1:56 a.m.; Location: Sector 214, Vallerio Forest, NH

Over the last seventeen months, Caplan had seen behemoths of all shapes and sizes. He'd marveled at their enormity and cowered at their wrath. But nothing—absolutely nothing—could've prepared him for Saber.

The beast had once stood some thirty feet tall. Now, it was roughly twice that height. The dark night and swirling snow kept him from seeing its entire body. But he caught glimpses of its tree-like legs and its nearly-invisible swishing tail. This was truly a behemoth among behemoths and perhaps the only creature that could've challenged—and defeated—the enormous ArcSim.

But it wasn't Saber's size that made his brain reel. After all, ArcSim had been just as tall until its untimely death. No, what really boggled his mind was the creature's growth.

He'd glimpsed plenty of behemoths over the last year and a half. And all of them were about ten times larger than their reborn megafauna counterparts. Saber had started out the same way. But now, it was some twenty times larger than a reborn saber. And that differential, quite possibly, was still growing.

Rising to his feet, he scrambled between trees, putting distance between himself and Saber. As he ran, he thought about Morgan's duffel bag back in the SUV. He thought about the logbook stowed within it. She'd known lots of information about the behemoths. She'd even figured out their usage of infrasound. And yet, she'd never mentioned anything about a mega behemoth.

What purpose did a mega behemoth serve anyway? What ecological niche did it fill? Was Saber the lone mega behemoth? Or did others walk the planet as well?

A short distance away, he spotted Mills. She lay at the edge of the tree line, her gaze focused on Saber.

He dropped to his belly next to her. "Howdy stranger."

She nodded at the mega behemoth. "It looks like Saber decided to crash the party."

"Actually, I sent it an invitation, etched in smoke." He arched an eyebrow at her. "What are you doing out here anyway? I told George to gather everyone in the vault."

"So I heard. But come on. Did you really expect me to let you have all the fun?"

Roaring, Saber strode through the forest, its monstrous paws driving tree trunks deep into the earth. It stopped on the opposite side of Savage Station and bared its horrible curving teeth for all to see. Its lava-orange eyes, hotter than a blazing inferno, took in the scene before it.

Abruptly, it charged down the old road, tearing up pavement and leaving deep impressions in the soil. Archaics, screaming and howling, vanished underfoot.

Saber slid to a halt on the opposite side of Savage City, tearing up even more pavement and soil. Its jaws plunged to the ground and it bit down on a bunch of fleeing archaics. Blood and gore splattered across the dirt.

Melted snow began to mix with the churned-up soil. Hard dirt turned into viscous sludge.

"I think Saber packed on a little mass," Caplan whispered.

"A little? It looks like it swallowed another behemoth whole."

Smacking its lips, Saber paced into the forest and stomped out Caplan's second fire. Then it began to feed on the dead archaics. In the process, its paws crushed down on more snow, causing it to melt and mix with the sludge. Before long, a giant mud trough ran through the center of Savage City's ruins.

The mega behemoth reached the other end of the ruins. Stopping short of the hatch, it rotated its head in both directions. Then it took a few sniffs at the air. A growl escaped its lips and it looked toward the forest.

All in all, this was going well, even better than Caplan's wildest dreams. The archaic army was dead or scattered. The vault remained intact. And Saber's attention, at least for the moment, was focused elsewhere.

"I think it smells the soldiers," Mills said.

"Just as long as it's not us."

Soft rustles rang out from the forest. The soldiers, moving in tight formation, advanced on the mega behemoth.

Her jaw fell agape. "Have they lost their minds?"

He rubbed his jaw. "They didn't have much of a choice. Like you said, Saber already sniffed them out."

"Then they should be running for their lives."

He cast a glance at Savage City, laying eyes on dozens of squashed archaics. "And end up like them?"

"Good point."

"We need to get to the vault." He sheathed his axe and returned it to his belt. "Start crawling as soon as the gunfire starts."

The wind picked up speed. The snowflakes fell faster. Peering through the blizzard, Caplan looked for the soldiers. He could no longer see them. But Saber's hulking mass was impossible to miss.

Rapid bursts of gunfire filled the dark, snowy sky. Caplan and Mills exchanged nods. They crawled forward, staying just inside the tree line. They snaked between trees and around small boulders, over hills and past dead bushes.

Roaring, Saber sprang at the soldiers. The gunfire intensified, then turned sporadic. Bone crunched. Flesh squished. Anguished screams floated into the snowy night.

Bile rose up in Caplan's throat. He crawled a little farther, dragging his body across the snow.

Metal shifted. A bright light poured out of the ground. Squinting at the hatch, he caught a glimpse of a single figure, cloaked in red. The figure grabbed hold of a ladder and descended into the hatch. Metal scraped softly against metal. The brightness vanished.

"Was that Chenoa?" Mills whispered.

He nodded. "She used her soldiers as a diversion."

"What a snake."

He continued to crawl through the forest. To his right, he recognized the blizzard-obscured ruins of Savage City. They weren't at the vault yet. But each second brought them closer to their destination.

The anguished screams died out. New sounds—thumping footsteps, splintering wood, deep-throated growls—started up.

Saber's hulking mass trotted out of the forest. It sniffed the air for a moment. Then it walked into Savage City.

Hide, Caplan mouthed.

Mills crouched behind a large rock. Meanwhile, he pulled up behind a thick cedar tree and pressed his back against the damp, mossy bark.

Mud splashed as Saber entered the trough. It surged forward, heading for the vehicles. The sounds of footsteps grew louder and louder. And then, inexplicably, they vanished. Sharp sniffs filled the air. A deafening growl pierced the dark, snowy night.

A shiver ran down Caplan's spine. The mega behemoth was close, about as close as it could get to him and Mills without leaving the trough.

It's got new scents, he realized. *Our scents.*

Gunshots punctured the air. Twisting his neck, Caplan saw three soldiers hobble out of the dense blizzard. Their faces were blotchy and full of ire. They stopped at the edge of the tree line, not far from his position. Shouts and curses, laced with lunacy, rang out.

The soldiers kept firing until they ran empty. Then they lowered their weapons. Their faces paled. Their ire gave way to fear. Twisting around, they bolted into the dying forest.

Caplan's body tensed up, ready to run as soon as Saber gave chase. But there were no sudden movements, no shockwaves coursing through the soil. After a few seconds, he snuck a peek around the edge of the tree.

The mega behemoth stood in the trough, showing no interest in the fleeing soldiers. It paid no attention to the blizzard, the forest or the ruins. Instead, it just stared.

At him.

Its nostrils flared. Its lava-orange eyes swirled and Caplan saw frenzied fury within them. But he saw something else, too. Something much more unnerving.

It knows me, he realized. *It remembers me.*

All of a sudden, he felt miniscule compared to the mighty beast. His feet moved on instinct, taking a few steps backward.

Saber climbed out of the trough. Its paws crashed down on the ruins of old stables, reducing them to dust and smithereens.

Some mammals, such as cows, were capable of holding grudges. But certainly not for seventeen months. That kind of petty ridiculousness was exclusive to humanity.

And mega behemoths, he thought.

Saber's eyes boiled with anger. Its lips spread into a strange, satisfied smile.

Caplan's brain shifted back to their previous encounter. Seventeen months ago, he'd fled from Saber. But without a helicopter, that wouldn't work this time.

"Get down," Mills whispered through clenched teeth. "It'll see you."

"It already did."

"Hang on." She reached for her quiver. "I'll give you a distraction."

"It won't work. Just get to the vault, okay?"

"Zach …"

"Get to the vault."

Caplan ran. But not into the depths of the dying forest. No, he ran straight at the mega behemoth.

Saber's lava-orange eyes flashed with confusion. Its head lunged toward the ground.

He dodged to the side. Saber's teeth slashed deep into the ruins of the stable, puncturing heaps of concrete and steel.

He smelled the creature's hot, rancid breath. He sensed its power, its confidence.

A dark shadow fell over Caplan as he darted underneath Saber's enormous head. The mega behemoth could no longer see him. But that didn't mean it would give up. Very soon, it would start to move, to search around. Its mighty paws would come crashing down again. Quite possibly, right on top of his head.

He sprinted to Saber's front right leg. Grabbing hold of fur, he pulled himself onto its paw.

The mega behemoth ripped its teeth out of the ruins, causing chunks of concrete to fly through the air. It curled its toes ever so slightly, sending fierce vibrations through its entire body.

Ignoring the vibrations, Caplan crawled to the ankle, then wrapped his fists around the coarse fur. Chuckling humorlessly, he shook his head.

Worst. Plan. Ever.

CHAPTER 64

Date: Dec. 3, 2017, 2:16 a.m.; Location: Sector 214, Vallerio Forest, NH

Saber's teeth gnashed together. Buckets of drool slipped out of its jaws and dripped down onto the snow.

Wind whistled as the mega behemoth twisted its shoulders from side to side. More vibrations stole through the behemoth's body and Caplan doubled up his grip on the fur.

He turned his gaze to the forest. Mills crouched at the edge of the tree line. Her eyes were big and round. Her jaw was wide open.

He turned back to the creature's massive ankle. He hadn't come up with a plan yet. But hey, there was no time like the present. And so, he quickly formulated an escape route. Eventually, Saber would start walking. He'd wait until it moved close to the vault. Then he'd drop to the ground and run for it.

He peered up. Saber's face, obscured by the heavy snow, was focused on the forest. Evidently, it didn't even feel his weight. And no wonder. Caplan was, for better or worse, an insect next to the mega behemoth.

Its head drifted downward. Down, down, down, all the way to its paws. Moving fast, Caplan crawled around the outside portion of the mega behemoth's ankle. Wrapping his fingers around fur, he braced himself against the creature's thick hide.

Saber sniffed its front right paw. Then its head lifted skyward again. Twisting around, Caplan crawled back to his original position. His breath turned bated as he regripped the coarse fur.

A growl filled the night as Saber backtracked. One by one, its paws splashed into the trough cutting through the center of Savage City, sending bits of mud flying onto Caplan's clothing.

Its front right paw was last to move. It curled backward with big, jolting movements. Caplan's body bounced off the paw and he swung wildly into the air, supported only by his grip on the fur. Abruptly, the paw descended and curled inward. He braced his feet again just as it struck mud. Shockwaves rocketed through his arms and all the way to his brain. He barely had time to recover before he found himself repeating the process all over again. *It's like a roller coaster*, he thought. *Just without the souvenir photo.*

Saber walked to the far side of town. It stopped short of the broken bridge and the dry creek bed. Releasing the fur, Caplan stretched his cold, aching fingers. Past the creek bed, he could see the vehicles, shrouded in snow. Ahh, what he wouldn't give to sit in one of them at that very moment. To relax in a nice seat, to warm his hands by the vents.

The mega behemoth dipped its head to the ground once again. Again, Caplan swung his body around the outside of the ankle. Saber sniffed the paw, then snorted. Hot air crested into Caplan, nearly blowing him off his perch.

It's still got my scent, he thought as he returned to his former position. *That's how it knows I'm here.*

Twisting around, the mega behemoth retraced its path, carefully sniffing along both sides of the old ruins. Meanwhile, more snow melted into the trough, mixing with the mud.

Sharp tingles ran through Caplan's fingers. His hands started to hurt. The pain quickly turned excruciating. Then it faded and his hands turned numb.

Fur slipped through his cold, stiff fingers. He grabbed more of it, but his grip continued to fail.

Saber's front right paw descended back to the mud. It crashed into the trough and he lost hold of the fur. He was still a good distance from the vault. But he knew he'd never last that long.

He slid off the paw. His boots landed on the two-foot deep mud and he sank into it.

Saber froze. Its head twisted downward.

It'll see you, Caplan thought. *It'll smell you, too.*

He dropped to the mud and rolled. The thick gooey, slop stuck fast to him. Grabbing up more mud, he caked it over his face, his arms, and his legs.

Saber peered down at him from high above. Then its head swooped to the trough. Its nostrils flared and it took a couple of sniffs.

Caplan held his breath. He didn't move a single muscle.

Saber's nostrils flared again. It took a few more sniffs. Then its head rose back into the sky.

And it walked away.

CHAPTER 65

Date: Dec. 3, 2017, 2:28 a.m.; Location: Sector 214, Vallerio Forest, NH

Move. Caplan's breaths came fast and furious. *You've got to move.*

Twisting onto his belly, he crawled through the trough. Slimy, cold mud slipped into his ears and mouth. It slid into his shirt and down his pants. It worked its way into his socks and shoes.

Saber stomped up to Savage Station. A deafening growl, angry and full of frustration, stormed out into the night.

Caplan crawled out of the trough and alongside the ruins of an old store. He hurried to the rear, then planted himself against a concrete wall.

Twisting around, Saber stomped back through the mud trough. Its head shot from side to side. Its lava-orange eyes blazed trails through the dark night.

It passed by Caplan. Rising to a crouch, he hustled to another set of ruins. He continued forward and the vault materialized in the dense blizzard.

Glancing over his shoulder, he saw Saber standing near the dry creek bed. With increasingly erratic movements, it shifted its paws, sniffing and growling at everything in sight.

He ran up to the vault and rapped on the door. "It's me," he whispered as loud as he dared.

The door opened. He darted past Mills and she shut the door behind him.

"Oh, I see how it is." Nose wrinkling, she turned to face him. "We're all cooped up in here. Meanwhile, you've been enjoying a mud bath."

"You know how I love to exfoliate."

She laughed and wrapped him into a fierce hug. Mud squished onto her clothes and skin, but she didn't complain. Taking his hand, she led him down the staircase.

Some forty people occupied the vault. They sat on the ground, quiet and still. Their stomachs rumbled. Their eyes looked hollow.

"You made it?" Aquila looked at him with dead eyes. "I figured you for a goner."

"We heard you hitched a ride on that monster," Tuffel added. "How was it?"

"Bumpy," Caplan replied.

"How'd you do it?" Ross shook his head. "How'd you make it back here in one piece?"

"Like this." He stared down at his mud-caked body. "Saber's tracking people by scent. Maybe by sight, too."

"That was Saber?" Dr. Sandy frowned. "It's bigger than you described. A lot bigger."

"It *is* bigger. It's a mega behemoth now." Caplan's adrenaline began to wane. The mud started to feel cold against his skin. Crossing his arms, he fought to control his chattering teeth. "Where's Sydney?"

Teo lifted a bruised arm. "Over here."

"Still think you can get us through that hatch?"

The ground rumbled. "Not with that thing out there."

Ross exhaled a tired sigh. "Then I guess we're stuck here until it leaves."

"It might not leave at all," Caplan replied. "Unfortunately, Saber seems to have the hots for me."

"Then maybe we should just feed you to it," Toland said matter-of-factly.

Mills stared at him in disbelief. "If anyone's getting fed to that monster, it's you."

"It doesn't want me." He looked at Caplan. "It wants him."

Caplan's look turned thoughtful.

"Shut up, Brian," Ross said.

"Why? Because I've got a point?"

"Because you're a jerk."

"No, he's right." Caplan furrowed his brow. "Saber definitely remembers me. Maybe we can use that to lure it away from Savage."

George gave him a dumbfounded look. "How?"

"I'll sneak back to the cars and start one up. It'll think it's me and give chase."

"It'll catch you."

"Not if I drive fast enough."

"What are we supposed to do once we get through the hatch?" Dr. Sandy asked. "We won't survive five minutes without you."

"She's right," George said. "Chenoa will be waiting for us with more soldiers. And you're a good fighter. Maybe our best one."

"What if Saber only thinks he's leaving?"

The voice, soft and wavering, caught Caplan by surprise. Twisting around, he looked at Elliott. "What do you mean?"

"What if we trick it? What if someone else takes your place instead?" She took a deep breath. "Someone like me."

"No." Teo shook her head. "Absolutely not."

"I can do this," Elliott told her.

"Yes, but—"

"I'm not a good fighter. You know that, I know that, everyone knows that. I'd be useless in that station. But I'm a darn good driver. Plus, I paid attention to our route. I can navigate it. I can stay ahead of Saber."

"Not forever."

"Don't worry. I'll find a way to escape it." She took Teo's hand. "I promise."

Teo's face screwed up. She turned her gaze to the floor.

"Well?" Elliott looked at Caplan. A rare look of defiance crossed her pale visage. "What do you say?"

He didn't like the idea. He didn't like it at all. But George and Dr. Sandy had made good points. Like it or not, the group needed him in Savage Station. "Are you sure about this?" he asked.

She nodded.

"Then do it."

CHAPTER 66

Date: Dec. 3, 2017, 2:52 a.m.; Location: Sector 214, Vallerio Forest, NH

"Okay, remember what I said." Caplan waited for Teo to finish plastering mud across Elliott's cheeks. "Get to the forest and don't be shy about it. Then head for your car. You've got the keys, right?"

Elliott held up a grubby keychain.

"Good. Wait until Saber crosses to the opposite end of Savage City. Then start up the engine."

"What if it doesn't come after me?"

"It will." He clasped her shoulders. Gave her a good, hard look. Her jaw quivered just a bit, which he chalked up to the cold mud. As for her eyes, they were tough and steady. "Good luck."

"Thanks, Zach. For everything." She surprised him by giving him a quick, tight hug before pulling away.

Elliott turned toward Teo. Their arms wrapped around each other. Their lips met in the middle and they embraced.

"Don't you dare die on me," Teo whispered to her.

"You either."

Reluctantly, they broke apart. Elliott twisted toward the cracked door and peeked out at Saber. She gave Caplan a brief nod. Her eyes met Teo's one last time. Then she slipped outside and ran to the forest.

Caplan turned his attention to Saber. For the next few minutes, he watched it swing through the ruins of Savage City, becoming more agitated by the second. It growled, it snarled. It stomped on old houses and swiped at trees, tearing them out by their withered roots.

When the coast was clear, Toland, Ross, and Tuffel slipped outside. They covered themselves with mud, then returned to the vault. Others took their place at the trough. Before long, the entire group was doused with muck.

An engine came to life.

Caplan shared a knowing look with Teo. "Here we go."

Saber's hulking shadow froze near the hatch. For a moment, it sat still, surrounded by snow and ice. Then it twisted around. Roaring, it raced toward the purring engine.

Teo and Caplan ran outside. Squinting over his shoulder, he stared into the blizzard. But he saw nothing. No trees, no cars, no hulking shadow. Nothing but a sheet of falling snow.

Teo tugged his arm. "She gave us this opportunity. Don't waste it."

They ran to the hatch with the others in close pursuit. Shaking snow out of her hair, Teo knelt down to study a control panel. "I need tools," she said. "The ones we took from the garage."

Caplan turned to Ross. "Take a couple of people to the cars. Get us every tool you can find."

Gathering together a half-dozen people, Ross hustled toward the vehicles. The snow quickly swallowed them up.

The temperature dropped a few degrees. The wind turned brutal. Fighting off shivers, Caplan rotated toward the others. "Half of you stay here and watch over Sydney. The rest of you come with me."

He darted into the forest. After a short run, he came upon dozens of soldiers, all dead. Their remains, chewed and drained of blood, were gruesome and he did his best not to look at them. "Grab their guns," he called out. "Plus anything else we can use."

Holding his breath, he scouted the area. He located a loose pistol and a couple of rifles. He kept the pistol and handed the rifles off to others. Then he led everyone back to the hatch and they placed all the extra guns and ammunition into a pile.

Facing west, he scanned the forest for surviving archaics and soldiers. Others followed his lead, taking up position all around Teo.

Ross' group raced back to the hatch, their hands full of bags and tools. They passed everything to Teo, picked up weapons from the pile, and joined the lookout.

Ross donned a rifle strap and joined Caplan. "What do we do once Sydney gets the hatch open?"

"Same thing we always do." He shrugged. "Wing it."

"No plan?"

He thought back to his original plan, the one he'd followed for so long. How had he put it to Ross? Oh, yes.

A big population also gets you noticed, he'd said. *And being noticed is tantamount to death. Staying small is a much better strategy.*

"What's the point?" A small smile crossed Caplan's face as he glanced at the rest of his group. "Plans change."

He chuckled. "Thank God for that."

Metal scraped against metal.

Glancing over his shoulder, Caplan watched as the hatch swung open. There was no light this time. Instead, he saw a well of blackness.

Tools in hand, Teo stood up. "We're in."

CHAPTER 67

Date: Dec. 3, 2017, 3:30 a.m.; Location: Savage Station, Vallerio Forest, NH

Kneeling next to the open hatch, Caplan squinted into the blackness. He waited for it to subside. For moonlight to penetrate the top floor of Savage Station. But it didn't happen.

Giving up, he perked his ears. He heard no murmurs, no movement. It was almost as if the top floor was completely deserted.

Almost.

He couldn't see them. He couldn't hear them. But he could still feel them. He could feel the warmth of their bodies and the slight shifts in air as they fought to control their breathing.

Ever so slowly, the blackness began to melt. It peeled away from the walls and he saw the ladders. Then the rotors, still and quiet, appeared. The helicopters were next, followed by the floor.

He crept along the edges of the gigantic hatch, looking for shadowy figures. But he didn't see anyone. Where were they hiding?

He tapped his pistol against one of the ladders. Metal dinged and vibrated. There were no sudden movements, no abrupt blaze of gunfire.

He turned his gaze to his team. Roughly forty armed and exhausted people stared back at him. They'd lost more than half their number in the last day or so. It was a staggering loss. And yet, it was but a drop in the bucket compared to the world's losses over the last seventeen months.

"They're down there," he whispered. "I can't see them, but they're definitely down there."

George slid to the side of the hatch and snuck a quick peek into Savage Station. "I don't know," he said doubtfully. "We can cover the entire floor from up here. Chenoa had to know that. She would've taken her soldiers to a more defensible location."

"I say we error on the side of caution," Tuffel said. "We take up position around the hatch. Then we send our people down the ladders. If soldiers pop up, we put them down."

"That only works if they actually pop up," Caplan said. "Which they won't. They'll stay in hiding and gun us down."

"Then we need to drive them out of their hiding spots." Mills twisted around. "I'll be back in a minute."

She ran into the snowstorm. Ross shot Caplan an inquisitive look. Caplan shrugged.

A few minutes later, a puttering engine came into earshot. Then an old sedan careened out of the dense blizzard. It drove along the west side of Savage City, on the relatively muck-free strip of land between the ruins and the surrounding forest.

It stopped near the hatch. The engine ceased and Mills hopped out of the driver's seat. "How do you feel about about causing a little chaos?"

"Sounds good to me." Caplan scanned the interior and noted one of the helicopters was positioned quite close to the east wall. He pointed at it. "Aim for that."

Mills moved the car into position. Meanwhile, Caplan sectioned a skinny tree and gathered more firewood and tinder. Returning to the car, he placed everything into the chassis. He used George's lighter to ignite the tinder. A small fire burst to life. It spread from the tinder to the wood. Then it spread to the upholstery.

Once the interior was aflame, Caplan checked on the others. They stood around the hatch, their guns focused on the interior. Satisfied, he gave Mills a nod.

She released the brake. Then she, Caplan, and Ross pushed the vehicle forward. Passing over the lip, it toppled into the station. It struck the helicopter, then smashed to the floor with a tremendous bang. The helicopter tipped toward the wreck. Flames exploded.

A helicopter door banged open in the center of the floor. A soldier raced out into the open.

"They're in the choppers," Caplan shouted. "Fire."

Loud blasts rang out. Glass exploded. More doors flew open and soldiers ran outside. Many of them fell under the onslaught. But a few managed to slip into a nearby stairwell.

Caplan ran to a ladder and slid down to the first floor. Grabbing his pistol, he whirled around. The floor was a mess of smoke, glass, falling snow, fire, and charred, twisted metal.

His group descended the other ladders. Grabbing fire extinguishers, they swept through the room, checking the fallen soldiers and dousing the flames with chemical foam.

Teo climbed down a ladder. Spotting a control panel, she hurried toward it. Her fingers flew over a keyboard.

Caplan gathered everyone into a tight group near the stairwell. "We got most of them," he whispered. "About a dozen escaped downstairs. There could be more of them down there as well."

Mills screwed up her face in thought. "The last thing we want is a long drawn-out battle. I say we concentrate on James. If we kill or capture him, Chenoa might surrender."

"Where do we find him?" Tuffel asked.

A memory of Corbotch's private room filled Caplan's brain. "On Level X. But he won't come quietly. Remember, he's got augmented genes now. He's practically a super-soldier."

Screeches, bellows, and whines drifted down from above. Wiping sweat from his brow, Caplan glanced up at the still-open hatch. He saw a shadowy archaic, framed by the falling snow. Other archaics rushed into view.

"Sydney?" he called out.

"The controls are damaged," she shouted. "I need a few more minutes."

"Aw, crap," Ross muttered.

A hefty archaic beat its chest and screamed at the sky. Other archaics grabbed hold of the ladders and lumbered down the rungs.

One archaic, a dark-haired female, grew impatient. It leaned closer and closer to the hatch. Finally, it stepped into open space and took the plunge. It crashed to the ground, dying upon impact. Caplan wondered if others would follow suit, lemming-style. Unfortunately, they seemed to learn from the dead archaic's mistake.

Rifles and pistols swung outward. They took aim at the ladders. Loud blasts echoed off the walls. Some archaics, shrieking and bloodied, fell victim to the gunfire. But others reached the floor safely. Vicious scuffling broke out.

Caplan fired his last bullet, then tossed his pistol to the ground. Grabbing his axes, he went on the attack. He chopped out the legs of one archaic. Swinging around, he sank his second axe into another archaic's chest.

Many archaics fell. But others continued to stream down the ladders in droves.

Ross clubbed down an archaic and shot Caplan a glance. "We'll hold them off for you."

"I'm not leaving."

"You have to." He wiped blood from his lip. "Find a way to stop these things. Otherwise, we're all dead."

Caplan met Ross' gaze. Then he ran to a door. Throwing it open, he entered the stairwell.

And began his descent into Savage Station.

CHAPTER 68

Date: Dec. 3, 2017, 3:58 a.m.; Location: Savage Station, Vallerio Forest, NH

Footsteps pounded on concrete. Hefting an axe, Caplan whirled around. He froze for a second, his eyes locked on a shadowy, feminine figure. "Bailey?"

She halted a few steps above him. One hand held her bow. The other one drifted to her forehead, brushing hair away from her eyes. "I figured you could use some back-up."

He lowered the axe. "We need to stop those archaics."

"How?"

An earlier conversation with Corbotch came to mind. *That bloodlust, as you call it, is a temporary condition,* the man had said. *We deliberately don't program it into the genomes. Instead, we artificially induce it via implanted microchips. I won't bore you with the details. But in essence, we have the ability to plague our archaics with a horrible ringing noise that only subsides with the consumption of blood.*

"By taking charge of their microchips," he replied.

"If we control the chips, we control the archaics?"

"That's the idea. Dr. Barden installs the chips in the clinic. Most likely, he controls them from there as well."

"Do you know how to operate the microchips?"

He shook his head. "Maybe Dr. Barden will help us."

"And if he refuses?"

Several stories up, a door banged open. Bellows, shrieks, and howls roared into the stairwell. "Then we'll have to convince him."

Twisting around, he ran down a few more flights. The sounds of the archaics faded a bit. How had they gotten into the stairwell? Where were Ross and the Pylors? What about Teo, Toland, Aquila, Tuffel, and all the rest? Were they still alive? Were they still fighting?

He reached the floor for the clinic. Mills fitted an arrow into her bow and gave him a nod. He tried the knob, then pushed the stairwell door open. The lobby was brightly lit and seemingly empty.

She stole outside. He followed her out and scanned the area. Seeing no one, he closed the door softly behind him. Then he crept to the clinic. Voices, barely audible, slipped through the doors.

"We have a breach," Dr. Barden announced. "The details are unimportant. All you need to know is that archaics are currently free inside of Savage."

A hushed silence followed.

"We won't be shutting down their desire for blood. We don't need to. Just follow protocol and evacuate to your quarters. Lock and barricade the doors. Stay absolutely quiet until you hear from us. Are there any questions?"

Another hushed silence filled the void.

"Well?" Roberts snarled. "What are you waiting for?"

Caplan pulled Mills to the wall. Hiding his axes, he turned away from the clinic. She caught on quickly and twisted her back to it as well.

The double doors flew open. Frantic murmurs rang out as footsteps thundered past their position. Caplan snuck a peek over his shoulder. He saw technicians, orderlies, and others. Their faces reflected confusion and terror.

Other doors, including the one leading to the stairwell, banged against stoppers. Soft, inhuman shrieks filtered into the lobby. The murmurs gave way to frightened whispers. Tempers flared.

A technician pushed an orderly. She lost her balance and careened to the floor. Someone jostled the technician and he fell as well. Screams rang out as the panicked crowd overran them.

Another orderly lost her balance. Pitching forward, she smacked into a couple of scientists. A whole heap of people crashed to the floor. The crowd didn't falter. It raced onward, crushing people with cruel indifference.

Gradually, the crowd vanished through the various doors. A few lucky folks picked themselves off the floor and limped after them. Others stayed where they lay, unconscious or worse.

The double doors swung shut. Other doors followed suit. Footsteps and voices faded away. The inhuman shrieks died out.

Caplan glanced at Mills. *Dr. Barden is still inside*, he mouthed.

So is Chenoa, she mouthed back.

Two birds, one stone.

He cracked one of the doors and looked into the dimly-lit interior. He saw a couple of figures—soldiers—hurrying among the beds. They appeared to be checking restraints.

He stepped into the clinic with Mills at his heel. Silently, she closed the door.

"I see three soldiers," he whispered. "No Chenoa or Dr. Barden. They must be in one of the back rooms."

"You find them." She studied the soldiers. "I'll take care of these guys."

"Are you sure?"

She arched an eyebrow as if to say, *Are you really asking me that?* Rising to a crouch, she darted along the wall. She turned at the corner, then silently made her way toward the soldiers.

Caplan turned in the opposite direction. He hustled to the left wall, then turned. Staying low, he crept past rows of beds. He tried not to look, but he couldn't help stealing the occasional glance. The pre-archaics, unconscious and sporting surgical scars, lay on the mattresses. Seeing them like that, ready to be transformed against their will, made him think of Morgan.

His jaw hardened. Continuing forward, he saw the beige drywall as well as the tables and chairs that had been pushed up against it. He caught glimpses of the corkboards, work schedules, and warning signs. And of course, he noticed those oddball posters. Especially the one depicting the beautiful couple toasting to the distant nuclear explosion. It made him think of the scientists, technicians, and orderlies who'd just raced out of the clinic. He recalled the fear and anxiety etched upon their faces.

It's not so great when it's happening to you, is it? he thought with disdain.

He reached the second set of double doors. They creaked open automatically. Cringing, he cast a quick glance over his shoulder. Fortunately, the soldiers hadn't noticed.

He stepped into the connecting hallway. Then he walked to a pairs of doors and peeked through the small windows. He saw the brightly-lit room filled with modules. Two people stood in the center of the room, surrounded by machines and computers. One was Dr. Barden.

His thoughts went to Ross and Toland and all the others still fighting the archaics. If properly motivated, Dr. Barden could save them. But first, Caplan had to deal with the room's other occupant.

Okay, Chenoa, he thought, shifting his gaze to her. *It's time to end this.*

CHAPTER 69

Date: Dec. 3, 2017, 4:12 a.m.; Location: Savage Station, Vallerio Forest, NH

The floor creaked under his boot. He froze, halfway through the doorway. His gaze stole to Roberts. She remained in the middle of the room, hands on hips, her gaze locked on Dr. Barden. Dr. Barden, in turn, was talking in a rush, his words coming out in a garbled mess.

Caplan's heartbeat remained steady. For whatever reason, Roberts and Dr. Barden had left the room unlocked. Perhaps they weren't planning on staying there. Perhaps they just hadn't locked the doors yet. Either way, he was taking advantage of the situation.

He slid into the room and the door closed silently behind him. His fingers tightened around the axe handle. He had no interest in a fair fight, not when so many lives were on the line. He just wanted to finish off Roberts. Then he'd force Dr. Barden to end the archaic threat.

He reared back. His arm whipped forward. His wrist snapped and the axe soared across the room.

Roberts whirled around, her red cloak twisting then unfurling. Her fingers, already adorned with the thick brass knuckles, shot upward. Bracing herself, she formed fists and brought them together in front of her face.

The metallic blade crashed against the brass. A ringing vibration rang out. Then the axe fell harmlessly to the floor.

Roberts, her visage steeled in concentration, dropped her hands to her sides. Gently, she covered the axe with a heeled boot. Shifting her leg, she slid the weapon across the floor. It bumped into the far wall, then came to a rest.

"Hello, Zach," she said, her lips tight.

"Chenoa. Dr. Barden." His body shook with anger. "I ran into Amanda outside."

Dr. Barden winced. Roberts smiled.

He could barely speak. "Why?"

"To square us up, of course," Roberts replied. "You took Kevin from me. So, I took Amanda from you."

His mind shot back to the North Maine Woods, to the musclebound freak who'd cornered him. He hadn't even killed the man. It had been the work of the Danter colony. Not that it mattered now.

"Let's set aside our personal differences for a moment." She gave him a withering look. "Tell me something. How does it feel to doom this planet to total extinction?"

His look turned incredulous. "Are you really blaming me for something that started millions of years ago?"

"James is this planet's only hope. And yet, you're trying to stop him. You're fighting on the side of mass extinction, Zach."

"I'm fighting to rescue my friends, to give them a better future."

"They won't have a future if you keep this up. Any victory you win will be a pyrrhic one."

"Not if we take up the cause."

"You can't fill James' shoes. No one can. He's a true visionary. He poured his life into the Apex Predator project. He saw it through every crisis, every miserable failure. He brought ancient creatures back to life. He created the colossi. In short, he's irreplaceable."

"He's also demented."

"True genius is never appreciated in its time."

"Enough." Caplan glanced at Dr. Barden. "It's over, Doc. I need you to stop the archaics."

"What?" Dr. Barden croaked.

"You control their microchips, right? That means you can release them from their bloodlust."

"Oh, I see." Realization dawned on Roberts' visage. "Your friends are fighting the archaics, aren't they? That's why you came down here alone."

"My friends aren't the only ones in danger." Caplan kept his gaze focused on Dr. Barden. "You can end this right now. Stop the bloodlust."

The doctor's face twisted with discomfort. He backed up against the far wall, as if trying to melt into it.

"He's not going to help you." Roberts took a step forward. "Shall we finish this?"

Caplan thought back to the torture he'd received at Roberts' hands. He recalled the beating, the electroshocks, and the sleep deprivation. But most of all, he thought about

Morgan. He thought about the transformation process, about the horror and pain she must've endured.

Quiet anger filled his soul. Twirling his axe, he circled around to his right. Holding her fists like a boxer, Roberts came out to meet him.

He took a few swings, measuring her up. She dodged his attacks and offered up a few jabs of her own. Slowly, she drove him back toward a module.

"Ever thought about joining our archaic program?" she asked. "We're always looking for new recruits."

"You first," he replied. "After all, you've already got the mentality for it."

She threw a jab. Caplan leapt out of the way. She followed it up with a vicious uppercut. He ducked and the fist whistled past his head.

Hoping to catch her off-balance, he swung his axe overhand. She lifted her forearm, cutting off his attack. With his right side exposed, she aimed a punch at his waist.

Searing pain ripped through his body as the brass knuckles sank into his side. She followed up with a jab to his kidney. More pain flooded through him. Gasping for air, he reeled backward. His legs struck the module and he spun away, narrowly eluding a third blow.

Choking and sputtering, he stumbled across the room. His free hand grabbed hold of another module and he fought to catch his breath.

She walked to the open module. Her fingers danced over a control panel. Lights flashed and a series of beeps rang out. A surge of electricity passed through the room as the module creaked open. "This is the module we used to transform Amanda. In fact, the program is still up." She twisted toward Caplan. "I really do like the idea of turning you into an archaic. You won't live long but at least Amanda won't have to die alone."

"And I really like the idea of killing you," he managed through light gasps. "That way Kevin won't be all alone in Hell."

She strode toward him, her red cloak scraping gently against the floor. Her smile was at full wattage. Her clenched fists were clearly itching for another round.

She shot a cross at his waist. He maneuvered to block it. Her brass knuckles slammed into his forearm. It exploded in pain and a tingling sensation shot down his fingertips.

She swung more fists at him, battering his sides. Gritting his teeth, he kept his arms low, blocking the shots as best as possible. Pressing hard, she turned him in a circle. Then she drove him back.

His legs brushed up against the module for a second time. But this time was different. This time, he could feel the yawning interior behind him. The module was wide open and ready to accept a new patient.

He swung his axe. She dodged it, but he didn't stop. Instead, he kept right on swinging, puncturing the floor with the sharp blade.

"You missed," she said.

"Did I?" He shoved her.

Her feet backpedaled. But her cloak, pinned to the floor by the axe, halted her momentum. Arms flailing, she fought to keep her balance.

He plowed into her. She toppled over. Her head struck the floor and her eyes bulged in pain.

Freeing herself from the cloak, she leapt to her feet. Her free hand reared back and she took a wild swing. He ducked. Her momentum carried her forward. Swinging behind her, Caplan gave her another shove.

She stumbled into the open module. Her head struck the interior and she fell awkwardly into the sloped, dentist-style chair.

Grabbing the open door, he slammed it shut. Electricity buzzed. Machinery whirred. A faint scream, full of intense agony, drifted out of the module.

Dr. Barden grimaced. "Don't do this."

"Why not?"

"Because she was telling the truth. That module was pre-programmed for Ms. Morgan."

"So?"

"Ms. Morgan's genetic profile, like all such profiles, is utterly unique. Subjecting Commander Roberts to this kind of transformation won't just kill her. It'll kill her in the most painful way possible."

Caplan thought back to Morgan, to the painful and terrifying changes she'd been forced to undergo. Changes that would, very soon, end her life. He couldn't save her. But at least he could punish the person responsible for hurting her.

"Good," he said. "It couldn't have happened to a nicer person."

CHAPTER 70

Date: Dec. 3, 2017, 4:24 a.m.; Location: Savage Station, Vallerio Forest, NH

"I'm sorry." Dr. Barden exhaled. "But I can't help you."

Caplan pushed the man up against a second module. "Do you want to end up like Chenoa?"

"If I could help you, I would. But I can't."

"Why not?"

"I only install the microchips. I don't control them."

Caplan's eyes cinched tight and he took a deep breath. "Let me guess. James?"

"James."

He released Dr. Barden and took a step back, his twin axes now jingling gently against his waist. In the process, he saw Roberts' module. Her vitals, listed on a small monitor, showed she'd already expired. But the machine remained in operation nonetheless, still performing its cruel pre-programmed genetic treatment.

It was one thing to subject Roberts to a forced transformation. It was something else to do it to innocent people. Could he and his friends really take Corbotch's place? Could they really create more archaics? And even if they could, could they ever fully fill the man's shoes? Or had Roberts been right about Caplan dooming the planet to certain extinction?

Mills, bow in one hand and a blood-soaked arrow in the other one, shifted on the balls of her feet. "Where's James now?"

"He maintains a bunker on Level X," the doctor replied. "He monitors and controls every aspect of the Apex Predator project from down there."

"I know the place." Caplan's mind skipped back to the hunting lodge room. To the animal heads. To Lucy, the first archaic he'd ever seen. "I assume he's got it locked up tight. How do we get inside?"

"I don't know."

Mills stared daggers at him.

"I'm telling the truth. I never went down there without an invitation."

"Do you know how to operate the microchips?" Caplan asked.

Dr. Barden shook his head. "I'm a doctor, not an electronics whiz. My work with the microchips began and ended with the transplant."

"Does anyone else around here know how to operate them?"

"I doubt it. James kept many things, including those chips, close to the vest."

Soft bellows and faint shrieks leaked through the ceiling. Caplan and Mills exchanged a knowing look. Clearly, the archaics were roaming the upper floors. It wouldn't be long before they reached the clinic.

A part of Caplan wanted to tell Mills to hunker down in the room, to wait with Dr. Barden. Not that she'd actually listen to him, but the desire to protect her hit him on a very deep level.

On the other hand, he'd felt Corbotch's freakish, genetically-engineered strength back in the North Maine Woods. Like it or not, he was no match for that. To defeat Corbotch, he would need her help.

He arched an eyebrow at Mills. "Up for another fight?"

"With James?" Her eyes glowered with barely-concealed pleasure. "I wouldn't miss it for the world."

CHAPTER 71

Date: Dec. 3, 2017, 4:46 a.m.; Location: Savage Station, Vallerio Forest, NH

"Don't be shy." Corbotch's loud voice boomed through the slightly-cracked elephant doors. "Come in. Make yourselves at home."

Caplan shared a glance with Mills. Then he pushed one of the doors open. The familiar wood-paneled room with its elaborate carpeting materialized before him. He saw the wall-mounted animal heads and the old-fashioned chairs and couches. He saw the dark wood tables along with the statues and figurines adorning their surfaces. And he took note of the glass cabinets, stocked with antique pistols, muskets, and rifles.

Corbotch, dressed in his usual tailored white shirt and gray sport coat, faced the monitor bank. On Caplan's prior visit, the screens had depicted feeds of behemoths. But now, they mostly showed images of Savage Station's interior.

One screen showed a close-up of Ross. The man lay on his back, desperately fighting off a frenzied archaic. Another screen depicted Teo. Back to a wall, she swung a broken propeller blindly at a crowd of clawing, scratching archaics. Toland took up a third screen. He'd climbed on top of a helicopter and was stomping away at four or five screeching archaics. Still other screens showed still other people. The Pylors, Tuffel, Aquila, and all of the rest. Some lay dead. The rest fought for their lives.

Just one screen was devoted to the world outside of Savage. It showed a top-down view of a behemoth trail. A car—Elliot's car—shot down the trail at high-speed, followed closely by the enormous Saber.

Caplan's fingers curled around the axe handles. He wanted to kill Corbotch. And yet, he couldn't do that. He needed the man. He needed him to help save his friends.

Corbotch walked to the door. He closed it and slid several bolts into place. Turning around, he offered Caplan and Mills an easy smile. "Hello, Zach. Hello to you as well, Bailey. Welcome back to Savage."

Caplan's gaze remained locked on the monitors. "Stop this," he said. "Now."

"I'm afraid I can't do that."

"It's not just us," Mills said. "Your own people are in danger."

"I know. But at least those who made it to their quarters will survive."

"Maybe for now. But not forever."

"The archaics will get bored once they finish off your friends. They'll leave and this station will return to normal."

Caplan knew Corbotch had a cruel side. Even so, he found himself startled by the man's lack of concern. His brain worked in overdrive as he sought about for a way to save his friends. "We can help you," he said at last.

Corbotch gave him a curious look.

"Chenoa is dead. So are her soldiers."

"And you want to replace them?" Corbotch shook his head. "I don't think so."

"You need people. We've got people."

"Dozens of survivor communities operate on this continent. They're in constant danger and exist on meager resources. If I so much as snapped my fingers, they'd come running." He shrugged. "I'll miss Chenoa. I'll miss the others as well. But replacing them will be an easy task."

Caplan rushed Corbotch. His right axe swept in a downward direction. His left axe curled back, ready to strike the follow-up blow.

Corbotch sidestepped the first blade. Jumping back, he dodged the second axe as well. His hand shot out. He grabbed Caplan's shoulder and yanked.

Caplan hurtled through the air. His back smashed into one of the chairs and he crumpled to the carpet.

Corbotch took a second to straighten out his shirt. "Do you think I like this?" he asked. "Do you think I enjoy watching people die?"

Caplan rubbed his aching jaw. "I know you do."

"Enemies, yes. But not innocent people. Not people who never tried to harm me. I'm not a monster, Zach. Perhaps I've done monstrous things, but I'm not a monster."

"Earth to James," Mills said. "Doing monstrous things makes you a monster."

"Monster don't hate themselves."

Caplan blinked. "What?"

"I may appear cold-blooded to you. But believe it or not, all of the lives I've ended have taken a toll on me." He sighed. "If I'd left well enough alone, the extinction would've wiped out our species. By then, this entire planet would've been dead. So, mankind was always doomed. I might've sped things up a bit, but our fate was written in stone long before any of us were born. That knowledge is the only thing that allows me to live with what I've done."

Still holding the axes, Caplan climbed to his feet. Noticing a sudden commotion, he glanced at a monitor. An archaic was in the process of tackling Tuffel to the ground. Other archaics swarmed the Danter resident. Their fists beat his chest. Their teeth sank into his flesh. Within seconds, he was a bloody corpse. Nausea roiled Caplan's gut and he had to grip the chair to keep from keeling over.

"So, I killed off our species," Corbotch continued. "And in the process gave this planet its only chance at survival."

"I get it. I do." Caplan swallowed hard. "But a few more people won't change anything. Let our friends live. We'll stay here. We'll help you."

"I can't. Even if I wanted to help you, it's impossible." He followed Caplan's gaze to the swarming archaics. Then he nodded at a large console beneath the monitors. "I control the microchips from that console. But my control is limited. I can't just turn their thirst for blood on and off like a light bulb. Once it's gone, it's gone for good."

"That's fine with us," Mills replied.

"But not with me. I didn't instill bloodlust in my creations because I want them to kill indiscriminately. I did it because they're new to this world. Without bloodlust, they won't survive."

"You don't know that."

"No, I don't," he acknowledged. "But I believe it."

"You can make more archaics." Caplan's tone turned desperate. "You can make them as bloodthirsty as you like. Just let our friends live."

"It's far too risky. The world needs archaics and it needs them now."

Mills shifted her gaze to one of the monitors. "Then at least stop Saber."

He arched an eyebrow. "Saber?"

"The saber-toothed tiger behemoth." She nodded at the massive creature chasing Elliott's car. "Or rather, mega behemoth. In case you haven't noticed, it's grown a bit."

"I'm aware of the situation."

Caplan tasted blood on his tongue. "Are you aware that it killed ArcSim, the short-faced bear behemoth?"

Corbotch's face twisted slightly with ... was that frustration? "Yes."

"And you haven't cut off its bloodthirst yet? It seems to me you wouldn't want a behemoth killing other behemoths before they get a chance to patch up the food chain."

Corbotch didn't respond.

"Wait a minute." Mills furrowed her brow. "You already cut off its thirst, didn't you?"

"That's not ..." He took a deep breath. "It doesn't matter. Plans are in place to deal with the situation."

The sudden gnashing of teeth caused Caplan's gaze to shift to another monitor. The upper-left screen showed Connie Aquila. Her head was tilted to the left and an archaic was biting down on her neck. Her eyes bulged with pain and her mouth was locked open in a silent scream. Then blood spilt forth and she slumped to the ground.

First, Tuffel. Now, Aquila. Unless he did something quick, everyone else would follow suit. He looked at other screens. Some contained data and diagrams. Presumably, that was how Corbotch controlled the microchips and thus, his creations.

But was Caplan willing to risk everything to save his friends? What if Corbotch was right? What if shutting down the bloodlust sealed the world's fate?

His brain waged a silent, internal war. Then he gave Mills a look. She met his gaze and he willed an unspoken message to her. *I'll play punching bag*, he thought. *You figure out those microchips.* She offered a slight nod in response.

Brandishing his axes, he stepped toward Corbotch. The man unleashed a quick jab at his chest. Caplan put up his defenses and the fist slammed into his arm with the force of a sledgehammer. His body erupted in horrible pain, then quickly numbed over.

Mills raced toward the monitor bank. Corbotch grabbed Caplan by the arms. With a mighty heave, he hurled the man across the room. Caplan slammed into Mills and they both fell to the ground.

"Don't waste your time," Corbotch said. "My system is completely proprietary. You'll never figure it out."

Mills retrieved her bow and fitted an arrow into the bowstring. She let it rip. Corbotch dropped to the floor, but the arrow still managed to nick his shoulder blade.

She readied another arrow. But he was already on top of her. His fist smacked her jaw. Her eyes flew to the back of her head and she sagged to the ground.

Caplan's body felt rubbery and tired. With great effort, he swung an axe at Corbotch. But the man parried the blow, then punched Caplan in the forehead. It was like being hit by a block of cement and Caplan flopped onto the ground.

A foot slammed into his stomach. His stomach muscles seized up and he gasped for air. But before he could breathe, Corbotch grabbed his throat. Dropping his axes, Caplan tried to pry the hand away. But it was far too powerful.

Corbotch pulled him off the ground and into the air. Struggling and choking, Caplan stretched his toes, trying to gain his footing. It didn't work so he started chopping at Corbotch's hand. But the man didn't even flinch.

"It's over, Zach," Corbotch said.

His cheeks started to burn. His eyesight dimmed and he felt himself drifting away to oblivion.

A loud crack, wood on flesh, rang out. Corbotch grunted. Releasing his grip on Caplan, he whirled around.

Caplan fell to the floor. Clawing at his throat, he struggled to breathe. Precious oxygen slipped into his lungs and his vision returned. Looking up, he saw Corbotch standing still, poised over a broken chair. Mills, her jaw bruised and bleeding, stood a few feet away.

Looking past them, Caplan saw the monitor bank. He saw Toland lying on top of a helicopter, an archaic's teeth chomping at his neck. He saw Teo, now weaponless and surrounded. And he saw Ross slumped on the ground, archaics piling on top of him. Everywhere he looked, he saw his friends on the verge of death.

Despair filled his chest. Even if he and Mills stopped Corbotch, they'd never figure out the system in time. The bloodthirst would continue to slip through the microchips.

A hard ridge crossed his brow. *Unless …*

Grabbing up an axe, he rose to his feet. His arm hurled back and he threw the bladed weapon with all of his might. It soared end over end, straight and true.

Corbotch sidestepped the weapon. The axe hurtled past him. Metal slammed into glass and metal.

"You missed," Corbotch said.

Caplan grinned. "That's what Chenoa thought, too."

Twisting around, he stared at the monitor bank. At the axe blade, embedded deep into the console. At the sparks, at the blinking images. "Oh, my God," he cried out. "Do you know what you've done?"

Caplan knew exactly what he'd done. Unable to seize control of the microchips, he'd severed the connection instead. Bloodlust and hunger would no longer flow through the archaics, the reborn megafauna, or the behemoths. For the first time in their miserable lives, they were free. Free from Corbotch, free from all forms of control.

The longer-term ramifications, of course, remained troubling. Would the archaics survive without bloodlust? How about the reborn megafauna or the behemoths? And if not, what would he do? How would he combat the Holocene extinction?

He knew those questions would need to be answered someday. But at least he wouldn't have to answer them alone.

Keeping his gaze locked on the blinking monitors, he watched confused expressions come over the archaics' faces. Their fists slowed, then stopped. Their bloodied teeth pulled away from flesh. They looked around, as if seeing the world for the first time.

Archaics climbed down from the helicopter. Toland twitched a few times, then rose to a sitting position. Other archaics backed away from Teo. Breathing heavily, she grabbed up her broken propeller.

Caplan shifted his gaze to another screen. He saw archaics pull themselves off of a thick pile. Ross came into view. His face looked bruised and he bled heavily. But he was moving.

Shifting his gaze to other monitors, Caplan watched as other archaics backed away from the rest of his friends. They headed for the walls and scaled the ladders. And then they were gone.

"You broke the connection." Corbotch's voice sounded hollow. "You—"

Caplan plowed a shoulder into the man's back. Grunting, Corbotch stumbled into the sparking, buzzing console. A sizzling sound rang out and his body stiffened. Then he collapsed in a heap.

Caplan limped across the room. He wrapped his arms around Mills and she embraced him in kind. They held tightly to each other, bound by equal parts love and horror. Love for each other. Horror for all that had happened. For the death of Perkins, Aquila, and all the others. For Morgan's transformation and imminent death. For everything they'd seen and done over the last week and a half.

"What now?" she whispered.

"This." He brushed hair away from her eyes. Then he lowered his head. His lips locked onto hers.

And they kissed.

CHAPTER 72

Date: Dec. 3, 2017, 8:04 p.m.; Location: Savage Station, Vallerio Forest, NH

Ross kicked off his dirty shoes and soiled socks. Carefully, he stepped onto the ornate carpet. A soft sigh of pleasure left his bruised lips. "Wow," he mumbled. "That feels amazing."

Caplan retrieved two tumblers from the bar. He dropped a few ice cubes into each one. Then he picked up a bottle of Hamron's Horror. Carefully, he poured copper-colored scotch into each tumbler.

Ross plopped down on one of the plush stools. He gave the alcohol a good sniff. Nodding in approval, he held the glass out to Caplan. "To the future," he said.

"To the future." They clinked tumblers. Then Caplan tipped the glass to his lips and allowed a bit of Hamron's Horror into his mouth. Like always, it tasted smoky and burnt his tongue.

Ross took a long draught. "I just checked with Sydney. She said the footage from that monitor cut out while the chase was still in progress. So, we still don't know what happened to Tricia."

"How's Sydney handling it?"

"About as well as can be expected." He sighed. "In other news, we buried the rest of the bodies. I figure we'll hold services in the morning. Do you want to say something?"

He nodded.

"I figured as such." Ross downed the rest of his liquor. Placing the tumbler on the bar, he tapped it with his finger. "One more thing. George told me James' people are starting to emerge from their rooms."

Caplan filled the man's glass. Then he downed his own tumbler and refilled it. "How are they taking the recent change in management?"

"Not great. It's going to take time to win them over."

"We've got plenty of that."

They drank in silence for several minutes. When Ross was finished, he pushed his tumbler toward Caplan. Caplan refilled it for a second time and Ross lifted the glass back to his lips. "They're not the only one who are peeved. Dr. Sandy and a few others, well, let's just say they're not pleased with your decision to spare James. They want him thrown to the behemoths, so to speak."

Thanks to his superior genetics, Corbotch had survived the electric shock. Now, he lay asleep in the concrete cell once used to hold Caplan, Mills, and Toland.

"We may need him," Caplan replied. "He knows more about the Apex Predator project than the rest of us put together."

"He'll never help us."

"He will if it'll help stop the extinction."

"We'll see." Ross took another drink, then looked around. "So, this is it, huh? This is where we're going to spend the rest of our lives?"

"Not necessarily."

He arched an eyebrow.

Caplan pulled Morgan's Apex Predator logbook out of a cupboard. He cracked the book open and retrieved a wad of paper from the interior. Unfolding it, he spread out the paper on top of the bar. It was a map of the United States. Little arrows and notes, scribbled in Corbotch's handwriting, decorated the map.

"What's this?" Ross asked.

"I found it on the console. It's James' record of the survivor settlements."

"What's that got to do with us?"

"Perhaps humanity wasn't meant to rule this planet with an iron fist. But I'm not sure we were intended to live underground like rats either." He stared at the map. "I'm going to find these survivor communities. I'm going to bring them together. Maybe, just maybe, we can carve out a role for humanity in this new world."

Ross arched an eyebrow. "It sounds like you're thinking about staying on as our leader."

Caplan nodded. "If you'll have me."

"You've got my vote." He glanced at the map. "So, do you need help with that?"

Caplan grinned. A song, familiar but different, came to mind. *Forget just surviving,* he sang in his head. *It's time to start thriving.* "Definitely."

APEX PREDATOR LOGBOOK

Apex Predator Memorandum
Date: July 14, 2013, 1:43 a.m.
To: Vallerio Foundation, Stage I Team
From: James Corbotch
RE: risk profile of a super-colossus

This email string has gotten quite heated over the last week and so I decided to step in and give my two cents on the matter. First and foremost, the work done by Dr. Grant is irrefutable. The risk of a "super-colossus," while slim, is undeniably real. And if a super-colossus does emerge, it will undoubtedly upset the very delicate changes we hope to make to the global food chain.

We must accept this and move on as best as possible. The truth is we need the colossi. Without them, Apex Predator will most assuredly fail.

With that said, I propose the following protocol to deal with the possibility of a super-colossus emergence:

1) Unmanned aerial vehicles will be used to track colossi at all times. Spot checks, conducted by approved and trained personnel, will be performed on a regular basis.

2) Monthly measurements will be taken for all colossi. These measurements will be compared to historical data in order to ascertain any irregular growth patterns.

3) If a super-colossus does emerge, Protocol Sixty-Four will be put into play. No effort will be spared to ensure the immediate destruction of this creature.

In closing, please remember that the risk of a super-colossus remains miniscule. However, the threat of such a creature is very real. Please keep your follow-up responses clean and your rhetoric polite. Remember, only the coolest of heads will be able to save this world from all that threatens it.

END OF BOOK TWO

Author's Note

Some ten months ago, I failed. And this wasn't some minor failure, either. No, I failed big-time.

On February 1, 2016, I published *FURY* (originally called *KNOX*), the fifth novel in the *Cy Reed Adventures*. I wrote *FURY* without an outline and enjoyed every second of the experience. I felt utterly confident it would be an enormous success. And indeed, it came roaring out of the gate … only to flop right on its face.

FURY was my first real commercial failure as an author. In the aftermath, I began questioning everything I thought I knew about books. I even returned to outlining and rewriting, processes that have proven highly destructive to my creativity.

So, what went wrong? With time, I've come to realize that *FURY*'s failure didn't result from a bad story but rather, a bad cover. A cover that, incidentally, I created. For years, I designed my own covers with, in retrospect, mixed success. Some covers were pretty good. Others, like the initial *FURY* cover, were rather poor. And unfortunately, a poor cover is the surest way to kill a good book.

But on a much deeper level, I failed because I insisted on doing everything—writing, cover design, formatting, publicity, and more—by myself. And that brings me to *SAVAGE*. On its surface, *SAVAGE* is about behemoths, the Holocene extinction, and desperate survival. But it's really about learning to accept help. Help from friends, loved ones, and even strangers. Help from people who can shore up our weaknesses. Help from people who bring encouragement and good cheer into our lives.

I recently contracted with a designer to produce new covers for all of my books. The process is ongoing but so far, I'm pleased with the results. And thanks to my wife's timely advice, I gave up outlining and rewriting all over again. I also asked my father to lend me a hand with marketing and production. His help has been invaluable in getting this book into your hands. Finally, your wonderful letters, emails, and social media comments inspired me to soldier through this period of debilitating self-doubt.

I hope all of you find the strength to accept help into your lives, especially during difficult times. And, of course, to offer that same help to others as well.

Thank you for reading *SAVAGE*. I hope you enjoyed it. If you want to be the first to know about my upcoming stories, make sure to sign up for my newsletter at **eepurl.com/CVjj5**.

Keep Adventuring!
David Meyer
February 2017

ABOUT THE AUTHOR

David Meyer is an adventurer and the international bestselling author of the *Cy Reed Adventures* and the *Apex Predator* series. He's been creating for as long as he can remember. As a kid, he made his own toys, invented games, and built elaborate cities with blocks and Legos. Before long, he was planning out murder mysteries and trap-filled treasure quests for his family and friends.

These days, his lifelong interests—lost treasure, mysteries of history, monsters, conspiracies, forgotten lands, exploration, and archaeology—fuel his personal adventures. Whether hunting for pirate treasure or exploring ancient ruins, he loves seeking out answers to the unknown. Over the years, Meyer has consulted on a variety of television shows. Most recently, he made an appearance on H2's #1 hit original series, *America Unearthed*.

Meyer lives in New Hampshire with his wife and son. For more information about him, his adventures, and his stories, please see the links below.

Connect with David!
Website: www.DavidMeyerCreations.com
Amazon Page: viewauthor.at/davidmeyer
Mailing List: eepurl.com/CVjj5
Facebook: www.facebook.com/GuerrillaExplorer
Twitter: www.twitter.com/DavidMeyer_

BOOKS BY DAVID MEYER

Made in the USA
San Bernardino, CA
31 December 2017